Great Australian
GHOST STORIES

Great Australian GHOST STORIES

Richard Davis

ABC
Books

First published in Australia in 2012
by HarperCollins*Publishers* Australia Pty Limited
ABN 36 009 913 517
harpercollins.com.au

HarperCollins*Publishers*
Level 13, 201 Elizabeth Street, Sydney NSW 2000, Australia
31 View Road, Glenfield, Auckland 0627, New Zealand
A 53, Sector 57, Noida, UP, India
77–85 Fulham Palace Road, London, W6 8JB, United Kingdom
2 Bloor Street East, 20th floor, Toronto, Ontario M4W 1A8, Canada
10 East 53rd Street, New York NY 10022, USA

National Library of Australia Cataloguing-in-Publication data:

Davis, Richard Michael.
Great Australian ghost stories / Richard Davis.
978 0 7333 3107 7 (pbk.)
Ghost stories, Australian.
Ghosts – Australia – Anecdotes.
398.250994

Cover design by Darren Holt, HarperCollins Design Studio
Cover image by John Donegan/Fairfax Syndication
Typeset in 10/16pt ITC Bookman by Kirby Jones
Printed and bound in Australia by Griffin Press
The papers used by HarperCollins in the manufacture of this book are a natural, recyclable product made from wood grown in sustainable plantation forests. The fibre source and manufacturing processes meet recognised international environmental standards, and carry certification.

5 4 3 2 1 12 13 14 15

Contents

Introduction

From ghoulies and ghosties and long-legged beasties
And things that go bump in the night, Good Lord deliver us!
Old English West Country Prayer, Anon

For most people the word 'ghost' conjures up images of transparent, white figures floating around ancient castles in Europe but, as the stories in this book prove, while Australia may be short on ancient castles, it has never been short on ghosts. Australia has its own rich heritage of ghost stories linked to our history and reflecting our unique national character.

Before sampling some of the best of these, let's take a moment to consider the question I have been asked most frequently since I began taking an interest in ghost stories, the answer to which might stir your curiosity and enhance your enjoyment of this book: 'What is a ghost?' Well, the only truthful answer to that is 'No one really knows', but there are plenty of theories.

Traditional believers hold that ghosts are the spirits of dead people, bound to the place they haunt by past anguish, unable to move on to the after-life until the place they haunt ceases to exist or they are exorcised by a religious ceremony. This view is enshrined in most world religions, including Christianity, and in the cultural heritage of most ethnic groupings.

Science has been very slow in coming forwards with more rational explanations to challenge this traditional view. The

English academic, Thomas Lethbridge, came up with one attractive 'scientific' alternative. He suggested that we all have an electromagnetic field surrounding us, its strength affected by emotional arousal, and that this force can linger in a suitable medium (water, earth, stone) long after the original source has departed — rather like a recording or a photograph. Then, when the witness' emotions are aroused by circumstances or surroundings and their electromagnetic fields are 'charged up', it can interact with the residual force — 'short it out' if you like. The result, Lethbridge claimed, is an image, a sound or an emotion 'played back' from a different time.

The diversity of theories and the absence of concrete proof make most people understandably sceptical about ghosts (and ghost stories) and that scepticism is fed by revelations of hoaxes, pranks, fraudulent mediums and sensational journalism. A good ghost story can also be cheap insurance against trespassers and burglars, the perfect deterrent for unwanted guests and a cover for clandestine activities. No doubt many ghost stories are the products of convenience rather than supernatural forces.

Some stories may also have their origins in natural phenomena being mistaken for the supernatural. Wind, for example, is capable of producing a remarkable range of sounds in nature and around human constructions; and light (especially when reflected off odd surfaces or seen through glass) can play cunning tricks with our eyes.

Then of course there are the multifarious capabilities of the human mind. Illness, exhaustion, shock, fear and exultation can all produce hallucinations, not to mention medication, illicit drugs and alcohol. *Alcohol.* Well, here we come to the sceptics' favourite explanation for ghosts. Especially in earlier times, when drink was the universal panacea for hardship, loneliness, boredom and pain, it must be admitted that many a ghostly spirit was conjured up from the fumes of real spirits, many an innocent object took on a sinister guise when judgment was clouded by drink and many a sufferer of delirium tremens imagined he saw a ghost instead of a pink elephant.

To balance this we have the testimony of thousands of sincere people — ordinary, intelligent, lucid and *sober* Australians — who genuinely believe they have had encounters with ghosts and many who have seen exactly the same thing in the same places simultaneously or repeatedly at different times: a vast body of evidence that cannot be denied and should not be discounted.

Maybe some day science will crack the mystery of ghosts, but in the meantime the absence of answers should certainly not prevent us from enjoying spine-tingling, spooky tales. So, dear reader, put aside your doubts, make sure the doors and windows are locked, turn the lights down low, settle in your favourite chair, keep a blanket handy (for when your blood runs cold) and join me on a journey behind the veil that separates the mortal from the eternal — right here in our own backyard.

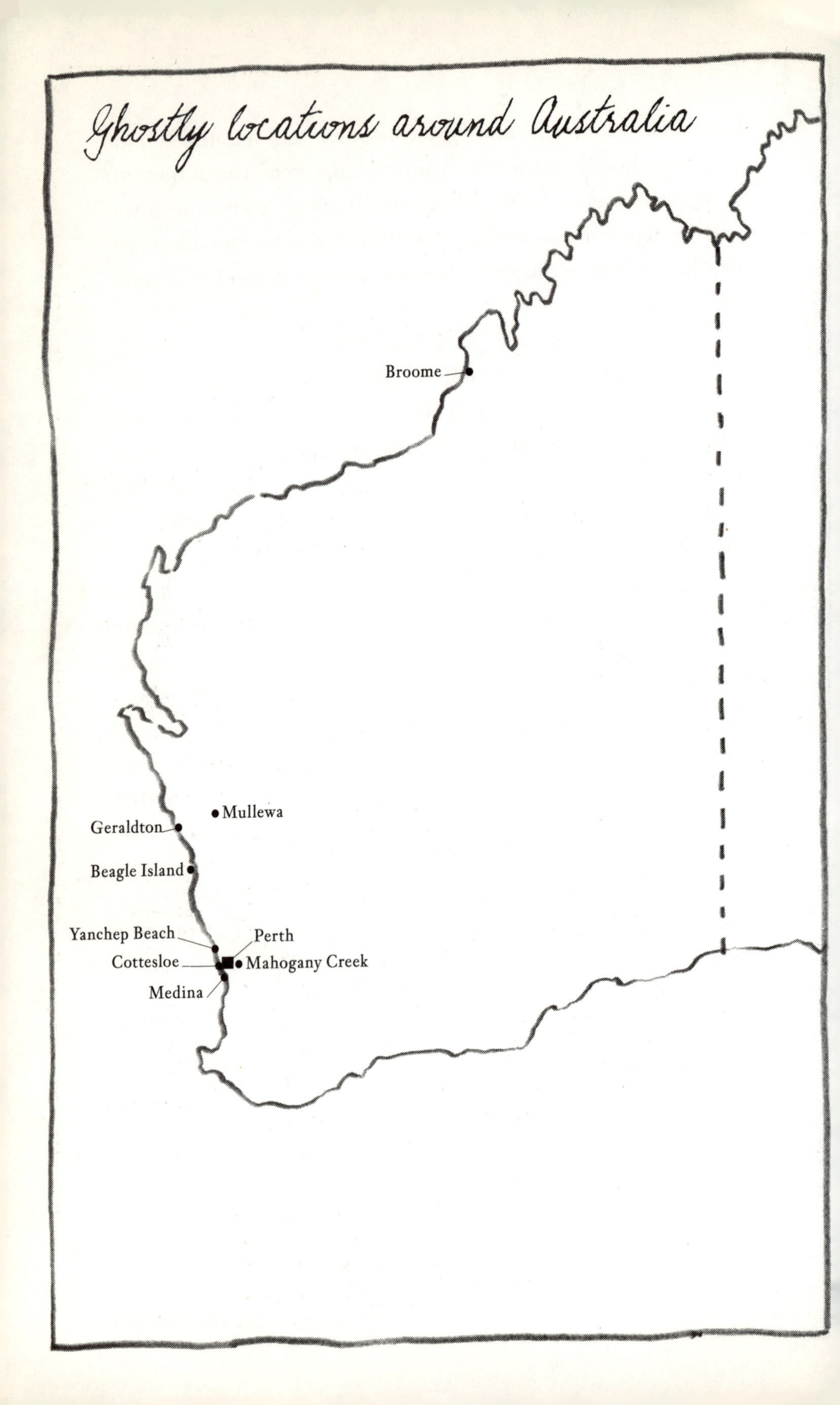
Ghostly locations around Australia
Broome
Mullewa
Geraldton
Beagle Island
Yanchep Beach
Perth
Cottesloe
Mahogany Creek
Medina

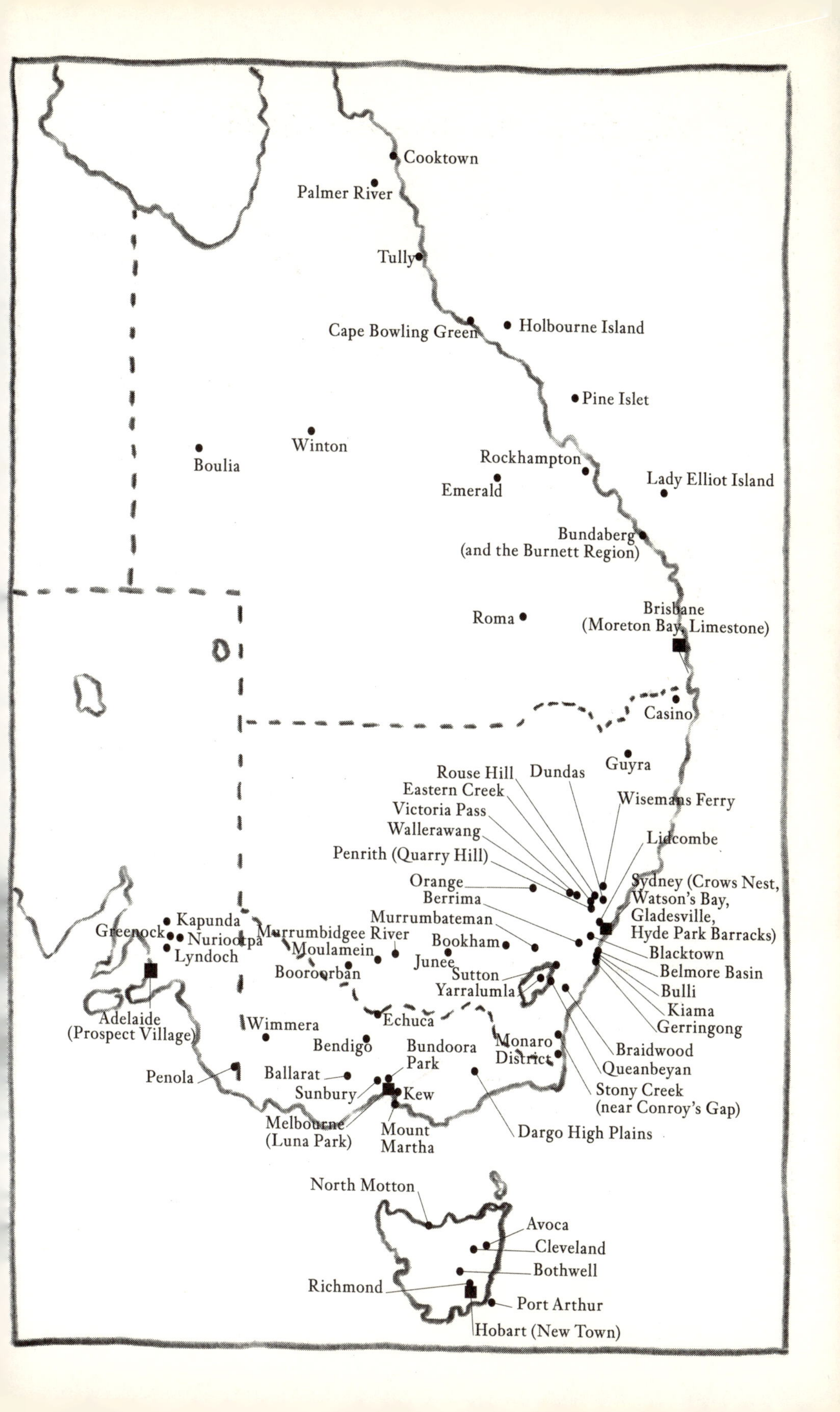

Cooktown
Palmer River
Tully
Cape Bowling Green
Holbourne Island
Pine Islet
Winton
Boulia
Rockhampton
Emerald
Lady Elliot Island
Bundaberg
(and the Burnett Region)
Roma
Brisbane
(Moreton Bay, Limestone)
Casino
Guyra
Rouse Hill
Dundas
Eastern Creek
Victoria Pass
Wisemans Ferry
Wallerawang
Lidcombe
Penrith (Quarry Hill)
Orange
Sydney (Crows Nest,
Watson's Bay,
Gladesville,
Hyde Park Barracks)
Berrima
Murrumbateman
Kapunda
Greenock
Nuriootpa
Murrumbidgee River
Moulamein
Bookham
Blacktown
Lyndoch
Junee
Belmore Basin
Booroorban
Sutton
Bulli
Yarralumla
Kiama
Adelaide
(Prospect Village)
Echuca
Wimmera
Gerringong
Bendigo
Bundoora
Park
Monaro
District
Braidwood
Queanbeyan
Penola
Ballarat
Sunbury
Kew
Stony Creek
(near Conroy's Gap)
Melbourne
(Luna Park)
Mount
Martha
Dargo High Plains
North Motton
Avoca
Cleveland
Bothwell
Richmond
Port Arthur
Hobart (New Town)

1.
A Trio of Headless Horrors

Like one, that on a lonesome road
Doth walk in fear and dread,
And having once turned round walks on
And turns no more his head;
Because he knows some fearsome fiend
Doth close behind him tread.

***The Rime of the Ancient Mariner*, Samuel Taylor Coleridge**
(English poet, 1772–1834)

The shapely, black-gowned figure always appeared (observers agreed) with arms raised and fingers outstretched — pale emaciated arms and long bony fingers — reaching, probing, searching for something apparently lost. Observers froze as the spectre moved, stumbling like a blind person on an unfamiliar path towards them. And sightless this spectre must surely have been, for where its head once joined its neck was a gory, seeping stump and nothing above it.

If the spectre's mutilation and its scrabbling motion were not enough to terrorise watchers, then the gurgling noises (described as 'strangled sobs' by some and 'gasps for breath' by others) which came from the neck stump were sufficient to curdle the blood of even the most stout-hearted.

If you had wandered in the cool of the evening among the whispering pines in front of Berrima Gaol in the southern highlands of New South Wales at any time in the last century and half, you too might have encountered this horrific spectre.

Dozens of others did and very few stayed around long enough to find out who it had once been or to learn its history. The few who did discovered a tale almost as shocking as and even bloodier than the spectre.

In 1833 Governor Bourke gave permission for Lucretia Davies to marry Henry Dunkley. The fact that vice-regal permission was needed indicates that the bride was under age or under sentence as a convict, or both. The marriage took place at Sutton Forest and the couple settled on a farm near Gunning, fifty kilometres west of Goulburn.

Lucretia was what we would call today 'sexy' and a ticket-of-leave man named Martin Beech who came to work at the Dunkley's farm in 1842 took a fancy to her. Lucretia quickly decided she preferred the young, virile Martin to her dull husband and a plot was hatched. One cold, moonless night in mid-September that year Lucretia slipped quietly from the bed she shared with her unsuspecting husband and unbarred the door to admit her lover. Martin carried a heavy axe and Lucretia watched impassively as he dealt the sleeping Henry one fatal blow that clove his head in two. The body was quickly wrapped in the blood-drenched bedding and the whole gory bundle carried out into the darkness.

Next morning when the other farm workers asked where the boss was, Lucretia told them he had gone to Berrima on business. For a week and a half it seemed as though the murderers had got away with their crime, but apparently not everyone believed their story. The police arrived one day and began asking awkward questions. They searched the property and found Henry's body in a shallow grave about 300 metres from the house.

Lucretia Dunkley and Martin Beech were arrested on suspicion of murder and taken to Berrima Gaol to await trial.

Almost a year passed while the police gathered evidence and the Crown Prosecutor assembled a watertight case against them. Finally, on 5 September 1843, they were marched under guard to Berrima Court House to appear before the Chief Justice of New South Wales, Sir James Dowling. The trial took just two days. Both defendants were found guilty and condemned to be 'hanged by their necks until they be dead'. The sentence was carried out at Berrima Gaol the same day.

As the first female to be executed by hanging in New South Wales, Lucretia Dunkley's fate was widely reported and she soon joined the ranks of infamous villainesses in colonial mythology — every bit as cruel, it was said, as her Borgia namesake — and the facts of her life soon became distorted. 'Farmer's wife' was not romantic enough for the public so the role of licensee of the Three Legs O' Man Inn at Berrima (which did exist) was invented for her. Her victim became a wealthy squatter staying at the inn whose throat she slit with a razor and whose blood she caught in a kitchen bowl before robbing him of 500 gold sovereigns but, truth to tell, the inventions were no more chilling than the facts.

There was much conjecture among the medical profession in the nineteenth century as to why people like Lucretia Dunkley and Martin Beech committed such heinous crimes. The science of psychology was in its infancy and it was thought that physical defects in the brain were the only possible cause of abnormal behaviour. The brains of many executed criminals were dissected in the vain hope of finding and identifying common defects. Lucretia's corpse suffered that fate. Soon after she was cut down from the gallows her head was sawn off with a surgical saw, placed in a box and sent to the study section of the Australian Museum in Sydney. There the hair and flesh were removed, the skull opened and the brain inspected without, needless to say, any significant aberrations being found.

It was not long before reports began to circulate about Lucretia's headless ghost appearing among the pine trees in front of Berrima Gaol — people of both sexes and all ages claimed to have seen her. A Berrima storekeeper claimed that his teenage daughter went mad after encountering Lucretia's ghost one summer night as she was passing the gaol; and the doctor who signed the papers admitting her to an asylum concurred that the young woman's reason had left her suddenly and unexpectedly, describing her as 'sane' one day and 'reduced to a state of idiocy' the next.

At Easter 1961 two students camping at Berrima claimed they were awakened in the night by the sounds of sobbing and laboured breathing and that when they scrambled from their tent they saw Lucretia's ghost wandering around the ruins of the Three Legs O' Man Inn. The location makes the student's claim a little dubious, but their description of the ghost and of the icy terror that gripped them as they watched it stumbling about accord with the evidence of Lucretia's other victims. That fifty-year-old sighting is the last on record although local ghost tour operators would have us believe Lucretia is still around and an old resident of Berrima reminds people: 'She may yet reappear. She's still searching, you know. She hasn't found her head yet.'

He's right: she hasn't. There are many relics of this gruesome story. Berrima Gaol, made famous in Rolf Boldrewood's novel *Robbery Under Arms*, and Berrima Court House, an imposing building in classical-revival style, still stand and, although the fact is not widely known, Lucretia Dunkley's skull remains to this day in the collection of the Australian Museum in William Street, Sydney, 120 kilometres beyond the reach of her ghost.

There isn't much about Lucretia Dunkley's story to raise a smile, but there are a few amusing aspects to the story of our second 'headless horror' and — take heart, squeamish readers — a blessed absence of gore.

Old-timers along the Murrumbidgee still talk about the 'The Headless Horseman of the Black Swamp' (or 'The Trotting Cob', to give the story its alternative title) and it's the main topic of conversation at the Royal Mail Hotel at Booroorban, on the Cobb Highway between Hay and Deniliquin. Tourist coaches stop at this colourful old pub and, while passengers tuck into a hearty meal and a cold beer, the publican and his wife are only too happy to tell them the region's most famous tale — as they and their predecessors have been doing for travellers on this route for nearly 150 years.

The swamp mentioned in the story is still there, a few kilometres down the highway in the middle of a dry saltbush plain and marked with an elaborate sculpture. In the early 1850s, a drover named Doyle either died of thirst or was murdered (versions differ) at what was then known as 'Black's Swamp', because it was a popular camping site for Aborigines, or 'Black Swamp', because of the infestation of rotting vegetation in the water (again versions differ). Thereafter, Doyle's ghost was said to appear mounted on a stocky, chestnut-coloured horse — 'the trotting cob' — circling around the swamp in the darkest hours of night.

Other drovers bringing herds down from Queensland to southern markets would water their cattle at the Black Swamp but avoided camping there for fear of the ghost. Many believed seeing it marked them for an early grave. A drover named Kelly and his offsider who knew nothing of this claim camped there with a small herd one night and Kelly told how they were visited by the ghost just before midnight.

'We thought it was a rider out late when we saw him first. He just appeared out of the shadows at the edge of our camp. We shouted a welcome, but it seemed he didn't hear us. He just kept circling, getting closer and closer until the light from our campfire showed his mount to be a neat, little, reddish-brown horse. His clothes were covered by a dusty cape and above the collar ... well, there was just *nothing* above his collar. It's no wonder the poor blighter couldn't hear us!'

Kelly had a near fatal fall from his own horse and his offsider drowned in a swollen creek soon after their encounter with the ghost. After Kelly testified to these events, wise heads nodded knowingly and the legend flourished.

Cobb & Co. established a coach service from Hay to Deniliquin in 1859 and a resourceful man named Edward Smith opened an inn at the Black Swamp. Mrs Smith became famous for the delicious scones she baked for coach travellers at all hours of the day and night and it was reported that these delicacies were much better received than the rot-gut liquor her husband brewed and served, which one wit said 'would stiffen a dog'.

Cobb & Co. drivers claimed that they often saw the headless horseman on his trotting cob and it became a tradition that they would regale their passengers with lurid stories of the ghost, then suggest a round of drinks (and a plate of scones) at Smith's inn for everyone (including themselves), at the passengers' expense — to fortify everyone, the drivers said, in case they encountered the galloping ghoul.

At least one Cobb & Co. driver genuinely believed in Doyle's ghost. Charlie Lee, who died at Deniliquin aged eighty-eight in 1929, was one of the company's most respected drivers. To his dying day Lee swore that he had seen the ghost and that it was no fraud.

A fraud, however, was exactly what most local people thought the ghost was. It was common knowledge in the district that a butcher from Moulamein, seventy-odd kilometres west of the Black Swamp, used to pretend to be the ghost so he could steal cattle from passing herds and sell the meat. The butcher built himself a wooden frame that fitted on his shoulders. He would then drape a blanket over the frame so that he appeared headless and run off a few head of cattle while the drovers cowered in fright. A load of buckshot in his backside was said to have ended the butcher's ghostly career but he, like Charlie Lee, lived to a ripe old age and died in his bed, still chuckling about his own craftiness.

Cynics dismiss the whole story of the 'Headless Horseman of the Black Swamp' as a hoax. Believers point out that Doyle's death and the earliest appearances of the ghost (without mention of cattle stealing) predate the butcher's escapades by a decade or more. Whatever the truth is, the headless horseman and his nifty nag have become one of Australia's most popular ghost stories and a profitable part of the folklore of the Riverina.

Our final 'headless horror' is much less well-known, but his story is perhaps the most touching of the three. Unlike Lucretia Dunkley, no one would suggest that he deserved his fate and, unlike the horseman at the Black Swamp, there has never been any conjecture about trickery or foul play associated with his story. On the contrary, what follows is testament to the perils of living in the most isolated regions of Australia and to the personal courage required to face them.

One of the great pastoral properties of the Channel Country in the south-western corner of Queensland is Hammond Downs. This giant cattle station (as large as a small European state) was established by the Hammond family in the middle of the nineteenth century. Hammond Downs can lay claim to several ghost stories, mostly concerned with victims of the flash floods that come roaring down Cooper Creek most years, turning the dry and dusty land into an inland sea.

The distinction of being the property's and the region's most famous ghost (and their only headless one) belongs to Edward 'Ned' Hammond, son of the first Hammonds to arrive in the district. Ned was an accomplished horseman; and he was strong, wiry and in the prime of his life when he went out alone one day during the dry season of 1889 to round up some stray horses. In what is still called the Wallaroo Paddock Ned's own horse slipped in a clay pan, throwing him heavily to the ground.

There are two versions of how Ned Hammond was found. The most likely tells of a search party finding him with a fractured spine trying to crawl home and his brother, John, riding 300 kilometres to fetch the nearest doctor but finding Ned dead on his return.

The other version claims that Ned managed to remount and the horse found its own way home. Along the way Ned collapsed and fell from the horse again, but one of his boots remained caught in a stirrup. Ned was dragged many kilometres, his head repeatedly hitting the stony ground until, by the time the horse limped into the homestead it was dragging a headless corpse.

Ned Hammond was buried near the homestead beside his infant daughter Mary, who had died eight years before, and some say that his ghost still rides the dusty plain where he suffered his fatal fall. The ghostly horse and rider have been seen in the beams of car headlights and heard galloping around camps at night. The story is passed from one generation of jackaroos to the next and the new chums are warned to watch out for the 'old boss'.

'So, how will we know him, then?' the youngsters invariably ask.

'Oh you'll *know* 'im all right,' the old hands reply. ''e ain't got no 'ead!'

2.
Fabulous Federici!

There are more things in heaven and earth, Horatio,

Than are dreamt of in your philosophy.

***Hamlet*, William Shakespeare**
(English playwright and poet, 1564–1616)

Theatres the world over claim to have resident ghosts and those in Australia are no exception. Australia's oldest surviving playhouse, the Theatre Royal in Hobart, for example, has 'Fred', a friendly, smiling phantom who is credited with having saved the little architectural gem he calls home by lowering the safety curtain when fire broke out backstage in 1984.

Even modern Sydney Opera House has its share of theatrical spirits, including 'Old Harry', who haunts the fly bridges above the stage, and 'Paddy', the meddlesome ghost of a derelict whose ashes are entombed in the building's foundations. Harry rattles ropes and pulleys and Paddy makes his presence known by taking noisy swipes at the instruments in the percussion section of the orchestra during performances.

Fascinating and frightening though Fred, Harry, Paddy and their counterparts in other theatres might be, the award for Australia's top theatrical ghost must go to Signor Federici — a true 'phantom of the opera' who manages to achieve maximum effect with minimum fuss and who has been alarming actors, singers, dancers, managers, technicians and patrons at Melbourne's Princess Theatre for more than 100 years.

Federici's story begins on a chilly autumn night in 1888 when the grand old Princess (which was then the grand *new* Princess) was packed to the rafters. Elegant ladies with bustles you could rest your beer on and gentlemen wearing tall silk hats lounged in the dress circle; merchants and their wives decked out in their Sunday best filled the stalls; and the 'gods' was crammed to overflowing with noisy housemaids in their smartest bonnets and apprentices in their shiniest boots. All had come to see and hear a new production of *Faust*, the most popular opera of the time, and, as the night sped on and the drama built to a climax, none doubted they had got their money's worth.

In the last act of the opera, while the deranged heroine Marguerite expires in a prison cell, the devil (Mephistopheles) claims the guilt-ridden hero (Faust) and drags him down into the fiery depths of hell. Melodramatic stuff indeed; and when elevated by Gounod's stirring music, guaranteed to move an impressionable audience like this one. There were sighs and gasps aplenty when this moment was reached and not a few of ladies in the audience suffered palpitations.

The hapless heroine was sung by Nellie Stewart, darling of the Australian stage for forty years, Faust by an English tenor, Clarence Leumane, and Mephistopheles by the celebrated basso Signor Federici. At the climax of the scene Federici threw his scarlet cloak around Mr Leumane, steam began to rise around their feet, coloured orange and red by flickering limelights, then the trapdoor on which they stood slowly descended, the two singers disappearing as if by magic beneath the stage.

A storm of applause and shouts of 'bravo' drowned the final chorus. The faces of the conductor and players in the pit glowed with unabashed pride, singers in the wings smiled with self-satisfaction and the promoters rubbed their hands together; a long and successful season seemed assured — but all was not well.

In the cellar beneath the stage the trapdoor came to a shuddering halt. Leumane stepped off and headed straight for the stairs to take his bows. Signor Federici seemed to hesitate then pitched forward into the arms of the steam machine operator, the victim of a massive heart attack.

The basso was carried upstairs unconscious (the pallor of death already on his face) and laid on a settee in the Green Room. Someone went for a doctor while others fussed over their colleague or stared in disbelief. His distraught wife arrived, closely followed by the doctor, who made a hasty examination then ordered that the patient be laid out, full length, on the carpet.

Two galvanic batteries were fetched and leads attached. The doctor frantically tore open Federici's costume and applied these to his barrel-like chest. Electric shocks sent spasms through the singer's limp body but failed to restart his heart.

It was, as the press reported, a scene both tragic and macabre. The red skullcap and false beard had been removed and the doublet ripped, but the cloak, the red silk tights, the sharp-pointed shoes and the rest of the satanic regalia the singer had worn on stage still clothed his now lifeless body. Stunned silence descended over the watchers, broken only by the sobbing of the widow and the moans of several swooning chorus girls.

'Federici' was the stage name of Frederick Baker, a thirty-eight-year-old Italian-born Englishman who enjoyed some success in London and New York before being signed up by J. C. Williamson Ltd for Australia. He had made his reputation in the comic operas of Gilbert and Sullivan, creating the role of the Pirate King in *The Pirates of Penzance* and making a speciality of the title role in *The Mikado*. When he arrived in Melbourne in June 1887 with his wife and two children he was already suffering from chronic heart disease. A certain hauteur in his manner and lack of abandon in his acting, remarked on by the press, may have been due to the precarious state of his health.

On the Monday following his death, Federici was buried in the Church of England section of Melbourne General Cemetery. The minister officiating collapsed at the grave side and had to be cared for by a doctor while the rest of the service was read by one of the mourners. The Princess Theatre remained closed that night as a mark of respect for its late star, but the *Faust* season recommenced the next night, a substitute singer taking the role of Mephistopheles.

When that performance ended and the cast assembled on stage for their curtain calls, some of them swore that Federici's ghost was with them — that two Mephistopheles in identical red costumes stepped forwards to take their bows that night. The substitute, Ernest St Clair, was not among those who claimed to have seen his ghostly counterpart but he did complain that invisible hands kept shoving him back into line every time he stepped up to the footlights. Such fanciful claims might be put down to overwrought emotions (or the desire for publicity) but it was not long before reports of Federici's ghost that could not be so easily dismissed began to emerge.

The impresario George Musgrove, a partner in the firm of J. C. Williamson Ltd and one of the most respected men in his profession, spotted a strange man sitting in the dress circle during a late night rehearsal and took one of his staff to task for allowing a visitor into the theatre. The employee was adamant that he had admitted no one. A search was made but by then the stranger had vanished. Musgrove never claimed it was Federici's ghost he had seen but others did and after that many claimed to have also seen it. Even more said that they had felt the ghost brush past them in the theatre's narrow corridors and any mishap or equipment failure that occurred was blamed on him. Never slow to capitalise on publicity, the theatre owners put it about that they were willing to pay 100 pounds to any member of the public prepared to spend a night alone in the theatre, but there is no record of anyone taking up their challenge or that they were really prepared to part with such a large sum.

Around 1900 a new fire alarm system was installed in the theatre. The resident fireman was required to punch a time clock every hour, which triggered a light on a switchboard at nearby Eastern Hill fire station. If the fireman failed to clock in the alarm was raised and a brigade despatched to the theatre. One night during a heat wave that happened. No message came through on the hour and within minutes a brigade set off, horses' hooves striking sparks off Nicholson Street and bells clanging frantically.

When they reached the theatre the station firemen could find no sign of a fire but did find their colleague — huddled in a corner, quaking with fear. When he recovered sufficiently the fireman explained that he had decided to open the sliding section of the theatre's roof to let the heat out and some fresh air in. As the panels opened, bright moonlight flooded the auditorium then the proscenium, revealing a figure standing, statue-like, on centre stage. It was, the shocked man said, a tall, well-built man with distinguished features, dressed in evening clothes with a long cloak and a top hat.

'A real toff 'e was, wiv' 'is hair parted in the middle an' all slicked down. But not a real man ... not flesh and blood. I could see *frough* 'im, I could,' the distressed fireman explained. 'Like looking frough dirty glass it was. An' 'is eyes? I shall never forget 'is *eyes* till the day I die. They glowed in the moonlight ... a bit like cat's eyes, but like no cat I ever seen!'

The most widely publicised sighting of Federici's ghost occurred in 1917. Betty Beddoes, the theatre's wardrobe mistress, was working round the clock to finish costumes for a production of Sheridan's *School for Scandal* which was about to open. At 2.30 in the morning another fireman knocked gently on her workroom door and stuck his head inside.

'Excuse me, Miss Beddoes,' he said, 'er ... would you like to see a ghost?' Curious but sceptical Betty said she would and followed the fireman up the side stairs to a landing beside the dress circle. The fireman pointed. Betty looked and could hardly believe her eyes. Federici was sitting in the middle of the second row of the dress circle, quite motionless and staring down at the empty stage. His face was in profile and although his features were indistinct Betty could see where his carefully groomed hair was greying. His immaculate white shirt front glowed in the half light and the studs that fastened it and the jewelled stick pin in the shape of a horseshoe securing his cravat sparkled like stars.

The wardrobe mistress and the fireman watched the spectre for a long time and it was still there when they returned to work. Fifty years later, Betty Beddoes could remember every detail of that experience and delighted in recounting what she called her 'only brush with the supernatural in nearly ninety years'.

Two years later another fireman, John Gange, spotted the ghost on two different occasions and Charlie White, chief machinist at the rival Her Majesty's Theatre, claimed that he had 'laid' the ghost in the 1930s, insisting that it was nothing more than a shaft of moonlight shining in through a small window above the dress circle, but earlier witnesses were not convinced and the sightings continued.

Irene Mitchell, proprietor of the St Martin's Theatre in South Yarra, reported seeing it while visiting the Princess one night and Kitty Carroll, wife of the impresario who took over the theatre after World War Two, claimed that she had come upon it suddenly in a side aisle during a rehearsal of the Ballet Rambert in 1947.

In 1966 June Bronhill, playing in the musical *Robert and Elizabeth*, observed a very peculiar light moving about at the back of the dress circle during a performance and told her colleagues: 'It was *very* strange, glowing in the centre and dull around the edge, with a sort of pinkish tinge to it. It moved slowly, backwards and forwards behind the last row of seats for three or four minutes then suddenly ... it was gone. At first I thought it was an usher with a torch searching for something or helping a member of the audience, but as I looked closer I swear there was *no figure* behind that light!'

Did she think she had seen Federici, the perennial star was asked. 'I'm not sure.' Bronhill laughed. 'Someone told me he died in a red costume, so maybe the pink colour is a faded version of that. I *really* don't know *what* I saw and certainly not *who* I saw, but I do know I saw it ... and I looked for it every night after that.'

By the early 1980s the Princess Theatre was closed and rapidly becoming derelict. Onto the scene came an enterprising couple, Elaine and David Marriner, who bought the old theatre and restored it to its former glory. The Victorian-berserk-style décor was refurbished inside and out, the wrought-iron-lace-capped cupolas repaired and the magnificent angel that crowns the central pediment given a new gold coating.

Mindful and proud of their theatre's famous phantom, the Marriners named their new foyer café 'Federici's' and Elaine was rewarded by a personal encounter with the ghost. While walking through the dress circle one day with a friend, the friend felt something brush past her, then Elaine turned to see a hinged seat that had been raised a moment before turned down. 'And they don't stay down unless someone is sitting on them!' Elaine told *Who* magazine in June 1996.

In the same magazine Rachael Beck, then starring in the musical *Beauty and the Beast*, recalled how a few months earlier she had spotted a stranger in the dress circle during a rehearsal who clapped silently after each number. Later she asked who he was but found no one else had seen him.

In 2004 Rob Guest told an ABC television crew how, during the run of *Les Misérables*, an usher had spotted him at the back of dress circle (in his nineteenth-century costume) and wondered why the show's star was there when he should have been backstage. As Guest explained, it was not him. He *was* backstage, waiting to make his entrance in the barricades scene.

And so the seemingly endless reports keep coming. And are they good for business? Of course they are. In the world of showbiz any publicity is good publicity and if stories of an elegant ghost add an extra ounce of romance and anticipation to a visit to the theatre, who would deny patrons that?

Before we leave Federici there is one interesting sidebar to this story that deserves to be mentioned. In 1972 film producers George Miller and Byron Kennedy (of *Mad Max* fame) shot a short documentary film about Federici. At 7.30 one morning the crew recreated Federici's funeral in Melbourne General Cemetery using nine actors. One of the crew took two still photographs of the scene while the cameras were rolling.

There is nothing out of the ordinary about the first shot but the second, taken just a few seconds later, shows a tenth figure standing among the 'mourners'.

That figure is not visible even in the out-takes of the moving film. It appears to be a tall, semi-transparent figure wearing a monk's black habit and cowl. Could it (opera-loving readers must now be wondering) be our old friend Federici in the disguise Mephistopheles wears in the church scene that preceded the last act of Faust?

3.
Ships of Doom

I looked upon the rotting sea
And drew my eyes away;
I looked upon the rotting deck
And there the dead men lay.

***The Rime of the Ancient Mariner*, Samuel Taylor Coleridge**

Most people have heard of the *Flying Dutchman*, that jinxed ship commanded by a tormented captain and condemned to sail the seven seas for eternity. The *Flying Dutchman* is said to pop up unexpectedly to this day and the lurid appearance of its blood-red sails and its phantom crew are said to be enough the scare the wits out of any seafarer. Equally well known is the *Mary Celeste*, the archetypical ghost ship, which was discovered sailing placidly along in the middle of the Atlantic Ocean in 1872 without a living soul aboard.

Much less well known are another pair of ghost ships, the wreckages of which lie just off the coast of Australia. Like the *Flying Dutchman* and the *Mary Celeste*, the first of these, the S.S. *Yongala*, appeared to a group of startled watchers, sailing the waters where it had met its doom a *decade* earlier. And the second? Well, the freighter *Alkimos* has a Greek name and its history is worthy of an Ancient Greek tragedy.

The Adelaide Steamship Company's 3700-tonne vessel *Yongala*, commanded by Captain William Knight, called at Mackay en route from Brisbane to Townsville. At 1.40 pm on 24 March 1911 it steamed out of Mackay harbour with forty-eight passengers, a crew of seventy-two and a thoroughbred racehorse named Moonshine on board. Minutes later the harbourmaster at Mackay received a report that a fierce tropical cyclone was bearing down on the coast, directly in the path of the *Yongala*. Without radio it was impossible to warn the ship.

At 6.30 that evening the *Yongala* was sighted battling mountainous seas and gale-force winds at the northern end of the Whitsunday Passage. Later that night or during the early hours of the next morning the *Yongala* sank with the loss of all on board.

Mailbags and wreckage (including the body of the racehorse) came ashore south of Townsville but the wreck was not located and identified until 1958, twenty-three kilometres east of Cape Bowling Green. In 1981 the *Yongala* was declared an historic wreck under the Commonwealth Shipwrecks Act. And so the official file closed on one of Queensland's worst shipping disasters, but long before then the ill-fated *Yongala* had entered the ghost lore of the sea.

In 1923 a party of local fishermen from Bowen were trying their luck in a small boat off tiny Holbourne Island (near the main shipping channel the *Yongala* would have used) when a large ship hove into view from the south. The fishermen had seen the ship before and they all recognised her — it was the *Yongala*, steaming steadily by in the bright sunshine twelve years *after* her sinking.

The steamship's sleek blue-and-red hull was now encrusted with millions of barnacles, the white-painted superstructure was rusted and draped with seaweed and the ship's once-proud funnel was twisted and stoved in. Of crew or passengers there was no sign. The bridge appeared unattended, but as the ship seemed to be bearing on a definite course, the watchers speculated that unseen hands must have been guiding it.

Wisps of smoke also trailed from the broken funnel, signalling the presence of phantom stokers toiling below decks.

The small boat bobbed dangerously in the swell caused by the larger vessel and the fishermen abandoned their fishing to watch the spectacle in amazement. Any doubts that it was a phantom ship they were observing were dispelled when the *Yongala* disappeared behind the southern tip of Holbourne Island then failed to reappear at the northern end. The fishermen raised anchor and sailed around the island, but could find no trace of any other vessel. The phantom ship had vanished as mysteriously as it had appeared.

Until the discovery of the wreck of the *Yongala* ninety kilometres further north in 1958, many believed the ghost ship had appeared to the fishermen to indicate that it lay off Holbourne Island. Today its location is beyond dispute; and if any of those fishermen were still around they would swear that their sighting of it was equally indisputable.

There are two interesting postscripts to this story. A Mrs Lowther, who lived in Mackay until 1969, recounted her own strange experience at the time of the wreck. She was booked to sail on the *Yongala* on its final voyage but at the last moment had a premonition of disaster and, although she was halfway out to the ship on a tender, refused to go aboard and demanded to be taken back to shore.

That same fateful night a family staying in a hotel at Eton, west of Mackay, also had a vision of the disaster. There was a kerosene lamp on the table in their room and suddenly one of the children pointed to it and said 'Look at the big ship!' The flame had blackened a portion of the glass creating the clear image of a large ship riding a mountainous sea. As the fascinated family watched, the picture faded and was replaced by another — the distressed face of a girl.

The next day news of the *Yongala*'s disappearance broke and, while the father was walking down a Mackay street he saw a poster for a touring theatrical company with the face of the young girl on it. He later learned that she had been among the unlucky passengers on the *Yongala*.

Prior to its sinking the S.S. *Yongala* had a long and proud history, but not so the ship that started life as the *George M. Shriver* and ended up as the *Alkimos*.

Any sailor will tell you some ships are jinxed, destined to an inglorious history of mishap and tragedy from the day they are launched. The *George M. Shriver* was such a ship. Built in the Kayser Shipyards in Baltimore in 1943, the 7300-tonne oil-powered freighter was one of the thousands, hastily assembled in American shipyards and called Liberty Ships, which ran the gauntlet of German U-boats in the Atlantic and carried much-needed supplies to worn-torn Britain.

The Kayser Shipyard prided itself on the speed with which it assembled hulls; ten days was the average. The *George M. Shriver* took *six weeks*. Its prefabricated sections didn't fit, equipment broke down and there were numerous accidents among the workers, who struggled to complete their task and rid their slipway of what was already being called a jinxed ship.

The *George M. Shriver*'s World War Two service record was largely undistinguished and it was in dry-dock more often than at sea. In 1943 the ship was sold to a Norwegian company and given a new name, *Viggo Hansteen*, but if it was hoped the change of name would bring a change of luck, that hope was never realised. In the years after the war when it passed into private hands, the ship was involved in all sorts of mishaps and needed constant repairs. In 1961, for example, it collided with another vessel in Bristol harbour and was out of service for eleven months while its bow and its superstructure were rebuilt. After that the Norwegian owners decided they had had enough of the costly ship and sold it to a Greek company who renamed it *Alkimos*, the name it carries to this day.

In March 1963 while en route from Jakarta to Bunbury in Western Australia the *Alkimos* struck a reef off lonely Beagle Island about 120 kilometres south of Geraldton. Local crayfishermen circled the stricken ship and reported its predicament to the maritime authorities in Perth but, inexplicably, the commander of the *Alkimos*, Captain Kassotakis, did not request assistance for three days. A tug was eventually sent to try to refloat the freighter but the captain decided the winches on *Alkimos* were more powerful. For two days the winches ground, the ship writhed and shuddered and moved not a centimetre. A salvage expert who was flown up from Perth flooded the stern of the vessel, raising the bow, and the *Alkimos* finally refloated.

Half-filled with seawater and in danger of sinking at any moment, the disabled ship was towed into Fremantle harbour but, if the captain thought his troubles were over, he was wrong. Repairs began immediately but, in May, a mysterious fire almost gutted the ship. The chief officer was fined 100 pounds for misleading an official inquiry into the grounding, writs for amounts totalling 25,000 pounds were served on the captain for failing to pay for earlier repairs and the ship was impounded. The owners paid up but cancelled plans to repair the battered and charred ship in Australia and engaged a local tug operator to tow it to Hong Kong.

The tug *Pacific Reserve* set out on 30 May with the *Alkimos* secured on a 600-metre towline. The sea was calm at first, but on the second day out an unforecast westerly gale whipped up mountainous seas. Fifty-seven kilometres north of Fremantle and twenty-four kilometres off the coast the towline snapped. The crew of the *Pacific Reserve* tried desperately to secure another line but the sea was too rough. The *Alkimos* began to drift helplessly towards the coast. For the second time in three months the ill-fated freighter ploughed into treacherous reefs and the boiling surf impaled it on Eglinton Rocks.

Several attempts to salvage the vessel were made but all ended in failure and the *Alkimos*'s jinx touched every one of them. Tugs were damaged, lines snapped, equipment failed, accidents and illness plagued the salvage crews and the crippled ship stayed wedged in rock and sand. Salvage attempts were abandoned when the winter storm season arrived, then in December a team from Manila arrived to try their luck, but the boilers on their tug, the *Pacific Star*, suddenly and unexpectedly showed signs of bursting and the owner of the company collapsed and died.

The help of a Roman Catholic priest was sought to dispel the jinx and it seemed for a time that his intervention had worked when a heavy swell lifted the crippled vessel and it miraculously floated. The *Pacific Star*, with its boilers repaired, took the *Alkimos* in tow but, a couple of kilometres from Eglinton Rocks, another vessel pulled alongside, arrested the tug's captain for unpaid debts in Manila and impounded his boat. Unable to give further aid to the *Alkimos*, the crew of the *Pacific Star* anchored the rusting freighter between the reefs off Eglinton Rocks but, true to form, it snapped its anchor chain in a heavy swell and drifted shorewards. The *Alkimos* finally came to rest about four kilometres south of Yanchep Beach, where it lies to this day, split apart, covered in barnacles, a home to fish and a very active, sinister ghost.

Two crew members from the *Pacific Star* were stationed on the *Alkimos* to guard the wreck. For the two men it promised to be a few weeks of light duties and relaxation at their company's expense while the legal wrangle over the *Pacific Star* was sorted out, but it turned out to be a living nightmare. After a day or two the men sensed they were not alone on the vessel. Tools left in one place would be found in another, a heavy hose they tried to move suddenly felt lighter as though another pair of hands was sharing the load. Strange smells of food cooking came wafting up from the disused galley and the sounds of pots and pans banging could be heard, but when they went to investigate the smells and sounds were gone. Finally, on a hot evening when the two men were on deck trying to catch the slight breeze that rose at sunset, they saw their fellow 'passenger': a giant of a man dressed in an oilskin coat and a sou'wester, who strode across the main deck then straight through a closed steel door.

The two Filipinos were replaced by other caretakers, all of whom had stories to tell about their encounters with the ghost. One pair claimed that it came charging towards them in a narrow gangway one day and that they felt the power of its baleful stare as it thrust them aside, knocking one unconscious. Another of the Filipino caretakers claimed that the ghost threw a kettle of boiling water at him.

No one had any idea who the ghost was and so, for want of a real one, he was given the name 'Henry'. A young American exchange student spent six days on board the *Alkimos* in July 1963 and recorded in his diary that he was stalked by terrifying footsteps the whole time and the door of the captain's cabin was slammed shut behind him by unseen hands. Sightseers and fishermen claimed to have seen Henry at night and in broad daylight moving about the decks of the ship in his oilskins and sou'wester. Local tour operators cashed in on the stories by organising ghost tours of the wreck; and a Dutch clairvoyant visited the ship. She spent half a day on board and reported the area beneath the foremast was 'a very evil place' where she believed someone had met a violent death.

A local identity, the late Jack Sue OAM, highly decorated by the US and Australian governments for his work with Z Force behind enemy lines during World War Two, was sceptical about the stories of the ghost and organised a party to spend a night aboard the *Alkimos*. The party comprised Jack, his wife and some local divers. Jack's scepticism was shattered when he heard footsteps, sneezing and coughing coming from a deserted section of the ship and one of the divers felt something brush past him. Moments later 'Henry' put in an appearance and, as the party watched in disbelief, the ghost strode purposefully across the deck and straight through a solid bulkhead.

The jinx on the *Alkimos* continued to reach out and touch the lives of all who came in contact with it. The pregnant wife of one caretaker slipped and fell on board and lost her baby. Two business partners, John Franetovich and Bob Hugal, bought the wreck for scrap but bad luck dogged them from that day: a tanker they owned collided with another ship and had to be scuttled; and Hugal, who until then had enjoyed perfect health, suddenly became seriously ill. Swimmers near the wreck were caught in currents that had not been there moments before, visitors to the wreck suffered injuries and motor vessels sailing near the wreck experienced engine troubles. Jack Sue became seriously ill soon after spending the night on the *Alkimos* and his wife died, tragically, in a car accident. One of the divers died suddenly and the fiancée of another was killed in a plane crash. The skull of a long-distance swimmer who had gone missing while trying to swim from the mainland to Rottnest Island was found in the hull of the *Alkimos* and identified by dental records.

One morning observers noticed smoke coming from the funnel of the hulk. It looked, they said, as though the old ship was preparing to sail away under its own power. Two newspaper reporters went on board to investigate and found that drums of tar stored in the ship had mysteriously ignited. This was just one of six unexplained fires on board.

Another party determined to lay the stories of the ghost set out to spend a weekend on the wreck. Their Land Rover broke down, the motor on their boat would not start and, when they finally put to sea, a single, huge wave that seemed to come from nowhere swamped their boat and soaked their expensive photographic equipment. Despite calm waters around the wreck the party's boat would not stay alongside. A line was tied securely to the *Alkimos* but mysteriously came undone. When they finally scrambled aboard in darkness none of their torches would work. They tried to set up camp on the solid bow area of the ship but their spirit stove blew up and, despite predictions of fine weather, heavy rain began to fall at around 2 am. As they huddled together in the rain, wishing they had never embarked on the expedition, they heard the incongruous sound of a dog yapping. The sound seemed to come from the stern of the ship but no dog could be seen. Despite being stressed out by their recent experiences, concern that an animal might be trapped or injured on the wreck set them searching, but each time they approached the source of the sound it retreated. No dog — or any other animal — was found, but the yapping continued through most of the night. (Strangely, the captain's logbook recorded the mysterious yapping of a dog in the engine room and other parts of the ship when the *Alkimos* was en route across the Atlantic during World War Two, a quarter of a century before.)

In an effort to find the truth, Jack Sue was persuaded to return to the ship with technicians from a television station, who set up cameras and recording equipment in the hope of catching 'Henry' on film or tape. Jack dossed down on an old steel bunk in one of the disused cabins, but was awakened during the night by strange noises. As his ears tuned to the sounds, he recognised heartrending groans (the sound one might expect from a person in agony), which seemed to be coming from the bunk next to his. Jack reached for his torch and snapped it on. The bright beam revealed that the bunk beside his was empty and when he shone the torch around the cabin there was nothing to be seen. Everything was in place and apparently undisturbed — but the terrible groans continued for several minutes more.

Jack admitted to being deeply affected by the sounds and not a little frightened on both his expeditions to the *Alkimos*; and as anyone who had the privilege of knowing Jack Sue would testify, he was not a man to imagine or exaggerate anything. And, after his wartime experiences, it took a *lot* to frighten him.

One of the technicians who went with Jack reported catching a brief glimpse of a strange, dark figure that disappeared into the salty night air. The recording equipment they used captured eerie rumbling sounds like distant drums or gunfire and a series of blood-curdling shrieks followed by coughing and heavy breathing, none of which was heard by the men on board.

Around 1991 in a heavy sea the bow of the *Alkimos* broke off and the twisted and torn wreck slowly began to disintegrate, disappearing from sight in recent years. To this day people stare out across the sea to where the two jagged halves of the hulk once towered above the water, recalling its grim history.

Fishermen circle round the spot swapping stories and divers occasionally explore what remains on the sea floor in the hope of catching a glimpse of 'Henry'. But the hundreds whose lives have been affected by the jinx know better and vow never again to go near the ill-fated *Alkimos*.

4.
Till Death Us Do Part

So, so, break off this last lamenting kiss
Which sucks two souls and vapours both away,
Turn thou ghost that way and let me turn this.

***The Expiration*, John Donne (English poet, 1572–1631)**

When personal relationships turn sour (or are soured by a third party), fertile ground for gruesome ghost stories is created. Here are two disturbing stories and one amusing story that prove that point. The first tells of a marital mismatch that resulted in both parties being condemned to haunt their former home. The second and third both tell of how obnoxious relatives wreaked havoc on other couples' relationships before and beyond the grave. All three stories have something else in common. They all originate from one of Australia's great wine-growing regions.

Commencing in the 1830s shiploads of Lutheran refugees from Germany migrated to South Australia and settled in the Barossa Valley. They modelled their settlements on the villages of their homeland, planted the hillsides with grapevines and established a wine-growing industry that flourishes to this day. They were dour and pious people with a culture, rooted in the Middle Ages, that acknowledged the powers of both light and darkness. For them, witches, goblins and sprites infested the hills of the Barossa region as surely as they did the Black Forest; and the devil incarnate was a real threat to their lives and souls. Ghost stories abound in this beautiful part of

Australia and perhaps the strangest and most compelling of all concerns a vineyard near the tiny village of Bethany.

One day in the middle of the nineteenth century a knife grinder came to the vineyard to ply his trade. The property belonged to a young spinster whose parents had died of dysentery when she was a child; since then she had been raised by Quakers. The young woman was endowed with property, good health and pleasant features. The only thing she lacked was a husband. The knife grinder was a personable young man more than content to pass the time of day with the young woman, especially when he learned that she was the sole owner of the neat cottage, all the livestock and the flourishing vineyard that stretched as far as the eye could see. A match was made; the spinster became a bride and the knife grinder became a prosperous farmer.

Soon after their marriage the husband discovered a side to his wife's character he had not reckoned on. Some nights she would disappear from their cottage without explanation. When she returned the next morning no amount of cajoling or threatening would make her reveal where she had been. At first he thought she was being unfaithful to him with another man in the village, but then strange rumours began to reach his ears. His wife, it was said, had rebelled against the strict teachings of the Quakers when still a child and had become a devotee of an elder who secretly practised the black arts. Now, rumour-mongers claimed, she regularly travelled in the company of twelve other women to the top of Kaiser Stuhl Mountain to perform witches' rites and dance naked under the full moon.

The husband by then had become a respected member of the local Lutheran Church and it was there he sought help. Before the whole congregation he declared that his wife had fallen into sin through idleness. The pastor advised him to keep his wife constantly pregnant to prevent her fornicating with the devil. The husband took the pastor's advice and bedded his wife as often as he could physically manage.

Two children were born within two years and after each birth the husband returned to his task with renewed vigour. Finally the wife protested and refused to submit to her husband's constant assaults. He then took a whip to her and beat her mercilessly until her back and buttocks were raw. In despair the young woman ran away from home — to Kaiser Stuhl Mountain.

When she returned a few days later she possessed strange new powers. She crept up on her husband while he was ploughing in the vineyard. She drew some cryptic designs in the dust and mumbled an evil incantation. When her husband saw her he reined in their white plough horse, but when he tried to remove his hands from the plough he found to his horror that he could not. His hands were as rigid as stone and his fingers were firmly locked to the handles of the plough. Try though he might he could not free himself.

The wife had placed a hex on her brutal husband and it seemed he was fated to spend the rest of his life endlessly ploughing the strips of ground between the vines in fair weather and foul. The wife cared for the horse, feeding it and stabling it at night. She brought food to her miserable husband and fed him with a spoon. She also took down his trousers each day so that he could relieve himself onto the soil. Unmoved by his tears and pleas she went about the business of running her own property once more and caring for the babies while he stumbled along behind that plough from dawn to sunset.

News of the husband's plight spread quickly through the village but no one dared come to his aid. It was not until he developed pneumonia and was close to death that his wife finally removed the hex and released him. He struggled to the cottage and crawled into bed where, just hours later, he died, cursing his wife. At her husband's funeral the young widow refused to don the traditional sackcloth and ashes or even wear black and while the rest of the congregation offered prayers for the soul of their departed *bruder* in their mother tongue, she was heard muttering incomprehensible words in a strange language.

After the funeral the widow was spat on and reviled by the old women of the village. Some said that, as well as her other sins, she conversed with her cat and grew herbs to concoct magic potions. She was blamed for every ill that befell the village. Finally, the elders of the church pronounced her to be 'the bride of the goat' (the Devil's bride) and ordered that she be tried by dunking. 'If she drowns her innocence will be proved,' they said, 'and if she does not, then God will have confirmed that she is a witch — and we shall burn her!'

The young woman was dragged, screaming, to the dam near the village and her head held under the water for more than an hour while the onlookers prayed fervently for her salvation. She struggled for a while but the strong hands of the self-righteous held her down. When they lifted her dripping body from the water, smeared with foul-smelling mud and weed, she was dead and two lifeless eyes stared accusingly at her judges.

Her innocence proven, the young woman was treated far better in death than she ever had been in life. The villagers gathered flowers from their gardens and the surrounding meadows to carpet the graveyard where her funeral was conducted. The pastor delivered an impassioned eulogy while his flock prayed and wept for her and themselves.

As the years passed the villagers tried to put the whole affair out of their minds but they could not, for the ghost of the young woman returned from the grave to take revenge on all those who had mistreated her. The story goes that the pastor, the church elders and each of the young woman's accusers were visited in turn by her vengeful ghost and that all met horrible deaths soon after.

True-believers claim that the ghosts of the young woman and her husband haunt the district to this day. Terrified witnesses have reported seeing the young woman dancing naked on her own grave when the moon is full, a wild and ferocious expression on her face, her body still streaked with mud and her hair matted with slimy russet-and-black weed.

The ghost of her unfortunate husband also appears in the old vineyard that was once theirs. He is seen at midnight and only when the moon is full: a ghastly spectral figure (little more than a skeleton), bowed and cowed, stumbling along behind a spectral plough drawn by a spectral horse.

When this story was made public some years ago the source quoted was a handwritten journal found by descendants of the young couple in a strongbox under the floorboards of the cottage. The vineyard is still there and so are the ghosts but the owners, not surprisingly, are reluctant to discuss this strange and dark episode in their family's history.

Another ghost whom locals can (and in this case will) put a name to haunts an abandoned farmhouse six kilometres from Greenock. Travus Klinkwort's story is well known in the district and very few feel sympathy for his ghost. A widower, Travus owned the farm many years ago and eked out a living growing vegetables, aided by his two daughters, Josia and Esther.

Travus was a cold and heartless man who worked his daughters hard and denied them any pleasures. He was also fanatical about protecting their virtue, but over-protection simply increased their curiosity and their desirability to the young men of the district.

Josia, the prettier of the two, invited a youth named Randall to meet her in the potato patch one night. Esther stood guard at a distance while Josia found out what she had been missing. Travus, suspecting deceit, grabbed his gun and ran to the potato patch. Esther screamed while Josia and Randall scrambled to their feet and tried to pull on their clothes. Travus fired both barrels of his gun.

The lovers were never seen again but it is said that Travus's potato crop the next year was the richest ever. Travus died a few years later and Esther went to her grave a crazed, crippled spinster, still hiding the secret of what had occurred that night.

As if condemned to endless punishment, Travus Klinkwort's ghost is trapped at the scene of his terrible crime. He has often been seen (and even photographed) standing in the doorway of the crumbling building. He wears a torn great coat, baggy trousers and a battered hat. He stares unrepentantly back at observers while they wonder if he still has his gun.

A real-estate agent (new to the district and knowing nothing about the house's history) ventured up the dusty driveway to the Klinkwort house one day a few years back, hoping to find a property to list and, to his dismay, discovered the answer to the question about Travus's gun.

Finding the house deserted and the front door ajar he ventured inside. At first he saw nothing but dust and cobwebs and heard nothing but the wind whistling through gaps in the roof. 'I was just doing a few calculations in my head about what it might cost to fix the place up when I heard a sound behind me,' the real-estate agent later explained. 'I thought I must have disturbed a dog because it sounded just like that deep growling sound dogs make in their throats. I turned around very warily and to my surprise found, not a dog, but an old man standing in the doorway of the front room. I was relieved that it was not a vicious dog, then terrified when the man raised an ancient shotgun and pointed the barrels at me.

'The old man's mouth was closed and the strange sound seemed to be coming from inside his body. The sound got louder and louder until it was a deafening roar and then I saw one crooked, bony finger begin to close around the trigger. I yelled "Don't shoot!" but it was too late. I saw the gun fire, but heard no explosion and in that instant the figure and the roaring sound vanished ... and so did I a split second later. Up until then I'd never believed in ghosts, but *real* guns go "bang" and *real* people don't vanish into thin air!'

The real-estate agent also recalled the awful stench of rotting potatoes in Travus Klinkwort's house ... and smells of an even worse kind figure in our final story of ruptured relationships from the Barossa Valley.

When a thirty-six-year-old shy spinster met a like-endowed bachelor in a café near Nuriootpa, love (or desperation) brought them together. Certain that the bride's tyrant of a mother, a widow herself, would not approve of the match, they eloped. Eventually the mother came round — or appeared to — and invited the couple to share her house, but it soon became apparent that all she really wanted was an unpaid labourer to tend her garden and a handmaid to wait on her. She also took every opportunity to drive a wedge between husband and wife, telling each the other was 'screwing around'.

The old woman had some other objectionable habits. She weighed 130 kilograms and consumed platefuls of spiced sausages, dill cucumber, pickled onions and sauerkraut at every meal. Dessert comprised dozens of cream cakes that she devoured with glee, cream dripping off her jowls. After these gargantuan feasts she would repair to the stone dunny in the yard, there to sit and fart thunderously for the best part of an hour.

The repugnant parent insisted the daughter sleep with her, so these times were the only opportunity the unhappily married couple had to be alone and to catch up on some of the pleasures they had missed out on in their youth. One night the husband and wife realised that Mother had been an unusually long time in the dunny and that they had not heard the results of her labours for some time. The daughter went down with a torch and found her mother slumped on the wooden seat, her voluminous red bloomers hanging around her bulbous ankles. The old woman's face was much the same colour as her bloomers and she was quite dead.

Daughter and son-in-law had a terrible time shifting her. Finally they dragged her out of the dunny and rolled her onto a sheet of corrugated iron. This they dragged under a stout tree branch then winched the body into a wheelbarrow with a block and tackle. When the doctor arrived the old woman was lying angelically composed on her bed and the couple were drooping with exhaustion.

During the old woman's wake the daughter excused herself from the guests and went down to the stone dunny. She was glad of a few minutes' rest and solitude but soon her relief turned to terror. The carefully bolted door was suddenly flung open then slammed, jamming securely. The daughter's screams attracted the guests, who came running to her aid. When they tried the door it swung open effortlessly.

Next time the daughter used the dunny the contents of the pan boiled up and splashed over her shoes, and when her husband was taking a pee the raised wooden seat was slammed down with dire consequences. That was too much for the couple; drastic remedies were required. They decided to demolish the old dunny and build a new one (with one of those newfangled flushing systems) attached to the house.

A team of workmen arrived a few days later to begin work. The husband thought the solid wooden door on the old dunny worth saving, so while the workman started removing the roof he went inside to unscrew it. The door slammed, trapping him. 'Let me out you bloody old bitch!' he screamed (or words to that effect). The workmen told him not to worry; they would pull him out through the roof. Then it happened. As the workmen watched, mouths agape, the large metal can rose from its spider-infested bed, hovered momentarily in mid-air then flipped upside down, pouring its stinking contents over the mortified husband's head.

'I copped nothing but *shit* from the old girl when she was alive, but I copped even more after she died,' the husband remembers. Rhubarb and flowers now grow where the haunted dunny once stood — and very well they grow too.

5.
Amityville, Australia

A ghost is the outward and visible sign of an inward fear

Ambrose Bierce (American short-story writer, 1842–1914)

In 1980 American husband and wife psychic investigators Ed and Lorraine Warren were invited to Melbourne to appear on a popular late-night television variety show. The Warrens had become world famous for their involvement with the Amityville Horror house (long before the book and film) and in the case that inspired the film *The Exorcist.*

On the night they appeared the program's host invited viewers to phone in if they had a supernatural problem the Warrens might be able to solve. A young couple called long distance from Sydney with a harrowing story. They told how they and their children moved into their Gladesville house three years before and had been tormented by strange and terrifying events ever since. They described how they all felt deeply oppressed by some strong, invisible force whenever they were inside the house. For the wife and children this produced mind-numbing lethargy and for the husband homicidal tendencies. 'I love my wife,' the distressed man explained, 'but I find myself reaching for a knife and barely able to control the urge to stab her ... it's as if some evil takes control of me and the only way I can escape is to leave the house.'

They told of loud, eerie laughter echoing through the house and robbing them of sleep night after night and strange symbols that looked as if they had been drawn in thick dust appearing on the interior walls. They also described how cadaverous faces suddenly appeared, reflected in windows and mirrors. The man described the faces of several ugly, evil-looking old men, two haggard crones and an attractive younger woman, all leering and scowling at them from within the glass. One particularly terrifying face that appeared on a mirror had an expression of such hatred and malevolence that it had turned their stomachs, they said. After three years of psychic persecution the family were at their wits' end and begged for assistance. The Warrens agreed to fly to Sydney the next day, visit the house and do what they could to help.

When they arrived (with a television crew in tow) they found a well-kept, split-level brick and tile house about forty years old and showing no outward signs of the tumult within. As soon as Lorraine Warren entered the house she said she could feel a great pressure bearing down on her, so strong that she could barely raise her arms. 'There is something very evil here,' she announced. When she lay on a bed in the room where she felt the force was centred, the television crew watched in amazement as her features changed and she seemed to visibly age before their eyes. Her back arched, her hands clenched and unclenched convulsively, her eyes blazed and they knew that she had entered into some kind of mental combat with whatever it was that held sway over the house.

In the meantime they were having problems of their own. A fully charged battery pack went dead after just a few minutes and their cameras failed, then worked, then failed again. When they tried to phone for back-up equipment they found the line was dead. Twenty minutes later it was working perfectly.

After five hours in the house the Warrens gathered the family and television crew together to deliver their verdict. The house, they were reported as saying, was cursed. An old woman had placed a hex on it and its occupants and it was now in an advanced state of demonic possession. If the family remained there any longer a psychic explosion would occur and their lives were at risk. 'Leave now,' was their advice.

The family fled, leaving most of their possessions behind. The press picked up the story and the headline 'FAMILY FLEE GHOST HOUSE' was splashed across the front pages of newspapers across the country. The orgy of publicity lasted (as such stories do) for about two days and has been followed by thirty years of silence. The Warrens went back to America and the family moved to another suburb. Someone else now lives in that house in Gladesville which, had the Warrens not intervened, might have become as famous as the one in Amityville.

Strange events that had a few years earlier overtaken a West Australian family, first in a small flat in Shoalwater then at Medina, also attracted national press and television coverage, keeping readers spellbound for several weeks.

The parents, Peter and Faye, and their three small children (the youngest a baby), were a very ordinary family in most ways: battlers trying hard to make ends meet. Peter had been out of work for some time then found a job in January 1973. Faye missed having him around all day and began to feel lonely and trapped in the little flat. Nerves were on edge and tempers probably flared, but the events that followed soon reunited the family, in fear for their sanity and their lives.

Some unseen force began throwing objects around inside the flat. The youngest member of the family seemed to be the main target. A large saucepan filled with boiling water and potatoes was hurled at the baby's cot moments after Faye had lifted her out. A loud bang in the bedroom brought both parents running just in time to see a heavy hairbrush rise from the dressing table and strike the baby's pillow just millimetres from her head. A mosquito net covering the cot was ripped down and tossed to the floor. When Peter was stepping out of the shower one day he watched, horrified, as a heavy pan came hurtling down the hallway, made a right-angle turn and crashed into the frame of the bathroom door, leaving a deep gouge.

When a reporter from the *Sunday Independent* visited the flat a heavy china mug crashed to the ground beside his feet and skidded across the floor. A kindly Methodist minister who called to offer comfort found himself the target of a flying drinking glass that shattered in mid-air just centimetres from his nose. Newspapers across the country picked up the story and the flat was besieged by well-meaning people offering help, the morbidly curious and many cranks including a couple who turned up in a black limousine saying they collected ghosts and were going to take the family's away in the boot of the limo!

After forty separate incidents in ten days both parents were at their wits' end. Two Catholic priests tried to exorcise the 'demon' without success. Faye collapsed and had to be hospitalised. The state Minister for Housing agreed to provide alternative accommodation for the family and they moved to another flat at Medina several kilometres away, but the mayhem started up there. Whatever it was that caused it had travelled with the family to their new home.

TVW7, who had covered the events at Shoalwater, sent a senior reporter, John Hudson, and a cameraman, Brian Dunne, to Medina to do a follow-up story. When they arrived they found the flat full of neighbours all testifying to having seen the latest freak events (cutlery, crockery and clothing flying about) but if the pair were at all sceptical about these accounts, what happened when they ushered the strangers out and set up their equipment removed any doubt from their minds.

They decided Faye was not in a fit state to stand up to a long interview so Hudson agreed to tell the story in front of the camera and lead the audience on a tour of the flat. At the moment the camera started to roll a tremendous crash was heard. Hudson and Dunne rushed to where the sound had come from and found a tangle of mops, brooms, buckets, tins of polish and bottles of cleaner strewn in a sticky mess on the laundry floor. There was no one in the laundry (which was freezing cold, although the rest of the flat was warm) and if anyone had left they would have had to pass the two men and would have been caught on camera.

Faye remained seated in the lounge during this commotion but was visibly upset by it. Before resuming filming the two men made a careful search of every room in the flat, ending in the kitchen which was separated from the lounge by a bench divider. The kitchen was scrupulously clean: everything in its place, cupboards and drawers firmly closed.

No sooner had they returned to the lounge than the whole kitchen seemed to explode. As Faye and the men watched in disbelief, the curtains billowed and all the cupboard doors flew open with a mighty *whoosh* and a deafening clatter. Drawers crashed to the floor spilling their contents, crockery and cooking utensils rattled, banged and broke and a steel colander fell from the wall hitting the floor with a crash like a cymbal. Next a container flew out of a cupboard and rose high in the air. It turned upside down and salt began to pour from it in a fine stream. The container moved slowly around the kitchen in loops, the trail of salt inscribing figure eights on the sink and floor until it was empty. Then it floated gently down and came to rest upright in an open drawer.

Hudson later described the destruction he had witnessed as the strangest and most frightening experience of his long career as a journalist.

He was reported as saying: 'Whatever it was that was causing all the banging, scattering and smashing must have had tremendous power. Things were happening all at once. It was like a storm roaring through the room — completely unstoppable. There was nothing we could do but watch in awe.'

Much has been written about this family's experiences and, as with the house at Gladesville, comparisons made with the events at Amityville in the United States. The mass of detailed corroborative evidence has been tested against theories about poltergeists (the term spiritualists use to describe mischievous disembodied spirits) and most investigators have concluded that some supernatural force, either external (a ghost) or internal (generated by one of the family) *was* involved. Some have suggested the mother, Faye, may, unknowingly, have been the source; that her mind, burdened by anxiety, could have developed the power to move objects or created a force that took on an existence of its own, which is, some theorists say, how all poltergeists come into being.

The family disappeared a few months later. I don't know whether the events stopped or the family decided to suffer them in silence. I hope it was the former. Thirty years have passed and Peter and Faye are probably grandparents now. Like the family in Gladesville, they may not wish to be remembered as the victims of one of Australia's most public ghost stories, but the supernatural is arbitrary in whom it chooses to involve and no blame should be laid on the victims. Wherever both families are I hope they have found peace and happiness.

6.
Australia's Most Famous Ghost

What beck'ning ghost, along the moonlight shade
Invites my step, and points to yonder glade?

Elegy to the Memory of an Unfortunate Lady,
Alexander Pope (English poet, 1688–1744)

It is a mystery why some ghost stories catch the public's imagination and survive while others, often more shocking and more credible, are forgotten. A perfect example is the story of Frederick Fisher, Australia's best-known ghost story, which has been the subject of hundreds of newspaper articles in many languages, books, poems, a film, a stage play, an opera and an annual folk festival held to this day in the town where his ghost appeared — to just one man on one occasion — 185 years ago.

Frederick Fisher was a ticket-of-leave man: that is, a well-behaved convict who had been released into the community to fend for himself. Fisher acquired thirty acres (twelve hectares) of land on the western side of Queen Street in Campbelltown and built himself a shack where the Campbelltown Post office now stands. Farmer Fisher prospered but preferred the company of his own kind — other ticket-of-leave men and itinerants who roamed the countryside. It was his custom to invite a few of these 'mates' over to celebrate his good fortune and most nights his table provided a bed for as many rum-soaked carousers as could fit on it or under it.

Fisher's best mate was his neighbour, another ticket-of-leave man named George Worrell, with whom it was said Fisher shared all his secrets. When Fisher got into debt and his arrest seemed imminent he signed over his property to George Worrell either to avoid having it seized or to give a false impression of his assets. Fisher did go to gaol and Worrell boasted how his own property increased by thirty acres: 'It's all mine now ... all that was Fred's ... he give it me afore he went t' prison,' he told everyone in Campbelltown but, when Fisher was released six months later and returned to reclaim his property, Worrell was, as we might say today, thoroughly pissed off; and the scene was set for a heinous crime.

On the night of 9 June 1826, Frederick Fisher disappeared. George Worrell resumed control of Fisher's farm and told anyone who asked that Fisher had decided on the spur of the moment to go home to search for his former family and had sailed from Sydney on the *Lady Saint Vincent* bound for London. Fisher had often spoken of his wish to return to England around the Campbelltown taverns so everyone accepted Worrell's story — for a time at least.

Suspicions began to arise, however, when Worrell tried to sell one of Fisher's horses and the prospective buyer demanded proof of ownership. Worrell produced an obviously forged receipt that he said he had been given when he bought the horse from Fisher. Worrell (not a very bright spark) also began to appear around town in Fisher's clothes and inquiries in Sydney revealed that the *Lady Saint Vincent* had not been in port on the day Worrell said his mate departed.

Foul play was suspected and the authorities began to take an interest in the case. *The Australian* of 23 September carried the following notice from the Colonial Secretary's Office:

SUPPOSED MURDER

WHEREAS FREDERICK FISHER BY THE ship Atlas, holding a Ticket of Leave, and lately residing at Campbell Town, has disappeared within these last three months — it is hereby notified that a reward of twenty pounds will be given for the discovery of the body of the said Frederick Fisher, or if he shall have quitted the Colony, a reward of five pounds will be given to any person or persons who shall produce proof of the same.

Circumstantial evidence weighed heavily against George Worrell. The police questioned him; he panicked and changed his story. He had, he now said, seen Fisher murdered but had taken no part in the crime. He named three of Fisher's other cronies as the murderers and they were arrested but soon released for lack of evidence. The absence of a body was hindering the police and Worrell might still have got away with the crime of murder had a local farmer named James Farley (or Hurley in some accounts) not gone for a stroll down Queen Street late one night.

About 400 metres from Fisher's shack Farley spotted a figure sitting on the top rail of a fence. As he drew closer he realised, to his horror, that it was Frederick Fisher — not the living, breathing man that he had seen and spoken to many times, but Fisher's ghost. The pale, 'fuzzy' form was bathed in an eerie white light and there was blood dripping from an open wound to its head. The ghost looked straight at James Farley, its dead eyes holding the living man's in a hypnotic stare. Next it let out a long and terrifying moan which Farley described as like the howl of a wounded beast. Then it raised its right arm, extended a quivering finger and pointed in the direction of the creek that flowed behind Fisher's farm.

Farley, by his own account, fainted at that point and when he came to the ghost was gone. Greatly distressed, Farley staggered home and collapsed again at his own front door. He was put to bed and there he lay in a state of shock for ten days. When his senses finally returned Farley sent for William Howe, the local police magistrate, and told him the story.

Knowing Farley to be a reliable man, Howe immediately ordered a search of the creek. Bloodstains were found on the fence where Farley said the ghost had appeared and a 'black tracker' led the police to a spot beside the creek where he said (after scraping the surface of the water with a gum leaf and tasting the scum for 'white man's fat') the body was buried. The police dug and, less than one metre down, came upon the body. It was identified by its height and build and by its clothing as the remains of Frederick Fisher. There was not enough of the face left to identify. The lower part was battered to a pulp, while the forehead and the back of the skull had been holed with some heavy, sharp implement like an axe or a pick. What the murderer had not finished decay had. The local doctor, Thomas Robinson, described how, when he lifted one of the corpse's hands, the flesh came away and stuck to his skin.

George Worrell was arrested for Fisher's murder and sent for trial by jury at the Supreme Court of New South Wales on 2 February 1827. The trial lasted just one day. Worrell was found guilty on a Friday and executed at the Dawes Point Battery the following Monday. On the morning of his execution Worrell confessed to a clergyman that he alone had killed, mutilated and buried Frederick Fisher.

There was no mention of a ghost at Worrell's trial or in the newspaper reports of the proceedings but, by then, the story of Fisher's ghost had entered the folklore of Campbelltown and would soon spread far and wide, across the colony and the world.

It was recorded in Martin's *History of the British Colonies*, published in London in 1835, and in Tegg's *Weekly*, a Sydney journal published in 1836. Tegg's version was attributed to a Mr Kerr, a tutor employed by Police Magistrate Howe. Charles Dickens included it in the journal he edited, *Household Words*, in 1853 and versions appeared in French and Italian.

From the beginning, distortions occurred — almost every aspect of the story was changed and romanticised so that truth became indistinguishable from fiction.

So, was there ever a ghost? Well, James Farley was a respected man, sober in his habits and God-fearing, according to his contemporaries. Sceptics suggest the ghost story was an invention by him to ensure Worrell got his just deserts but that would mean that Farley knew the whereabouts of the body, which implicates him.

A Campbelltown barber claimed responsibility for the ghost some years after these events, saying he had been tipped off about the location of the body and had felt an obligation to point the authorities in the right direction. The barber claimed he had donned a white cloak to create the appearance of a ghost and a black cloak to make it disappear, but others dismissed his claims as an insult to Farley's intelligence.

James Farley lived to a ripe old age and a little known sequel to the story tells of a friend named Chisholm asking Farley on his deathbed whether he really saw Fisher's ghost. Farley is reported to have raised himself up on one elbow, looked his friend straight in the eye and said: 'I'm a dying man, Mr Chisholm. I'll speak only the truth. I saw that ghost as plainly as I see you now.'

7.
The Mystery of the Min Min

But now the lonely diggers say,
That sometimes at the close of day,
They see a misty wraith flash by,
With the faint echo of a cry.
It may be true; perhaps they do.
I doubt it much; but what say you?

***The Demon Snow-shoes*, Barcroft Boake**
(Australian bush poet, 1866–1892)

There have been reports of 'ghost' lights appearing all over rural Australia since the beginning of white settlement (and probably before), but the 'Min Min' is the grand-daddy of all such lights — the one everybody's heard of and every bushman claims to have seen. 'Min Min' is an Aboriginal word (for what no one is absolutely sure) but the light was not named by Aborigines. According to legend, it was named after the Min Min Hotel on the old coach road between Winton and Boulia in central western Queensland, where it first appeared. There is, however, some doubt as to whether the light was named after the hotel or the hotel after the light.

'Hotel' is far too grand a title for the timber and corrugated iron shanty built about a century and a quarter ago to serve as a way-station for Cobb & Co. coaches. Most such places had bad reputations but the Min Min had the worst of any in the region. It reputedly served rot-gut liquor at exorbitant prices, doubled as a brothel and was the haunt of thieves, cattle rustlers and other assorted villains. Legend insists that many travellers and naïve jackaroos disappeared there and that the small cemetery behind the hotel was conveniently provided to bury the evidence. So infamous did the Min Min become that someone put a match to it one dark night in 1917 and it burned to the ground ... or so the legend goes.

Reliable records, if they existed, would probably disprove most of the above and reveal a much more mundane history for this miserable little hostelry. Records do show the name of the last proprietor — a Mrs Hasted — but there is no real evidence that she presided over a branch office of Sodom or Gomorrah. Records also show that there were devastating bushfires in the district in 1917 (Mrs Hasted's brother was badly burned fighting one), so it seems more likely that nature disposed of the Min Min Hotel than a human avenger.

The generally accepted story of the first sighting of the Min Min Light belongs to later the same year, when a hysterical stockman burst into Boulia police station at around midnight one night gabbling about being chased by a ghost. After the local constable calmed him down, the stockman told how he had been riding past the ruins of the Min Min Hotel at about 10 pm when a ball of light suddenly rose from the middle of the cemetery, hovered as if getting its bearings, then darted towards him. The stockman panicked, dug his boots in and galloped towards Boulia. Several times he looked over his shoulder and the light was still there. It followed him to the outskirts of the town then disappeared. (Sceptics who know the region may well wonder how the horse and rider managed to cover 100 kilometres in two hours — but let's not spoil a good story.)

In 1961, a reported sighting from 1912, predating the above (and the destruction of the hotel) by five years came to light. Henry Lamond, one-time manager of Warenda station on whose land the hotel stood, claimed that he had seen the light in the winter of that year. Its appearance had at first alarmed him, but when he realised his horse was quite unperturbed by it Lamond decided his own fear was unwarranted.

There have been so many reported sightings since then that it would take most of this book to recount them all. Station owners and managers, policemen, ministers of religion, school teachers, shopkeepers and no-nonsense bushman have seen the Min Min Light — most of them intelligent and honest people whose credibility is unquestionable. All describe it as a round or oval ball of light glowing so it illuminates its surroundings, travelling between one and two metres above the ground either in a straight or undulating line. Sometimes it appears to stop and hover; sometimes it bobs about and usually dives towards the earth as it disappears.

There are almost as many theories about its origin as there are sightings. The supernatural school claim that such lights are spirits of the dead: ghosts in inhuman form. Sceptics with some knowledge of the bush suggest that the lights may emanate from fluorescent fungi (such are quite common) or from birds who have brushed their wings against the fungi. Fireflies are also cited as are swarms of moths, their wings reflecting moonlight. None of these is likely. Personally, I've never seen a mobile mushroom and the only common bush birds that hover (eagles and hawks) are not nocturnal. A swarm of moths would not be visible at any great distance. And fireflies? Well, there's no doubting their ability to emit light but as one bushman put it: 'You'd need about ten million of the little buggers, standing shoulder to shoulder, to produce a light *that* bright.'

Traditional science groups the Min Min and other similar Australian lights along with European and North American

Will-o'-the-wisps and Jack-o'-lanterns into the category *ignis fatuus* which simply means 'foolish fire' and attributes them to marsh gas (methane) or phosphoretted hydrogen, the gas that escapes from decaying animal matter. As the Min Min Light was said to originate in a cemetery the presence of the latter was possible once, but its domain is far too arid to produce marsh gas. Subterranean gas escaping through fissures or drill holes is more likely and records show the Min Min Hotel was built beside a water bore, but all theories involving gas rely on the premise that the gas somehow self-ignites, which is impossible.

That very rare natural phenomenon, 'ball' lightning, which travels across the landscape at high speed, has also been suggested as an explanation but, like all lightning, it dissipates quickly and never remains visible for as long as these lights are claimed to.

Some very distinguished scientists have studied the phenomenon, arriving in Boulia in a flurry of publicity and making claims of infallible theories, but most have not even managed to see the light let alone explain it. The famous novelist H. G. Wells (*The Time Machine* and *The War of the Worlds*) took an interest in it while visiting Australia, but even his fertile mind could not come up with an explanation. Probably the first plausible explanation came in the 1990s from Colin Croft of Charleville, who discovered that he could see a grass fire at night that was at least eighty kilometres away and below the horizon. Croft claimed that what he saw was a reflection of the fire on a layer of dense air. This tied in with an old theory that said the light only appeared when a lighted lamp was placed in a window at Lucknow, the nearest station homestead to the Min Min Hotel.

An even more cogent and convincing argument for this theory came in 2003 when a University of Queensland neuroscientist, Professor Jack Pettigrew, published a paper in the journal of the Australian Association of Optometrists. Professor Pettigrew, who knows his way around Western Queensland and has seen the light, concluded that what he saw was an inverted mirage — the image of a distant bright light carried on a cold, dense layer of air — and that the terrain of the Channel Country makes the area ideal for this phenomenon to occur. Professor Pettigrew also cited another famous case where this phenomenon had produced an image of the Irish coast 'floating' above the calm Atlantic and observed by the crew of a ship more than 1000 kilometres from land.

While scientists puzzle and country folk speculate, the sightings continue. Tourists report the light following their cars and campers put the kettle on in readiness to offer a cuppa to the rider of the motorcycle they think is approaching. A group of station hands on horseback claimed they cornered the light one night a few years back and played phantom polo with it!

The Min Min has also proved good for business in Boulia in recent times. The town now hosts the 'Min Min Light Big Sky Festival' every September and during the tourist season visitors can view the 'Min Min Encounter', a high-tech display in the town's centre.

If the reader feels inclined to go Min Min Light–watching, I suggest you take the Kennedy Development Road from Boulia. Cross the Hamilton River, then just west of the boundary between Warenda and Lucknow is the site of the old Min Min Hotel. The old coach road is about 500 metres north of the present thoroughfare; and there's not much left of the ruins, just a scattering of broken glass and some rusting rails around the cemetery. It's not the most pleasant place to be after dark, but your perseverance just might be rewarded with a glimpse of the legendary light.

Something most Australian 'ghost' lights, including the Min Min, have in common is that they give rise to curiosity rather than fear. By and large, those who witness their transit across the landscape feel privileged rather than petrified — but not all. A light which appears in the Burnett region of Queensland has been dubbed 'The Blairmore Ghost' because local legend has it that this mysterious light has enshrined the tormented spirits of a succession of murder victims.

The Blairmore Ghost first appeared on Christmas Eve about ninety years ago, the day after a mailman met his death on Blairmore station. When the unfortunate mailman was buried, rigor mortis had not set in and the local Aborigines believed he was still alive and would return as a *debil debil*. It seemed their prophesy came true when the mysterious light appeared. Many people have seen the light since including Jim Matheson JP, former Government Stock Inspector and Brisbane City Councillor, who published details of his encounter with the Blairmore Ghost in 1957. It makes spine-chilling reading.

Matheson was driving along the boundary road of Blairmore station on a humid, stormy night when his car became bogged in a wide patch of mud. Unable to free the vehicle, Matheson settled down in the back seat to sleep until morning. Minutes later another car came along the road travelling fast and, before Matheson could give warning, ploughed into the mud up to its axles. The second car contained a commercial traveller and his wife. The three chatted for a while then returned to their cars to sleep.

Matheson was just dozing off when he heard distant pitiful cries of 'Help! Help! Help!' He scrambled out of his car and cupped his hands behind his ears. The cries seemed to be coming from the middle of a nearby paddock. Matheson hastily pulled on his boots and set off in the direction of the cries, which were still coming at brief intervals. Before he had gone ten paces Matheson recalls there was 'half a stone' of sticky black mud clinging to each of his boots, but he struggled on. Then he saw the flickering light. It wasn't any shape you could put a name to: it swirled and changed, swelled and shrank, like a formless, luminous blob of jelly.

When Matheson moved towards the light it began to dribble towards him like a fat, phosphorescent slug. The cries for help grew louder and seemed, Matheson recalled with lingering horror, to be all around him and *inside* him, entering through the pores of his skin.

'I was absolutely terrified,' Matheson admitted. 'I couldn't move ... my legs seemed to be frozen, but worse, I couldn't *think* straight. All I knew for certain was that I was in the grip of some deadly struggle and that something no longer alive and just feet away was robbing me of my own life force!'

Then mercifully, just as Matheson felt himself being sucked — body and soul — *into* the light another sound intruded on what was left of his consciousness: the sound of the commercial traveller's wife screaming. The instinctive urge to go to the aid of woman in distress made Matheson turn and run back to the cars. He believed his life was saved at that moment.

The three travellers quickly gathered some sticks, paper and petrol and started a fire, then huddled in its cheerful light all night, listening to the distant, terrifying and increasingly desperate cries of 'Help! Help!' drifting towards them on the wind. As dawn approached the sound faded and finally could be heard no more.

Jim Matheson searched the paddock in daylight but could find nothing remarkable. Later he related his experience to a local cattleman. 'You were lucky,' the cattleman said. 'A stockman once heard the ghost crying for help and went to it. He was dead when they found him and his face was not a pretty sight. Some people believe his spirit took the original ghost's place and that the stockman has been trying to catch another victim ever since. It could have been *you* out there tonight, Jim, crying for help.'

8.
The Ghosts in the Glen

Over a pitfall, the moon dew is thawing,
And with never a body two shadows stand sawing,
The wraiths of two sawyers (step under and under),
Who did a foul murder, and were blackened by thunder.
Whenever the storm-wind comes driven and driving,
Through the blood-spattered timber you may see the saw striving,
You may see the saw heaving and falling and heaving,
Whenever the sea-creek is chafing and grieving.

***Ghost Glen*, Henry Kendall (Australian poet, 1839-1882)**

Australian red cedar was often referred to as red gold in the nineteenth century. Its durability, fine grain and lustrous colour made it a favoured timber for panelling and furniture-making. Cedar cutters were the first white men to arrive in many areas and fortunes were made from its export while irreparable damage was done to the continent's native forests.

Cedar cutters were a rough, tough breed and there were none rougher or tougher than those who pillaged the dense forests of the south coast of New South Wales. Since 1802 it had been necessary to obtain the governor's permission to log cedar, but most of the cutters who established a base at what is now Kiama around 1815 were convicts holding tickets-of-leave, who did not give a toss for the governor or his laws. There is no better illustration of the types of men that roamed this wild country in those far-off days than the story of the

Ghosts in the Glen — one of Australia's most durable ghost stories. It's survived almost 200 years; a gruesome real-life melodrama in which the characters are divided into good and evil, innocent and corrupt, with biblical clarity.

The story begins one wet and windy night in the mid-1820s when a young Englishman accompanied by a large, brindled sheepdog entered the inn at the tiny settlement of Kiama. The young man had just arrived from England and was on his way to take up work on Alexander Berry's property, Coolangatta, at the mouth of the Shoalhaven River. The bar room in the inn was filled with rough characters in various stages of drunkenness. A wiser man might have kept his own counsel and his money concealed but the naïve young Englishman offered to shout drinks for the whole company and displayed a purse fat with gold sovereigns. As the night wore on the young man became drunk and only two ruffians remained to keep him company. Eventually he rose unsteadily to his feet, whistled his dog and announced he had to be on his way.

'Now listen, chum,' said one of his devious companions, 'me an' me mate 'ere, we wouldn't let ya go off on your own on such a night ... there's some real *bad* lots in these parts. Ya never know what might 'appen to ya! As you're goin' south an' we're goin' south, we'll keep ya company an' show ya tha way.'

'Very kind of you, sirs,' (or some such polite words) replied the innocent and the three men and the brindled dog disappeared into the night. The young man never turned up at Alexander Berry's and his two erstwhile companions disappeared without trace. Months passed and the fate of all three might never have been known had one of Berry's assigned convict servants not become lost in the wild country around the present-day township of Gerringong. Search parties found the servant after four or five days, cold, wet and hungry. Despite his ordeal the man appeared to be in full control of his faculties and had a incredible story to tell.

In dense fog he had wandered from the track that ran south between Kiama and his master's property and had become hopelessly lost in the drearily uniform grey bush. Without food he soon tired; and as night closed in and rain began to fall he built a rough shelter out of branches and curled up on the cold ground to sleep.

The second day was spent fruitlessly searching for the track and another night, even wetter than the first, huddled in the rude shelter. Sleep was long in coming and short lived. A distinct tap on the man's shoulder woke him. He raised his head to find a bloodstained hand and forearm, raggedly severed at the elbow, on the ground beside his head and from the distance he could hear the faint sound of a saw cutting timber. The ghastly limb twitched just centimetres from his nose and the fingers stretched and clenched as if trying to reach for him, but the man was so terrified he could not move a muscle. After a few seconds the gruesome sight vanished and the sound ceased.

The man lay shivering with fear and cold through the rest of that long night, finally dropping back to sleep just an hour before dawn. But again, he was rudely awakened, this time by an agonising human scream that echoed through the bush. The sound of the sawing returned, too. He peered in the direction the sound was coming from and caught a glimpse of two tall figures sawing a log over a sawpit that he was sure had not been there in daylight. One figure was down inside the pit with only his head and shoulders visible and the other stood on the rim. Their clothes appeared dry but their faces were wet with perspiration and their hair and eyes clogged with sawdust. Their lips were drawn back in painful grimaces as they strained at their work and the long two-man cross-cut saw flew up and down as it bit into the timber, its rasp ringing loudly now through the bush.

Morning came but not the sun. The wind picked up to gale force and icy rain pelted down. Terror, tiredness and hunger reduced the lost man to a state where he could only crawl about fifty metres to a large hollow log and ease himself inside (where it was blessedly dry) before collapsing into a deep but troubled sleep.

Night returned and with it came a violent electrical storm. One deafening crash of thunder woke the man. He rolled over inside the log and looked towards the open end. There, to his horror, he saw a head, blood-spattered and with terrifying, blood-shot eyes, staring back at him. In the distance he could see a dark shape lying on the ground with what looked like a dog beside it, but the horrific head held his attention. Its battered, blackened mouth was moving as if speaking, but its words were lost in the fury of the storm.

To the terrified man's relief the head vanished after a few seconds and he was able to climb out of the log. Shielding his eyes from the rain he stepped closer to the dark shape on the ground and realised it was the body of a man to whose neck the ghastly head was now attached. Beside the body cowered a brindled sheepdog, nudging the lifeless hand that lay nearest to it and licking the bloodied face.

A flash of lightning and a peal of thunder signalled the return of the spectral sawyers, now both at ground level and engaged in conversation. Between gusts of wind the man caught a few foul curses and a few callous words.

'He's still got about fifty sovereigns on 'im ... we'll cut 'im up and burn the bastard.'

'I'll 'ave 'is boots.'

'I'll 'ave 'is breeches.'

'We'll have to slit that bloody cur's throat, too. It ain't no good to no one an' I'm sick of its bloody whining!'

Both figures then strolled towards the body, each drawing vicious-looking knives from their belts. Another scream, so loud and terrifying that the lost man had to put his hands over his ears, then resounded through the bush, followed by a lightning flash close by that lit the area like the noon-day sun and temporarily blinded him. Deafening thunder shook the air. The poor man closed his eyes and fell to his knees, overwhelmed by the natural and unnatural forces that were assailing him. When silence returned, broken only by the pattering of rain and the rustle of the wind as the storm receded, he slowly opened his eyes. The body was gone. So was the dog. The vision of the sawyers and their sawpit had vanished. The lost man was quite alone, surrounded by dark, dripping bush.

If someone came forwards with a story like that today we would probably say it was caused by delirium, but the search party who found the man wandering several kilometres from the scene of his ordeal believed him. He was taken back to Berry's property and cared for until his strength returned, then he guided a party back to the gully he described as a 'glen', where they found the remains of the shelter and the hollow log he had spoken of. Nearby they found signs of an old campfire and in it the broken and partially burned bones of a man with a shattered skull. Under a bush a few metres away was the skeleton of a large dog, the vertebrae of its neck savagely scored with a knife.

The story of these ghostly visions quickly entered the folklore of the district, told and retold around cosy firesides and memorialised in the poem quoted at the beginning of this chapter. Farmers in the Gerringong region for decades after swore that the lost man was not the only one who saw the spectral sawyers and their human and canine victims. Whenever a violent storm coursed through the coastal ranges settlers trapped in it reported catching glimpses of the ghoulish tableau and hearing the scrape of that ghostly saw carried on the wind.

The story of the spectral sawyers also became a popular moral tale, told to generations of children in the region as warning against trusting strangers and in a few cases to curb the antics of mischievous offspring. Many a child went to bed with the remonstration: 'If you're not good, them ghostly sawyers'll cut you up into little bits!'; and many a child's dreams were plagued with visions of severed heads, severed hands and saw blades spattered with blood.

There is a curious codicil that gives credibility to this tale. About ten years after the murder an Irish timber splitter named Pat McAnnally shared a hut with another man called Jem Hicks at Bulli, forty kilometres up the coast. Hicks was a morose man with a reputation for violence. One stormy night when the two sat alone in their hut McAnnally commented to his mate that it was a good night for a ghost story and mentioned the ghosts in the glen at Gerringong. The reaction from his companion stunned the little Irishman. The much larger Hicks turned on him: 'You hold your gab about that there Gerry-gong business ... d'ya hear?' Hicks shouted above the wind.

The two men sat without speaking for several minutes. A gust of wind blew open the door and howled through the hut. Jem Hicks jumped to his feet, put his hands to his temples and screamed: 'Curse the money! Curse the dog! Will a fella never get no peace?'

The little Irishman made an obvious deduction. 'You black-hearted hound! You're one o' them moiderin' bastards, ain't ya?'

Jem Hicks scowled. He grabbed a piece of firewood and hurled it at McAnnally, then ran out into the night. Next day McAnnally reported his suspicion to the police, but Jem Hicks was never seen again.

180 years on there's not much other evidence to test the veracity of this famous and compelling story. The modern holiday village of Gerringong and the surrounding farmlands bear no resemblance to the wild settings of the story, however, there is a fact most chroniclers seem to have overlooked. On a historic property called Alne Bank near Gerringong there is a gully that has always been called (though no one remembers why) 'the glen'. Perhaps if, with the permission of the owners of Alne Bank of course, you were to camp there on a stormy night you might yet hear that spectral saw and catch a glimpse of those ghastly 'Ghosts in the Glen'.

9.
The Spectral Bridegroom

> *I know that ghosts have wandered on earth, so be*
> *with me always — take any form — drive me mad!*
> *Only do not leave me in this abyss, where I cannot find you!*
> ***Wuthering Heights*, Emily Brontë (English novelist, 1818–1848)**

This disturbing story has found a permanent place in the folklore of the flat, dusty Wimmera region of north-western Victoria where the events took place on a hot Saturday afternoon in the not-too-distant past. The story begins at an old weather-beaten wooden church on the outskirts of a small town where most of the district's residents had gathered to witness a marriage.

Both bride and groom were well-known locals — she the daughter of a local businessman, he a wheat farmer with a modest spread about twenty kilometres out of town. The stark little church had been brightened up with bunches of wildflowers and sheaths of pungent eucalyptus leaves, the minister was robed up, the elderly organist was seated at her harmonium ready to strike up 'The Bridal March' and the congregation sat on hard wooden pews, excitedly chattering, swapping compliments on one another's outfits and awaiting the arrival of the wedding party.

Showing the practical spirit that characterises people who live in such remote and harsh regions, the bride drove herself to the church in her own little Morris car with her Dad sitting beside her and her Mum and her sister (the only bridesmaid) in the back. They arrived punctually at the wicket gate of the church to be greeted by a worried-looking best man and no sign of the groom. 'Sorry, love, he isn't here yet,' the best man explained. 'He was gonna meet me here half an hour ago, but he hasn't showed up yet … reckon he's had a spot o' car trouble, eh? I'm sure he'll be along in a minute.'

That minute passed and so did about thirty more and there was still no sign of the missing bridegroom. The congregation got restless, the bride got worried, her father got angry and her mother, fearing scandal, shook her head and sniffled into her handkerchief. Finally, half an hour after the service was to have begun, the bridegroom appeared, not driving his car as expected, but on foot and running up the street towards the church. As he drew closer the waiting group saw that his suit was torn and covered in red dirt and a makeshift bandage wound around his head was clotted with dried blood.

'What happened to you?' the bride asked, relieved that her intended had turned up but concerned about the state he was in.

'I had a bit of an accident on the road, love. This bloody big roo bounded across in front of me. I couldn't miss it and I lost control of the car. It's smashed up, but I'm OK. I had to wait till someone came along so I could hitch a ride,' the groom explained. 'Anyhow I'm here now, so let's get on with the wedding, eh?' he said, giving his future wife a squeeze and adding in a whisper: 'Cor, you look bonzer, love!'

The minister was concerned about the injury to the young man's head and suggested the local doctor should take a look at it before the ceremony.

'I'm all right, Reverend,' the bridegroom insisted. 'I've held everybody up too long now … I'll get the doc to have a look at me later. Let's get on with it, eh?'

And so the ceremony took place. The bride and groom exchanged their vows, the groom placed a gold ring on the bride's finger, the men in the church mused over what 'a lucky bastard' the groom was and how soon they could get at the beer, the women had a jolly good cry and the minister finally pronounced the couple 'man and wife'.

A spread of ham sandwiches, fruit cake, hot tea and cold beer had been arranged at the local pub and most of the thirsty guests trekked off to get stuck into that, but as the newlyweds were leaving the church, the groom asked his new wife if she would drive him out to pick up his damaged car before they went to the wedding breakfast.

'I'm a bit worried someone might pinch me tools out of the back,' he said. 'I'd be able to enjoy meself better if I knew the car was safe.'

'*Men!*' muttered the bride, but at that moment if her new husband had asked her to walk over hot coals she would have agreed just to please to him.

Excuses and promises to return within the hour were made and the bride's father promised to save his new 'son' some beer. The best man, the bridesmaid and three of the groom's closest mates were recruited to go with the couple in case help was needed to tow the car into town.

Reluctantly, the bride hitched up her wedding dress and climbed into the driver's seat of her own little car. While she removed her veil and tossed it onto the rear seat, the groom slid in beside her, wincing with pain as he ducked his head down and again when he settled on the passenger seat.

'You sure you're all right?' the bride asked.

'I'm fine, love. You know me ... me head's like a block o' wood. We'll pick up the car then go to the pub for a while and *then ...*' The groom put his hand on his bride's knee, but she pushed it away.

'One thing at a time, eh?' she remonstrated. 'As soon as we get back here, the doctor needs to take a look at that bang on your head. I don't want you passing out on me tonight, do I?' The couple laughed as the bride drove off. The rest of the group followed in two cars and years later one of the men testified to the mystifying and terrifying events that followed.

'What I'm gonna tell you will be hard to believe, I know,' he explained, 'but as God is my witness, it's the truth. And it was not just me but *all* of us who went off after the wedding that day that saw what happened.

'All the roads were unsealed then and the dust was fierce. I was riding in the second car with the best man and the bride's sister was in the back. There was another car following us with the other two blokes in it. We couldn't see the bride's little Morris — she was a few minutes ahead of us — but we knew where she was heading and we could see the cloud of dust she was making. We drove on for miles and then, all of a sudden, the weird stuff started to happen.

'Now, I can tell you 'cause I've lived in the Wimmera all me life, bends are as rare as hen's teeth on the roads out there. You can drive 100 miles in some places without turning the steering wheel, but, anyhow, we came to what must have been the only bend in that road — a right-angle turn where the boundaries of two properties met. The country all around was covered in thick, stunted scrub and we couldn't see what was around the bend as we came up to it.

'The best man was just saying to me that maybe this was where the accident had happened when he stopped in mid-sentence and shouted out "Bloody hell!" As we came around the bend we saw the little Morris stalled in the middle of the road. The best man jammed his foot on the brakes and we just managed to stop in time — just a yard from the other car. But that was not what gave us the biggest shock. The bride was out of her car, standing beside it screaming her head off!'

A more incongruous sight could hardly be imagined than a bride dressed in her long white wedding gown, standing quite alone in the middle of a dusty road in a dusty landscape miles from anywhere; especially one who had been deliriously happy just half an hour before and who was now wringing her hands in a frenzy and screaming with horror and dismay.

Our witness continued his account. 'We all piled out and ran to her. Her sister grabbed the bride's arms and held her. "What is it? Tell me," she begged. But, by then, me and the best man knew what was wrong. Both of us had glanced into the little car and it was *empty*.

'"He's gone!" wailed the bride. "He was sitting next to me one minute and we were talking. We were going along fine ... he said we were nearly there ... then suddenly, he just *vanished*. He's *gone*!" she repeated, then collapsed, sobbing hysterically into her sister's arms.

'"He can't be gorn," the best man whispered to me. "He *is*," I said. "He must've wandered orf," said the best man, loud enough for the bride to hear. "He didn't *wander off* ... how *could* he?" she screamed. "We were going twenty miles an hour!"

'At that moment the third car that had been following pulled up and the best man explained what had happened. He and the two from the third car insisted on making a search of the scrub on both sides of the road. I didn't bother. I believed the bride. You don't make up stories like *that*. The three returned after about ten minutes and the best man whispered to me "He's gorn all right ... there's no one out there." I didn't bother to answer and a terrible explanation for what had happened began to dawn on me. "We need to go to crash site," I said to the other men.

'I suggested the bridesmaid bundle her sister into our car and wait for us, while the rest of us drove on to find where the groom had crashed his car. The man who had insisted on the useless search tried to reassure the bride by saying that her new husband had probably wandered up to crash site ahead of them and that we would bring him back. The bride simply stared at him, her eyes like tear-stained saucers. It broke me up, I can tell you. I turned away.

'We got into the third car and drove carefully around the other two. "It's bloody weird," said the best man. "He couldn't just disappear out of a moving car ... could he?" I kept silent while the others tossed the idea about. I believed I knew the explanation and it scared the hell out of me. Half a mile further up the road, the best man who was sitting next to me, shouted: "There! Up ahead! There's his car ... Oh *Jesus*!"

'I parked a few yards from the groom's car. Lying on the opposite side of the road was the kangaroo he had hit — a large male, unmarked but dead, with a trickle of blood oozing out of its nose. We ran up to the wreck. The sand all around was soaked with petrol and oil. The car was overturned and lying with its wheels sticking up in the air. The roof of the car was crushed and almost flattened. I dropped to my knees at the passenger side window, knowing full well what I would see through the jagged, broken glass. I prayed I would be wrong, but I wasn't. The bridegroom was still in his car where he had been trapped since the crash, his lifeless body wedged between the dashboard and roof. His head had gone through the windscreen and a swarm of flies buzzed around a terrible, bloody injury to his forehead.'

The witness's account ends at that point and I am tempted to end the retelling of this story on the same dramatic note, but I can hear a chorus of complaint from readers wanting to know how these strange events played out and what happened to the unfortunate bride. Well, the local constable filed an accident report which tactfully avoided mentioning the time of death and a coroner's inquest concluded that the bridegroom had met his death by misadventure. The local newspaper (showing more consideration than the press generally do today) reported the 'tragic death of a local man on his wedding day' very briefly and left the details to the imagination of its readers. Most of those readers had been present at the wedding and they knew what they had seen, as did those of the party who had gone out to the wreck. The bridegroom's signature was written boldly in the church registry and the ring he had given his now widow rested on her finger for all to see. She attended her husband's funeral in the same church they had married in a week earlier then moved away from the district. As far as I know she never received another visit from her spectral bridegroom.

10.
The Wisdom of Solomon

The existence of a liar is more probable than the existence of a ghost.

George Bernard Shaw (Irish playwright, 1856–1950)

Every period in Australian history has had its Alan Bonds and Christopher Skases: opportunists in the right place at the right time prepared to risk their shirts on long odds and exploit weaknesses in the system. In the 1820s and 30s such a man was Solomon Wiseman, known far and wide as 'The King of the Hawkesbury' and who, witnesses swear, still haunts his former home in the company of a collection of colourful and terrifying spooks.

As a young man Solomon Wiseman worked as a lighterman on the River Thames in London carrying cargo from ship to shore. A little less usually reached the shore than left the ship and the profit went into Solomon's pocket. He was caught red-handed one night transferring some valuable Brazilian Redwood from his lighter to an accomplice's boat. The next morning he was arraigned before a magistrate at the Old Bailey, who promptly sentenced him to death. This was later commuted to transportation to the penal colony of New South Wales — for life.

Solomon's young wife and infant son accompanied him on the convict transport *Alexander* and Mrs Wiseman gave birth to a second son as the ship was passing Cape Town. On arrival in Sydney in August 1806 Jane Wiseman, being a free woman, applied to have her husband assigned to her as a convict servant and the authorities agreed. Less than a year after being sentenced Solomon was, effectively, a free man and able to devote himself to making his fortune. On his wife's recommendation he soon had a ticket-of-leave and a year after that a full pardon.

Solomon used the profits from his Thames exploits as a deposit on two trading vessels that plied the coast from Newcastle to the Shoalhaven River, and was granted land in several places around the fringes of the colony. One parcel of eighty hectares was on the banks of the Hawkesbury River, opposite the mouth of the Macdonald River. Solomon established a tavern there in 1821 which he called 'The Packet', but so remote was the spot and so few the customers that he allowed the licence to lapse. That same year Jane Wiseman became ill, died and was interred in a vault on the Hawkesbury property. Solomon was left with four sons and two daughters to care for although, by then, he was on the way to becoming a very rich man.

In 1826 providence smiled twice on Solomon Wiseman: a comely widow agreed to become his second wife and stepmother to his brood and Governor Darling announced that a road connecting Newcastle with Sydney was to be built — running right past Solomon's Hawkesbury property. Solomon wasted no time. He tendered for and won a contract to supply fresh meat to the convict road gangs, built a new tavern and obtained a licence to operate a ferry across the Hawkesbury, which became an integral part of the new Great Northern Road. Profits poured into Solomon's coffers and within months he was able to set about building himself a fine two-storey stone residence, Cobham Hall, on a hillside overlooking the tavern and the ferry. In less than twenty years Solomon Wiseman had progressed from being a felon to a man spoken of in government circles as 'our wealthy and respected contractor' and from a convict to 'King of the Hawkesbury' complete with his own castle.

In 1832 the government decided it could no longer allow a private individual to control the ferry and purchased it (for a generous sum) from Solomon, retaining the name Wisemans Ferry — which it bears to this day. In that year Solomon also divested himself of the running of the tavern to one of his sons-in-law and spent the six years of life that remained to him living like a country squire, holding grand social entertainments at Cobham Hall, including one attended by Governor Bourke.

In October 1838 Solomon Wiseman died. His body was laid to rest temporarily beside his first wife's in the grounds of Cobham Hall. His obituary described him as 'a respected old colonist' (which was a common euphemism for an ex-convict) and rather wishfully as 'a friend to the poor'.

Shortly before his death Solomon had promised the community in the small village that had grown up around his ferry and taken its name that he would donate a piece of his land and 300 pounds to build them a church, which was also to house his and his family's remains. Construction had just begun when Solomon died. Scrutiny of his estate revealed that he had never owned the land he so freely gave away and his executors refused to hand over the 300 pounds. A scandal ensued and, although the church was eventually completed, the disenchanted community shunned it.

Notwithstanding, Solomon and Jane Wiseman's remains were duly installed in a vault in the church but Solomon was not allowed to rest there very long either. There were rumours that he had been entombed in a swallowtail coat and expensive boots, with a court sword at his side, a diamond ring on his finger, gold stickpin in his cravat and his gold watch and chain strung across his ample belly. ('It would be just like old Sol to try to take his riches with him!' the locals said.) When the disused church fell into disrepair, thieves broke in and raided Solomon's tomb. They didn't find any of the aforementioned booty, just the old man's teeth and bones, which they scattered. According to one story, youths in the village used his skull as a football, kicking it around in the dust. Eventually the local postmaster paid to have what remained of Solomon gathered and buried in the local cemetery. Jane's body was also removed to the cemetery and the couple were laid to rest for the third and final time.

Perhaps no man's mortal remains deserve the fate that befell Solomon Wiseman's but there is plenty of evidence (apart from the debacle over the church) to suggest that he gave the villagers at Wisemans Ferry little reason to respect him. He was not the benevolent country squire he liked people to think he was nor the charitable sage his obituary described. Solomon started and ended his life as a rogue. Only his bank balance improved. Such men are the stuff legends are made of and in no time at all wild stories about the King of the Hawkesbury's character and his lifestyle became part of local folklore. So too did a whole collection of ghost stories centred on Cobham Hall, which became, in the 1880s, the Wisemans Ferry Hotel.

The most oft-reported ghost was (and still is) that of a female whose appearances are sometimes heralded by the rustle of fabric, footsteps or gentle coughing. Guests staying in the hotel in the 1890s and early 1900s reported visits to their rooms in the middle of the night by a pale figure dressed in a long, gossamer-like nightgown; it would float across the floor, sometimes pausing to look at them lying, quaking with fear, in their beds. The ghost seemed to some observers to be crying.

The same pathetic figure was also seen leaving the kitchen and climbing the main staircase, floating about in the garden and on the road between the hotel and the ferry. One lady in her eighties described to the press in 1974 how as a small girl out walking with her mother one evening she encountered the ghost 'just up from the ferry and surrounded by grey mist'.

'She was quite beautiful — if a dead person can be said to be beautiful — with a long, slender neck and graceful arms. The features of her face were indistinct as if they had been worn away or faded, but her expression was very sad. In fact, a sort of overpowering sadness seemed to ooze out of her whole body which we could feel and which made me want to cry. I was scared, of course, wondering why she had shown herself to us and worried what she might *do* to us, but I was also fascinated by her. My mother grabbed me and folded me in her arms to protect me; I could feel Mother's body trembling through her skirts.

'The ghost just stood in front of us, blocking our way, for maybe three or four minutes, then she sighed — a deep, mournful sigh that sounded like a rush of wind — then she faded until only her outline was visible, then that disappeared into the strange mist ... and the mist itself just evaporated, leaving bright moonlight. Five minutes after she appeared, she was gone. Mother grabbed my hand and we ran back up the hill as fast as our legs could carry us!'

Most people believe that this footloose phantom is the ghost of Jane Wiseman. Sceptics argue, quite rightly, that Jane died a full five years before construction began on Cobham Hall but forget that she was originally buried close by and that some reports of the ghost refer to it rising from Jane's original tomb and hurrying towards the house. Where legend and history do clash is concerning Jane's death. Legend would have us believe she was thrown from the balcony at Cobham Hall by Solomon and died when her head struck the semi-circular steps below. History, of course, proves that impossible. Springing from this story was a claim, still repeated, that bloodstains appear on those steps from time to time. If they do, the blood was never Jane Wiseman's.

Another contender in the identity stakes is Rosanna White, a housemaid whom Solomon found one day in bed with another servant, Richard Maddox. Stories tell of Solomon ordering Rosanna's hair shaved off and Maddox heavily flogged. Rosanna was reported as cursing her employer and swearing that she would one day come back to haunt his house. Perhaps it is she, not Jane Wiseman, who haunts the building and its surroundings.

The shade of Solomon himself is said to wander his former home and the cemetery where his bones were finally interred. A European traveller staying in the hotel room that was once Solomon's bedroom claimed to have been awakened in the night by a strange scraping noise ('like rats' he said) and when he opened his eyes a 'most singular-looking old gentleman' was standing by the window.

'His face was the colour of parchment, crowned with a mass of white curls, his eyes small and his jaw prominent and lantern-shaped. He wore an old-fashioned coat of dark-coloured velvet and tight knee breeches. He had large buckles on his shoes and a heavy gold watch chain was fixed to his waistcoat and glinted in the moonlight. Under his arm he carried a brass telescope — like those used by ship's captains — and I fancied that before I had woken he had been using the instrument to look out the window. Now, however, his gaze rested squarely on me in a piercing and accusing stare. He was scowling at me as he would if he had come upon an intruder.' The traveller reached for his walking cane and the apparition vanished. Next morning when he described his nocturnal visitor it fitted the description old-timers gave of the King of the Hawkesbury.

The ghosts of three different convicts are also said to haunt the house. One, according to a popular but unlikely story, was Jane Wiseman's lover whom Solomon caught, tied in chains and dumped in the river. The second is an old lag who was supposed to have been flogged to death at Cobham Hall and the third a young convict-servant who came to Solomon one day begging to be allowed to go to Sydney to visit his dying mother. Solomon, the story goes, refused his request, saying there was too much work to do. The young man ran away and tried to swim across the river (which is odd considering Sydney is in the opposite direction), but his leg-irons dragged him under.

This convict was said to appear regularly at the door of Cobham Hall in ghostly form searching for his former master and still begging for permission to go to his mother. A witness described him as covered in weed and slime and with tears coursing down his ashen face: 'His hands were raised and held together, like he was prayin' or beggin'. There weren't much flesh on him ... maybe like he'd been eaten by the fishes, but his leg-irons was still on his ankles. I ain't never seen anything so bloody terrifying in all me life!'

One, or both, of the other convicts have been heard slowly dragging their leg-irons and chains across the yard, into the house and up the stairs — an eerie clanking sound that is all the more frightening because it has no visible source.

In the spring of 1961 Jane's ghost was blamed for a farcical sequence of events while the hotel was being renovated. An old wall was deliberately knocked down and, at the moment it fell, thunder boomed overhead and another wall collapsed spontaneously. An embankment close by gave way, allowing 5000 gallons (22 cubic metres) of water to rush like a tsunami through the ground floor of the hotel, smashing furniture and making what the appalled owner at the time called 'a horrid mess'.

In 1967 a well-known psychic and her assistants spent a night in the hotel with photographic and sound-recording equipment. At around midnight the temperature in the kitchen plummeted and a black cloud ('like smoke, but not smoke') enveloped half the room, obscuring everything it covered. Photographs taken then reveal a dark haziness over the affected area.

The expressway now linking Sydney and Newcastle takes a different route from the old Great Northern Road. There's not much traffic through Wisemans Ferry any longer but it is a popular spot for campers and visitors to nearby national parks. There is a cable-operated vehicular ferry where Solomon's ferry ran, and Cobham Hall under its Wisemans Ferry Hotel guise is still there — much altered but intact. To this day if you ask staff about the ghosts they will tell you stories of doors mysteriously opening and closing just last week, of strange noises heard the week before, of items moved by unseen hands and of the shadowy figure seen 'not long ago'. Whoever the restless spirits are that haunt Wisemans Ferry, they don't seem to show any inclination to depart.

11.
The Guyra Ghost: A Touchy Subject

'Oh, Sir, Sir, there are more tricks done in the village than make a noise!'

***Don Quixote*, Miguel de Cervantes (Spanish writer, 1547–1616)**

In the autumn of 1921 the town of Guyra in northern New South Wales found itself in the international spotlight. For a period of about six weeks the world watched with morbid curiosity as a worker's cottage about a kilometre from the town centre was assaulted by a destructive, invisible force, the occupants were driven to despair and the rest of the community tottered on the brink of mass hysteria.

It all began one morning when Bill Bowen, a gang foreman who worked for the Guyra Shire Council, walked into the town's police station and complained to Sergeant Ridge that during the night someone had placed a heavy wooden railway sleeper up against a window of the cottage he and his family rented. Putty, he said, had also been removed from around the pane of glass in the window.

The sergeant sent his two constables out to investigate. One, Roy Stennett, recalled fifty years later that when they got to the Bowens' house they inspected the window and removed the railway sleeper, leaving it fifty metres from the house. As the previous day had been April Fool's Day, the police concluded that the whole incident had been either a prank played on the Bowens by someone else or played on *them* by Bill Bowen. Mild amusement turned to annoyance when Bowen turned up at the police station the next morning complaining that the sleeper was back and more putty gone. Sergeant Ridge was now convinced that Bowen was pulling his leg. He told his constables to go back and shift the sleeper then return, secretly, after dark, to keep watch on the house.

Stennett and his colleague arrived at the Bowens' for the second time that day at dusk and settled down behind some bushes to watch — confidently expecting to catch Bill Bowen setting them up again. Less than an hour later they heard the crack of a .22-calibre rifle close by and the sound of a bullet ricocheting off the house. They ran towards where the shot had come from but could find no one. They returned to the house, where Bowen, his wife and three children were huddled in the kitchen, clearly frightened.

The next day the police and most of the townspeople were distracted by another problem. An eighty-year-old Irish woman, Mrs Doran, had been seen wandering around a paddock the day before with a potato in each hand. She had not returned home that night, so a full-scale search was undertaken. No trace of the old lady was found and the search was called off when darkness fell.

The two constables returned to the Bowens' home for another night vigil, this time inside the house. Soon after their arrival loud thumping was heard on the walls near the window where the railway sleeper had been placed and in one bedroom. From inside it sounded as though the thumping was coming from outside, but nothing could be seen through the windows. When the police went outside to investigate, the sound seemed to be coming from the inside. These unexplained noises continued for another two nights, then stones ranging in diameter from three to eight centimetres began to rain down on the corrugated iron roof of the house — singly and in deafening showers.

By then everyone in town and the surrounding district had heard what was going on. Crowds gathered around the Bowens' house each night to witness the strange to-do. Sergeant Ridge recruited volunteers to stand guard in each of the four rooms in the house and around the outside. Motorcars were lined up in a cordon with their headlights trained on the house, ready to flood the area with light as soon as anything happened. And happen it did, just after dark. The thumping began, rocks crashed into the walls and roof of the house and window panes were smashed. No one could have broken through the cordon without being caught, which meant that either someone within the house was responsible for the thumping and someone in the crowd had managed to throw the rocks without being seen, or that invisible forces were at work.

That weekend the story broke in the national press and curiosity seekers jammed the roads into Guyra and poured off the Sydney trains. There were journalists and photographers from city newspapers and a flock of self-styled experts on the paranormal. One of the latter, Ben Davey, described as 'a student of spiritualism and theosophy', told the press he had been called in by the authorities to subject the phenomenon to 'the acid test of spiritualism'. Sergeant Ridge (who was showing signs of stress) and his two constables had more or less moved in with the Bowens and were only too willing to allow anyone who offered a possible solution to join them.

Davey announced that the cause was almost certainly the spirit of Mrs Bowen's daughter by a previous marriage, a young woman named May, who had died just three months earlier. May, he said, was trying to contact her stepsister Minnie, Bill Bowen's twelve-year-old daughter, who occupied the bedroom where the thumping was loudest, and that Minnie was refusing to allow her to 'come through'. This theory implicated Minnie Bowen and thereafter she was the focus of official and public attention.

Minnie Bowen was a tall, thin girl with straight, dark hair and plain features, described by different newspapers as 'a normal girl', 'not clever', 'introspective' and 'backward for her age'. They all agreed she didn't smile very much and her eyes had a penetrating quality. An uncanny ability to anticipate questions was also remarked on. Davey took Minnie, her mother and a local sawmiller (just one of the troop of vigilantes who were stomping all over the Bowens' house) into Minnie's bedroom and told the girl that when the knocking started she was to ask the spirit if it was her stepsister. The noise began and, reluctantly, Minnie asked. Davey told the press, proudly, that Minnie then fell to her knees, crossed herself and raised her hands in supplication. The rest of the family and the policemen had crammed into the small room by then and they watched as the distressed child staggered to the bed where Mrs Bowen was sitting and laid her head in her mother's lap.

'It *was* May,' she stammered. 'She said: "Tell Mother I am perfectly happy where I am, and that your prayers when I was sick brought me where I am and made me happy. Tell Mother not to worry. I'll watch and guard over you all."' There was not a dry eye in the room when Minnie finished.

Poor Minnie. Those present believed her, but second — and third-hand retellings of what occurred in that room robbed it of sincerity. Minnie was accused of being the cause of the whole affair. She, sceptics said, banged on the walls with a stick and threw the stones. A local doctor secretly coated the walls of Minnie's bedroom with liquorice powder to detect the marks of blows and drilled a hole through the wall so he could keep her under observation. The paranormal fraternity said Minnie was conjuring up evil spirits. Ordinary folk simply got the wind up.

It was census time while all this was happening and the census collectors found themselves staring down a gun barrel whenever they knocked at a door. A small girl in town found the loaded revolver a parent had hidden under a pillow, fired it and wounded herself in the head. Unsubstantiated reports came in of a farmer's wife committing suicide for fear of the 'ghost'. Some claimed it was the shade of poor old Mrs Doran (who had been found dead) come back to haunt them. Lights burned long through the night, nerves strained and tempers quickened. A team of carpenters put heavy shutters over the Bowens' windows, but one morning while the family were away someone or something ripped them all down and smashed every window in the house. A cocoa merchant from Samoa, Mr Moors, who claimed to be a personal friend of Sir Arthur Conan Doyle (the creator of 'Sherlock Holmes'), insisted on removing much of the roof so that he and his entourage of five fully-grown men could hide in the ceiling overnight.

Sergeant Ridge finally cracked and was sent away for a rest cure. A tough Sydney cop named Hardy was sent up to clean up what was fast becoming a very public embarrassment for the police and after sorting out a notorious gang of Sydney hoodlums the year before, Hardy vowed he was not going to let some hick kid make a fool of him. He was much less gentle than the country police had been when he interviewed Minnie, and he succeeded in wringing a confession out of her. 'Yes,' she cried, she had thumped on the walls just like everyone said she had and yes, she had thrown all the stones. A very cocky Hardy wired his superiors in Sydney that the case was closed. That night, for the first time in almost a month, there were no thumping noises and no stones thrown. Hardy, the hero of the moment, caught the train back to Sydney the next day. The following night the whole terrifying business started up again.

At their wits' end, the Bowens packed Minnie off to stay with her grandmother in Glen Innes for their peace of mind and to protect her from vilification and further harassment — and the noises and the stone-throwing immediately stopped. Minnie settled in contentedly with her gran in a cosy house in Church Street, Glen Innes and it seemed as though the Bowens' problems were over. However, ten days after her arrival, to everyone's amazement and horror, stones began hitting the house in Glen Innes. Windows were smashed and solid walls shook under heavy blows. Ornaments crashed to the floor. The police were called, crowds gathered and the whole cycle seemed about to repeat itself. The grandmother wired Minnie's parents begging them to take their daughter back. Minnie packed her bags again and her parents reluctantly collected her.

Back home in Guyra the family sat on the edges of their chairs each night, ears straining and nerves tensed for the sounds to begin and the stones to rain down, but they didn't. Days went by, then weeks and nothing happened. The Bowens began to breathe easily, but the scars of the past were deep. A short time later they packed up and moved on.

Much has been written about poltergeist activity and how it often occurs in a household where there is a girl approaching puberty. One widely held theory claims that such girls are able to use the powers of their burgeoning sexuality to move physical objects and whip up psychic storms. Some believe that young women whose emotions are deeply repressed have the same powers. Minnie Bowen might well qualify as proof of either or both theories. She may truly have been, deliberately or innocently, conjuring up powerful forces. Equally likely, it could be argued, the Guyra ghost was not a poltergeist at all but a clever man-made plot to discredit the Bowens and drive them from their home, or simply a prank that got horribly out of hand.

When researching this story back in the mid-1990s I got some very strange responses from my inquiries made in Guyra. So strange, in fact, that I concluded the original published version of the story with the observation: *Readers are advised not to go asking questions around Guyra about the ghost: they may be surprised at the hostile response they get. Three quarters of a century after these events the people of Guyra still get annoyed when strangers pry into the affair. The Bowens' house is still there, but the current occupants do not take kindly to curious visitors. Descendents of the Bowens who live in the district get quite belligerent when anyone mentions the subject, and the local historical society declines to answer inquiries about it.*

I concluded at the time that perhaps they were all simply fed up with the whole business and made the observation that, as there is a vast amount of documentary evidence about the affair available, it seemed futile for the good folk of Guyra to close ranks so late in the day. That opinion has not altered and in fact, has been reinforced by a few more recent revelations.

When another researcher attempted to piece the mystery together in 2010 he found that archived copies of the *Guyra Argus* of the time were missing from the collections of both the State Library of New South Wales and the National Library in Canberra. Other inquiries in recent years prompted a few locals to come forwards with some facts that far from clarifying the situation confuse it further. One claimed that the house in Guyra that had been identified for decades as being the Bowens' was, in fact, not — their true house had been

200 metres away in a different street. The same informant suggested that the real house was subjected to thumping and stone attacks after the Bowens departed and up until it was demolished some years later.

A little of Minnie Bowen's later life has also recently been revealed. When she grew up she married, becoming Mrs Inks and living a long and peaceful life in Armidale, before being struck down and killed by a car in her eightieth year. Apparently she spoke little about her childhood, but did show evidence of having psychic powers and it was said that she could always make objects move without touching them.

12.
Saucy Spirits

I believe in a ghost, I believe in a ha'nt,
Good God a-mighty, I ain't no saint,
Ain't got no arms, ain't got no haid,
Don't stop to count them tracks I made.

Traditional African-American Song (untitled)

The theme of the dead returning to avenge themselves on those responsible for their deaths belongs more to popular fiction than genuine ghost lore. Leaving aside gruesome appearances, the ghosts in most of these stories seem a fairly respectable lot and as puzzled as their victims to find themselves where they are — but not all. There's an old story from the Monaro district of New South Wales about an enraged spirit who returned almost immediately to take his revenge on his persecutor in some very peculiar ways.

The story concerns a retired army major turned farmer and one of his convict labourers. The Major, according to the story, was a priggish bachelor with a quick temper who took sadistic pleasure in meting out rough justice with lash and noose. A loaded pistol was kept on his dining room table during meals and beside his bed each night. It was said that if any convict walked behind him, swore or blasphemed, the Major would have him flogged and serious offenders were hanged from one of two large gum trees in the homestead garden — four men in one day, it is claimed.

The convict in the story was an Irishman, transported for political crimes, who considered himself a cut above the rest and complained about having to work and sleep with riff-raff. When the Major showed no sympathy the convict threw a stone at him. According to the story, the Major tried the convict, condemned him to death and presided over his hanging that very afternoon but, if summary justice had rid the Major of problems before, it failed this time. A few nights after the hanging strange things began to happen on the farm: milk pails were knocked over, animals were let out of enclosures and a haystack burned down. The barracks that housed the convicts at night was a sturdy building from which they could not escape, so the Major blamed his free servants and the local Aborigines. His overseer was told to be more vigilant but the incidents continued and then, one dark and windy night, the Major himself discovered the culprit.

The incongruous sound of a man singing in the middle of the night woke him. Night-gowned and tassel-capped in the fashion of the time, the Major sat up in his giant four-poster bed and reached for his gun. He fumbled with candle and matches, but before he could strike a light the room began to fill with a lurid glow and the figure of the dead convict materialised at the foot of the bed. As the Major watched, horrified and scandalised, the ghost began to dance an Irish jig and sing a particularly bawdy song about the whores of Sydney Town. The Major fired his pistol at the figure but the bullet passed straight through and smashed an expensive vase on the mantel.

Now the Major had many unlikeable qualities but he was not a coward. He ordered the spectre to desist, cursed it and inveigled heavenly support. He hurled the pistol at it but all to no avail. The ghost of the Irish convict just chuckled, bowed obsequiously, kicked up its heels and launched into another, even more ribald song. Finally the Major closed his eyes and put his hands over his ears and that was how the servants found him when they came to his aid — but no trace of the ghost did they see.

The Major, being the practical man that he was, probably put the first night's experience down to indigestion or overwork but, when it was repeated night after night for weeks on end, he finally broke. Fearing that he would go mad if he stayed a night longer, the Major packed his possessions, sold his farm and moved back to England.

Well, that's how the story goes. History, however, tells it a little differently. Major William Sandys Elrington retired from the British Army aged forty-three in 1824. He was tall, red-haired and carried a large sabre scar across his forehead, a legacy of the Peninsula Wars where he served under the Duke of Wellington.

When he arrived in Australia in 1827 he was not a bachelor but a widower. His son Richard and the Major's old nanny, Mary Smith, aged seventy-three, accompanied him. Governor Darling granted the Major 200 hectares of fine land on the banks of the Shoalhaven River near the present town of Braidwood. He called the property 'Mount Elrington'. The census of 1828 shows his labour force comprising five assigned convicts and two emancipated convicts. Thomas Clarke, father of the notorious bushranging Clarke Brothers, also worked for the Major at one time. The Major had an elder son, also in the British Army, Lieutenant Clement Elrington, who sold his commission and joined his father for a time.

Major Elrington prospered. He was older, more experienced and had more capital than most settlers. He also lived on his property and supervised its running (many wealthy landowners preferred to live in the relative comfort of Sydney and left their properties in the hands of unscrupulous managers). He was respected in the district and appointed the local magistrate soon after his arrival.

Major Elrington was often cited as a model free settler but the model was flawed. The Major was subject to rapid changes of temperament and may have suffered from what we call today bipolar disorder. He quarrelled openly with his son Richard, disinheriting him and challenging him to a duel on at least one occasion, although there is no evidence of a duel taking place. His relationship with his other son, Clement, a would-be poet, was probably not much better. The Major also had a mania for discipline. The convicts at Mount Elrington were driven mercilessly and the lash and other brutal forms of physical punishment applied with alacrity.

There is official correspondence between the Major and the colonial secretary that confirms his power as a magistrate did not extend to pronouncing death sentences on convicts (or anyone else), but two trees, fitting the description of the infamous 'hanging' trees, stood until fairly recently at Mount Elrington in the location described in the story.

So, what of the ghost? There were many Irishmen among the convicts at Mount Elrington at different times; and a lad of about fifteen did throw a stone at the Major. This was probably not the youth's only crime, for he was brought before a senior magistrate. The Major, apparently in a benevolent mood, spoke in the young man's defence and tried, unsuccessfully, to save him from the noose.

Major Elrington did sell up, suddenly and unexpectedly, in 1845, and returned to England, but whether the reason was a ghost or simply the desire to spend his last days in his native Northumberland no one knows. So legend and history agree on some things, disagree on others and we must make up our own minds whether the Major was a maligned man and whether one of his convicts did enjoy a gleeful, ghostly revenge.

The Irish spook with his nimble feet and his bawdy songs is not the only saucy spirit in the annals of Australian ghost lore. A few of those ladies mentioned in his songs also feature in other stories and not only in Sydney. Take for example the ghost of the prostitute that used to appear on foggy nights on Princes Bridge in Melbourne in our great-grandfathers' time. She was a grotesque, aging creature with a painted face and threadbare finery who would stand under one of the street lamps, twirling a tattered pink parasol. As men passed she would smile at them and if any took a fancy to her and stopped, she would reach out a hand as cold as the grave and hold their arm in an icy grip. Then she would stretch back her head to show off her breasts, revealing a broad, jagged and livid scar running from her right ear to her left shoulder. While the observer gasped and recoiled in horror the wanton wraith would laugh — a staccato cackle that blended with the rattle of carriage wheels on the bridge. She would then try to shove her victim onto the busy carriageway. Most managed to regain their balance before falling or being run over and when they looked back their tormenter had disappeared, leaving only the smell of cheap violet scent lingering on the damp air.

Another of the 'sisters' features in a story about a lesson in manners that went horribly wrong in the Murray River town of Echuca around the same time. The story goes that this *fille de joie* picked up two sawmill workers in an Echuca pub one night and allowed them to buy her drinks. Later when the trio were strolling along the river bank near the sawmillers' cottage the men suggested the lady should repay their generosity with some free sex.

The prostitute got on her high horse and told the men her company was ample reward for the drinks. If they wanted sex, she said, they would have to pay for it. Just then they were approaching the old tramway bridge over Southern Cross Creek, so the men suggested that if the prostitute didn't co-operate they'd dangle her over the bridge until she learned how to show her gratitude properly.

The lady was still adamant: no pay, no pleasure. So the men carried out their threat. It was then that things went horribly wrong. As she dangled over the water, the prostitute's tight-fitting clothing bunched up around her neck, stopping her breathing. Her face suffused with blood and her eyes bulged. After five minutes the men dragged her limp body back onto the bridge but it was too late; the lady never again gave pleasure, with or without payment.

For the next thirty years or so, until the bridge was destroyed by flood, the ghost of this prostitute used to appear there when the full moon was setting (as it was when she died), waiting to take revenge on her unprincipled companions. The ghost's face was described as 'beetroot coloured' with either rage or the effect of strangulation, and its eyes bulged hideously. Witnesses claimed it would materialise in front of males crossing the bridge in pairs and block their way. It would stare at each pair until satisfied they were not the murderers, then howl with frustration and slowly 'evaporate'.

And then there's Sabrina — no, *not* that blonde bombshell whose mammaries used to fill our screen in the early days of television — but a lithesome young spectre of more recent times, given that name by the companion she adopted. Sabrina's story (surely one of the most bizarre in this collection) has its origins at the scene of a fatal road accident in the Sydney suburb of Blacktown. An unemployed artist told his part in the story to the *National Enquirer* in 1993.

The artist was the proud owner of a 1974 Triumph 2500 with a red body and white top. When he went driving alone one day and had car trouble a reassuring voice from the back seat told him not to panic — there was a garage one kilometre up the road. When the artist swung round there was a 'passenger' sitting in the back seat. The figure was hazy but clearly female, young and very attractive. He yelled: 'Who the hell are you?' (or words to that effect). The figure vanished — but not for good. She appeared six times more, lighting her finger like a candle on one occasion, according to the informant, so he could read a road map in the dark.

The young man told the *National Enquirer* the ghost usually appeared dressed in the same clothes — very short red shorts and a very tight white tank top — but, on one memorable day, appeared *stark naked.* He finally got an answer to his question after the two got to know each other better. Sabrina, as he decided to call her, told him she had been riding her bicycle in Blacktown one day when she was run down by a car and killed. It was not the Triumph that hit her and it did not then belong to the artist, but it was being driven past at the time. It was so new and bright and shiny and painted in her favourite colours that she decided to 'move in' — permanently. The artist said he didn't mind 'Sabrina' living in his car but he did try to avoid having friends sit in the back seat in case they took up her space or, worse, *sat on her.*

Another decidedly 'saucy' spectre which might, like Sabrina, still be around haunts Saint Andrews Inn at Cleveland in Tasmania. The old inn dates from 1825 and offers excellent accommodation and fine food. In its heyday, the hotel served travellers on the road from Hobart to Launceston and was popular with cut-throats and vagabonds. History tells of Tasmania's most notorious bushranger, Martin Cash, trading shots with the police there one day while holding the innkeeper's daughter hostage and stealing some bacon.

History records that a girl was also murdered in an upstairs room at the inn in the 1860s. Perhaps it is her ghost, or that of the young lady affronted by Martin Cash, who stalks the staircase, exacting revenge on the opposite sex.

Legend has it that the spirit accosts males of all ages, sidles up to them and begins to unbutton their clothes. Transfixed with fear (or delight) the victims allow themselves to be stripped completely naked after which the ghost vanishes leaving them mortified with embarrassment and, if it happens to be winter, shivering with cold.

The owners in the 1970s told the press the ghost had been very active in their time (following people up and down the stairs), but when they sold out she seemed to go to ground. The third owners saw her frequently, but the fourth did not, suggesting that perhaps the ghost skips a 'generation' of owners. The next owners (the fifth in this cycle) took over in the 1990s and reported hearing murmuring voices in one room and complained of clothes being put away mysteriously, so maybe it won't be long before this clothes-stripping, saucy spirit (like Freddy Krueger) is ba-a-ck.

13.
The Mourning Bull

No man can deny the many honest and credible people who affirm they have seen ghosts

Ludwig Lavater (Swiss theologian, 1527–1586)

Few ghost stories are as reliably attested to as the one known as 'The White Bull of Yeumburra'. The prime witness to the strange events in this story was one of the most respected policemen in the New South Wales police force.

When Senior Superintendent Martin Brennan wrote his memoirs in 1907 he devoted a whole chapter to a murder investigation he had been involved in during the winter of 1876 and its strange, supernatural sequel.* Martin Brennan was then a senior sergeant in charge of the Queanbeyan district of New South Wales. On 28 June Brennan received word that a shepherd named Jeremiah McCarthy had been murdered at a remote spot near the boundary of the Queanbeyan and Yass police districts. By arrangement, Senior Sergeant Brennan and one of his troopers met with an inspector and another trooper from Yass, the local coroner and a hastily recruited jury at the scene of the crime. The place was called the Washpool, an isolated spot on the banks of the Murrumbidgee River a few kilometres from the present

* *Reminiscences of the Gold Fields*, by Martin Brennan, published by William Brooks, Sydney, 1907. Brennan's account of these events has a policeman's thoroughness and concern for detail but his memory fails him on the names of some people and places. This account is drawn from Brennan's work, contemporary newspaper reports and private sources.

town of Murrumbateman. Steep hills surrounded the area on three sides and the only signs of human habitation were some old sheep-washing pens belonging to Nanima station and the shepherd's tiny hut. The nearest homestead was Yeumburra, a few kilometres away.

McCarthy's body was recovered from where it had been found, partly concealed in sparse scrub. It was carried back to the hut, where the coroner examined it and conducted an inquest. The shepherd had been shot in the head, then the front half of his skull hacked away with a sharp implement. Thirty-two pieces of lead shot were removed from what was left of his brain. The jury brought down a verdict of 'Wilful murder, by person or persons unknown' and the gruesome corpse was hastily wrapped in two blankets found inside the hut and buried close by.

The inside of the shepherd's hut was disordered. Several religious books that the victim had been fond of reading were scattered about. Three possums had taken up residence in the cold fireplace and a large goanna had devoured the contents of the meat bag and gone to sleep amongst the stinking remains of its feast. The flour and sugar bags had also been tampered with. At first it was thought the animals were to blame, but when an empty strychnine tin was found and large amounts of the deadly poison detected in the flour and sugar the evidence pointed to the murderer. There were also clear boot marks on the dirt floor, one pair belonging to McCarthy and another, much larger set made by someone wearing two left boots.

The policemen then rode to Nanima station to speak to James Ramsey, McCarthy's employer. Ramsey confirmed that McCarthy had been forty-five years old, single, sober and well read and had worked on Nanima for many years. Good shepherds prepared to live in wild and lonely spots with only their flock and a sheepdog for company were rare. Ramsey was very sorry, he said, to lose such a reliable one.

Next the police called at Yeumburra, where Charles Hall could give them little information, and at Ginninderra, another local station, where William Davis had some startling news. On the evening of McCarthy's murder Davis had found a villainous character called Mad Tom the Soldier in his kitchen. Mad Tom, despite his sixty years, was tall and powerful, one sinister eye staring out of a battered face framed with a grisly beard and lank hair. Mad Tom was well known to Senior Sergeant Brennan; his real name was William Hutton but he used many aliases, including 'Tom Robertson' and 'Waterloo Tom'. He claimed to have been a soldier in the British Army and to have lost his eye and been injured in the leg at the Battle of Waterloo, none of which was true. He had never been in any army and had sustained his injuries when attacked by Aborigines in Tasmania while trying to carry off a young Aboriginal girl. He had roamed the Murrumbidgee region for years, begging, stealing and intimidating people with his six-foot long-barrelled rifle and a bayonet-like knife. The police suspected him of many crimes but had not been able to convict him.

Davis said that Mad Tom had asked whether the shepherd McCarthy was still at the Washpool. The station owner and his men sent him packing, but discovered the next morning that a blanket, a left boot and a tin of strychnine were missing. The police had their culprit. Mad Tom the Soldier was tracked down and let off one shot from his murderous gun before being overpowered and taken into custody. He was wearing two left boots. The police were determined to get a conviction this time and decided the victim's body should be exhumed and the blankets retrieved as evidence. Senior Sergeant Brennan, the Inspector from Yass and two troopers returned to the

Washpool a few days later to carry out this gruesome task. What happened that day is stranger than fiction. Brennan takes up the story:

It was a beautiful clear day, the sun's rays shining on the river, but this changed as we stood beside the grave. Suddenly an extraordinary cumulo stratus [sic] *cloud, or 'woolpack', descended enveloping the mountains and casting deep shadows over the Washpool. We commenced the work of exhumation but just as the spade touched the timber slab that covered the body there was the sound of a terrific explosion. The ground trembled and seemed to sink beneath our feet. A great rumbling sound reverberated through the valley for some seconds followed by a tremendous roar from the hilltop above us. Suddenly we observed through the gloom a huge bull of immaculate whiteness rushing down the slope towards us. We promptly sought the protection of some trees close by, drew revolvers and stood in readiness for defence, but this was unnecessary, as the animal on reaching the open grave, stopped suddenly, and with head erect, surveyed the surroundings, pawed the earth for a few seconds then lay down beside the grave, moaned piteously and expired.*

The policemen emerged from their cover and after making sure the animal was dead, inspected it. The great beast was 'of marvellous symmetry' and in perfect condition. There seemed no apparent reason for its strange behaviour and sudden death. By this time, the four policemen were thoroughly unnerved. They hastily completed their task but had neither the energy nor the inclination to bury the huge carcass of the bull.

Two days later Senior Sergeant Brennan sent one of his troopers back to the Washpool to bury the poisoned flour and sugar and to make an inventory of the contents of the hut. William Davis of Ginninderra accompanied the trooper, saying he had a special interest in the white bull and wanted to take a look at the carcass. When the two men arrived at the shepherd's hut everything was just as the police had left it two days earlier, except for one thing — the bull had vanished. There were no marks where it had fallen beside the grave, no tracks to suggest it had been moved and no trace of blood, bone or hide to indicate that it had been butchered on the spot or eaten by dingoes or goannas. In fact, as the trooper remarked to Davis, it was as if the huge animal had never existed.

This strange sequence of events puzzled Martin Brennan for the rest of his days and, when he came to write about it thirty years later, he was no closer to finding an explanation than he had been in the winter of 1876. Some elements in the story can be explained by natural phenomena combined with coincidence. The sudden appearance of a cumulonimbus stormhead and a single crash of thunder would account for the mysterious cloud and the 'explosion'. If the area was then shaken by an earth tremor the dramatic prelude to the appearance of the bull could be explained, but the animal itself cannot. No one in the district owned such a distinctive (and valuable) beast. No cattle had been driven through the district for months and it had been a hot, dry year along the Murrumbidgee without any rain, so there was very little green vegetation for a stray animal to survive on let alone maintain such perfect condition. Martin Brennan believed that the animal was supernatural and admitted so, using the terminology of his time:

I am aware (he wrote) *that those who allege to have seen ghosts, apparitions and mysterious manifestations are looked upon as weak-minded and superstitious but, unable to account for what four police officers, in perfect health and with all their faculties unimpaired, witnessed, I conclude it to have been a 'psychological' phenomenon.*

Many years after Brennan published his account of these events, some new pieces of evidence came to light that had not been known to Brennan. William Davis's interest in seeing the carcass of the bull, which Brennan puts down to curiosity, was more than that. Some time before the murder of Jeremiah McCarthy, Davis had been out shooting with friends on Hall's property, Yeumburra, when they were charged by a large bull. Davis, a crack shot, raised his rifle, fired once and dropped the animal in its tracks. The bull died instantly a few metres from his feet. Later when he heard about the appearance of a ghostly-white bull at the murder scene, Davis wanted to see if it bore any resemblance to the animal he had shot. Perhaps he was less surprised than the trooper when they found it had vanished into thin air.

The second twist to this story belongs to more recent times. A descendent of Charles Hall of Yeumburra asked his aged aunt about the story of the ghost bull. The old lady told her nephew that there was no doubt about the bull's existence. She had, she said, seen it herself.

'Oh, I've seen it a few times,' she said, as though seeing the ghost of a massive pure white bull was nothing special to remark on. 'It comes back every time one of the family dies. I remember it suddenly appeared on a ridge near the homestead at sunset one evening during the last war. There was a brilliant, pink sunset and at first it was just a big, dark silhouette against the sky. The thing stood still for maybe two or three minutes and we all watched it. Then it raised its head, shook its horns and let out a tremendous roar that echoed around the valley. It turned then, and the light caught its hide and for a moment it shone, a bright, glowing white. Then it was gone. Next day we found out an uncle ... he was a soldier fighting in the Middle East somewhere ... had been killed in a battle.'

Finally, if you're wondering what happened to that other 'soldier', Mad Tom, he was sent for trial before a judge who happened to be a real old soldier: a retired lieutenant colonel with a soft spot for ex-servicemen. The prosecution pointed out that Tom was a liar, a thief and a murderer and that he had not even been born when the Battle of Waterloo took place, but the gullible judge could not bring himself to send Tom to the gallows and gave him a prison sentence instead. Mad Tom died in prison, delirious and crying out that he was being trampled by an invisible white bull.

14.
Suffer the Little Children

While yet a boy I sought for ghosts, and sped
Through many a listening chamber, cave and ruin,
And straight wood, with fearful steps pursuing
Hopes of high talk with a departed dead.

***Hymn to Intellectual Beauty*, Percy Bysshe Shelley**
(English poet, 1792-1822)

Pathos is a key element in many ghost stories. It is natural for us to feel sad for the terrified victims of haunting, but equally true that we can't avoid feeling sorry for the plight of many of the ghosts — even while they are chilling our blood and making the our hair stand on end. When the ghost in a story is that of a child whose young life has been cruelly snatched away by fate then the pathos can be almost unbearable, as the next story illustrates.

This tale begins one evening in the late nineteenth century when two stockmen were travelling across the Dargo High Plains in the rugged alpine country of eastern Victoria. It was almost dark when they stumbled upon a deserted hut deep in the bush and decided to camp there for the night. They lit a fire in the crumbling fireplace and spread their bedrolls on the floor among broken furniture and mice-eaten newspapers.

During the night they were awakened by the sound of sobbing and were startled to see a little girl, dripping wet and crying piteously, standing in the doorway. The men called to the little girl to come inside to the fire and made to get up, but before they could she vanished. They went outside, coo-eed and searched but couldn't find her.

Still thinking a living child must be lost in the bush, they widened their search the next day but could find no trace of the little girl. By daylight the stockmen could see that the hut and its surroundings were a melancholy sight. There was a dried-up well, some stunted fruit trees, the remains of a garden choked with weeds, broken fences and a scattered woodpile all overgrown with a tangle of scrub.

Finally they gave up their search and moved on to the nearest town, where they reported the incident to the local constable and learned that they had seen a ghost. Some years ago (they were told) a couple with a large family had tried to make a go of it in the bush but failed. Eventually they were forced to walk off, leaving everything they had laboured for behind. They took ship from Lakes Entrance, bound for Sydney, and it was not until the ship was well out to sea that they realised the youngest of their brood was missing. The little girl, it seemed, had wandered away from the wharf. The captain of the ship would not turn back and by the time a search was organised no trace of the child remained. Where her body lay no one knew, but her ghost made its way back to the little hut in the bush and there it remained, crying bitterly for its mother. The stockmen were not the first and would not be the last to see and hear this heart-rending little spirit — and once experienced it was never forgotten.

Also from Victoria (this time from the comfortable Melbourne suburb of Kew) comes another touching story of the ghost of a dead child — in this case a small boy. An old house that still stands in Barkers Road was the home of a prosperous family in the 1890s and is still, legend has it, the haunt of the tiny ghost. The father of the family was strict (even by Victorian standards) and imposed rules on every member of his household — spouse, offspring and servants — and meted out stiff punishment when anyone defied them.

Exactly how the youngest son in the family (aged around six years) managed to stir the wrath of his father one day is unclear — perhaps he spoke out of turn or slid down a banister — but the punishment he suffered is a matter of record. The father locked the child in his upstairs bedroom, denied him his supper and threatened to deny him his breakfast if he didn't bow to his will.

The little lad apparently had an adventurous streak and decided he would escape from his bedroom window and run away from home. His head was likely filled with exciting plans about joining a circus, becoming a midshipman in the navy or a daring bushranger, while he carefully knotted his bed sheets together to form a rope. One end of the makeshift rope was then tied to a bedpost and the other lowered out of the window. The little boy swung his body over the window ledge and began to descend the rope, hand over hand. Then disaster struck. The child slipped, the sheets tangled around his slender neck and he died gasping for breath, his feet just thirty centimetres from the ground.

A contrite father, a broken-hearted mother and a collection of distressed siblings accompanied the little boy's coffin to a local cemetery then promptly sold the house and moved away. The house remained untenanted for many years after the tragedy and rumours spread that the child's ghost could be seen climbing out of the window and hanging by the neck at around midnight on the anniversary of his death.

An old resident of Kew recalled seeing this terrible tableau when she was a young probationary nurse. 'I couldn't believe my eyes,' she said. 'I was walking up Barkers Road from the tram depot and some slight movement at the front of the darkened house caught my attention. I stopped, I remember, and put my hand on the fence and peered through the overgrown garden — and there it was! I could see plainly a small child's body with knee-length pants but no shirt or shoes or socks, swinging slowly back and forth from a knotted tangle of snowy white bed linen. His head was twisted, his little face contorted and his tongue lolled out of his mouth. For a moment I thought I was witnessing a tragedy that was happening then — at that exact moment. I screamed and felt along the fence for a gate so I could go to the child's aid. My hand touched an old rose bush and a thorn dug into my palm. The pain was intense. I looked at my hand; there was already a drop of blood on it, and when I looked back at the front of the house there was nothing there — no trail of white linen and no dead child. Every night after that, whenever I passed the house on my way home from the hospital, I looked for the little ghost, but I never saw him again and, do you know, I'm not sure whether I was disappointed or relieved.'

Victoria does not have a monopoly on child ghosts. Another whose story has become famous once resided (and may still do) in the Barossa Valley town of Kapunda, South Australia. On a hilltop a few kilometres from the town stand the ruins of the Kapunda Reformatory, a grim and eerie relic of harsher times, reduced now to foundations and a few bricks. Children, from infants to adolescents, were confined there in the nineteenth century under appalling conditions. Most were accused of petty crimes they may or may not have committed and a few were put there simply for convenience by parents who did not want to acknowledge them. Underfed, poorly clothed and seldom allowed to enjoy sunlight and fresh air, dozens of short and miserable lives ended in suffering within the reformatory's cold stone walls.

At the bottom of the hill below the ruins is an old graveyard. Many of the old headstones are crumbling, the fences are rusted and weeds grow in profusion. Local residents will not venture near the ruins on the hill or the graveyard at night. Both, they claim, are the haunt of the ghost of a young girl called Vera.

Vera was an inmate in the reformatory and her grave stands in the cemetery but, as many people who have seen her will testify, she often leaves her grave at night carrying a lighted hurricane lamp and goes searching for something or someone. She appears dressed in a white shift too large for her gaunt body and her feet are bare. She can be seen rising from her grave and climbing the hill to the reformatory ruins. In earlier times before the ruins crumbled, she would enter and her lamp could be seen moving from window to window as though she were pacing the length of the building. Today it is said she looks about, confused and mystified that the building is no longer there.

Observers who have had the courage to remain have watched her return to the cemetery, stop at her grave, condense into a thin strip of intense light then slide, noiselessly, back into the earth. The letters 'V', 'e', 'r' and 'a' (inverted so the 'e' looks like a '9') were often found scratched on the walls of the reformatory and are still occasionally spotted drawn in the hard-baked earth of the graveyard.

History records the story of another girl whose ghost haunts bushland near North Motton in Tasmania. Residents of this small town (near Ulverstone) don't like to talk about 'their' ghost because its presence is a reminder of a brutal event that took place in the early years of the twentieth century and which they do not care to recall. A small girl was murdered on a road that runs through a thickly wooded area just outside town and her lifeless body jammed into a hollow tree. Police reports also show that a piece of jewellery she had been wearing had been forced down her throat.

The little girl's spirit is said to wander the road where her life was so callously snuffed out. It appears unexpectedly in front of cars and has almost caused several accidents. 'One moment the road was empty,' one driver reported, 'and the next this kid was standing in the middle of the road! I slammed on the brakes and jammed my hand down hard on the horn, knowing there would not be time to stop before I hit her. It all happened so quickly, but I can still see the little figure that seemed to be rushing towards the car. At any moment I expected to hear the crunch as I hit her and I expected her to come flying through the windscreen ... but *nothing* happened. At the moment when the impact should have occurred she was just *gone*. I stopped and jumped out of the car and ran back, but I was alone on an empty road. When I got back in my car it was filled with a kind of grey fog so I opened the windows to let the breeze through. Next I heard a faint sound coming from far off in the bush. It was an unearthly wailing noise like I *had* never and *have* never heard coming from a human throat. I hit the ignition and the accelerator, putting as much distance as I could between me and whatever it was I had seen and heard.'

Of all these stories about the ghosts of children perhaps the most touching comes from another part of Tasmania — the Hobart suburb of New Town, where a charming little spirit was said to occupy St John's Anglican Church, the oldest church still in use in the city.

Picture if you will, this gaunt, Gothic chapel on a Sabbath morning in winter around the middle of the nineteenth century. In a cosy, boxed-in pew close to a large fireplace where logs blazed brightly sits the governor and his family, decked out in their winter finery. Arrayed in similar pews behind the viceroy sit his aides, officers and their ladies and the local gentry. Sputtering whale oil candles fixed to the pews light their hymnals and prayer books. Merchants, tradesmen and seamen with their plump wives and well-scrubbed children rugged up against the bitter cold fill the farthest reaches of the gloomy nave.

High above the rest of the congregation in a gallery on the southern side of the church, 100 or so emaciated convicts (male and female) huddle together on hard benches under the watchful eye of their gaolers. Admission to this bare and draughty eyrie is by way of a narrow, enclosed staircase barred by three doors, unlocked and locked in succession as the convicts pass through. The great doors of the church are also securely fastened in case some rash individual should attempt to escape.

Opposite the convicts' gallery runs a second gallery and here, shivering in threadbare uniforms, are the miserable and perpetually hungry inmates of St John's School for Orphans (located next door to the church) — the abandoned offspring of convicts and paupers, unwanted children of mixed parentage and the small, confused survivors of disease and accident.

On the preacher's command the congregation begin to sing ('Rock of Ages' perhaps, or the Twenty-third Psalm) and above the cultured voices from the nave and the gruff mutterings from the convicts' gallery rise the tremulous voices of the orphans, intoning words they barely understand, fearful that any lapse of memory or volume will earn them a box around the ears.

It is said that if you happened to be alone in St John's Church at dusk at any time in the last century you might have heard one of those tiny, plaintive voices still singing 100 years on. Parishioners called her 'Gwennie' for want of a better name and because the eerie disembodied voice was surely that of a little girl. It is also claimed that a cloud of chill air, like cold mist, enveloped the orphans' gallery when Gwennie sang:

'Goodness and mercy all my life
Shall surely follow me,
And in God's house for evermore
My dwelling place shall be.'

There have been no reports of Gwennie in recent years. Perhaps she has found peace and somewhere warmer to dwell. The same wish might be made for all the little ghosts in this chapter.

15.
Sportin' Types

Now about those ghosts. I'm sure they're there and I'm not half so alarmed at meeting up with any of them as I am at having to meet the live nuts I have to see every day.

Bess Truman (wife the 33rd President of the United States)

It is inevitable that in a country as sport-obsessed as Australia our folklore should include some spirit sportsmen and spirit sportswomen. One of the most remarkable of these stories concerns a now-retired senior public servant who had a nerve-jangling experience on Royal Perth Golf Course many years ago.

The future bureaucrat was just fifteen at the time and employed as a part-time caddie. He and another lad were accompanying two intrepid, middle-aged golfers around eighteen holes on a wet and windy afternoon when another party appeared out of the mist ahead of them. The second party was made up of two men and two women and one of the men had clearly lost his golf ball in the rough. He was searching for it while the others waited in the middle of the fairway.

One of the two players with our narrator called out 'fore', expecting the party ahead to move and signal back to play through, but his call seemed to go unheeded. A chorus of 'fore' echoed down the fairway but the party ahead seemed not to hear. Our narrator was told to 'Go and wake 'em up, lad.' He set off towards the other group and, as he drew closer, noticed that their clothes were old-fashioned and their clubs antiquated. At about fifty paces he opened his mouth to call out 'Excuse me', but the sound never left his throat. The three figures on the fairway had vanished. Instinctively he looked to where the fourth figure had been, in the rough, just in time to see it fade slowly away.

The two middle-aged golfers and the other caddie were as mystified as our narrator. From the greater distance of their vantage point they were able to convince themselves that the other party had just wandered off into the mist but the future public servant knew exactly what he had seen. Back at the clubhouse he asked if two men and two women fitting the description of the mystery party had signed on that day and he was assured that they had not. Later he went back to the spot and poked around in the rough where the solitary figure had been searching. Buried beneath fifteen centimetres of leaf mould he found an old golf ball — of a type and brand that had not been manufactured for fifty years. The ball is now almost a century old and the retired public servant still has it.

A group of youths had a similarly unnerving experience when they went to do a 'bit o' kickin'' on the Rugby Oval in Mulgoa Road, Penrith, at dusk on a summer evening a few years ago. The youths were having a fine time, ducking and dodging and planting easy goals between the white-painted posts. The sun had set behind the mountains across the river, but the warmth of the day lingered and there was not a breath of wind.

Suddenly everything changed. The youths heard footsteps pounding across the ground and they all turned expecting to find someone approaching but apart from them, the field was empty. At the same moment a narrow tunnel of strong, icy cold wind roared across the playing field, making their clothing flap and knocking the football from one youth's hands — but not disturbing trees just ten metres away. As quickly as the phenomenon had arrived it passed, leaving the group shivering with cold and shock. The boy who had been in possession of the ball was the first to find his tongue. 'What the fuck was that?' he asked, but none of his mates could offer an answer.

The youths told their parents then thought nothing more about the incident — until it happened again in the same place at the same time of day a couple of weeks later. No explanation was found for this strange phenomenon. History shows that a man murdered his wife at nearby Peach Tree Creek and a rower died on the Nepean River in a boating accident long ago. Perhaps it is connected with the murder (the unseen ghost of a running victim or a chasing killer), or the unfortunate rower wanting to join in the fun — or maybe it's the spirit of some long-dead Penrith Panther still adding goals to his score.

A visible ghost put in an appearance during a cricket match in the New South Wales town of Orange about forty years back. This happened on another balmy summer day when half the town gathered to watch the local team compete against a visiting eleven. The visitors won the toss and chose to bat first. Their opening batsmen were both professional shearers — tough men with powerful arms and broad shoulders conditioned by years of back-breaking labour. Between them the two amassed a score of 160 before their captain declared. The local team came stumbling off the field, drenched in perspiration and dazed by two hours of standing in the hot sun.

While wives, mothers and sisters served tea and the smell of sandwiches and cakes wafted through the pavilion, the coach of the local team tried to motivate his batsmen into pulling off a miracle in the second half. Among them was a young shop assistant playing his first game for his hometown team. He was slight in build and an unproven player but his cricketing pedigree was impressive. His late grandfather had been captain of New South Wales and a crack batsman who had demolished the attacks of many celebrated bowlers. The coach took the novice aside and said: 'Listen, kid, I'm gonna put you on at the end of the tail. Just do your best.'

The bad luck that had plagued the home team continued when they stood at the crease. By the end of eight overs their best batsmen were back in the pavilion and their score stood at six for forty-one. The middle order stood their ground and amassed another seventy runs between them, but when the young man's turn to bat came, the deficit still stood at fifty.

The novice batsman's mother and his kid sister were seated on a bench beside the railing and cheered him as he strode out onto the field. His mother was a war widow and ever since her husband had fallen to a Japanese sniper's bullet in the jungle of New Guinea, she had doted on her 'boy'. 'You show 'em, love!' she shouted proudly as he passed. Then she added as an afterthought: 'Remember your grandpa!'

The man of the moment reached the pitch and if the opposing team had known how much he was quaking in his shoes and sweating under his cap, they could have dismissed him with one curly ball. Instead the opposing batsman lobbed him a short ball. The batsman stepped up to it and struck it squarely. The ball raced away and the novice had his first runs on the board. Fears of being out for a duck were dispelled and the runs kept coming until just six more were needed for victory. Then a vicious ball rose off the hard, dusty pitch and struck him hard on the elbow. The frustrated bowler shouted for an 'LBW' dismissal, but the umpire shook his head. Meanwhile our hero was suffering excruciating pain in his arm. The limb hung limp at his side and when he tried to grip the bat again his hand felt numb.

While the bowler strode off to commence his run, the batsman closed his eyes to try to block out the pain and when he opened them again he glanced across to where his mother and his sister were seated. What he saw made him blink again. Sitting between them was an elderly man in a dark suit with a black waistcoat. A broad-brimmed Panama hat obscured most of his face but a drooping white moustache was visible below it and the studs that secured his old-fashioned starched collar glinted in the sunlight.

The novice batsman had never met his famous cricketing grandfather, but he had no doubt that it was he who was sitting beside his mother at that crucial moment. As if by some form of telepathy he heard the old man's voice speaking in his ear: 'You can do it, lad. I'm with you.'

Our hero faced up at the crease, the crowd held its communal breath and the bowler delivered a fast 'Yorker' that sped down the pitch like a bullet, hit the ground at the batsman's feet and spun off to the side. Just how he managed to get into a position to strike the ball, the young man never knew, but strike it he did, straight off the middle of his bat. The ball soared skywards and a fielder on the boundary positioned himself to catch it — but failed. The ball flew over the fielder's head, over the boundary and over the clubhouse, finally coming to earth beside a startled cow in a neighbouring paddock.

The crowd roared their approval and the rest of the Orange team ran onto the field to congratulate the hero of the moment. They hoisted him onto their shoulders and carried him back to the pavilion. The young man himself was in a daze brought on by surprise, relief, pride and the realisation that he had had an uncanny experience. He saw his mum clapping so hard her hat had toppled off and his sister jumping up and down with excitement, but the figure that had been sitting between them was gone.

Amid the handshakes, the slaps on the back, the hugs and the kisses, the young man kept his own counsel about what he had seen and heard. Neither his mother nor his sister mentioned it so our hero concluded that he alone had been privileged to see the ghost of his late grandfather. That is until he was packing up his gear in the pavilion half an hour later and the coach sauntered over. 'Well done again, mate,' he said. 'You saved our bacon. Oh, and by the way, who was that old geezer sitting next to your mum when you hit that six?'

Our final sporting story proves that the supernatural (like sport) breaches international boundaries and ghosts are not limited by distance.

It concerns the Sydney Olympic Games of 2000 and recent events in Japan — and a more thought-provoking story would be hard to find.

Juan Antonio Samaranch, President of the International Olympic Committee at the time, pronounced the Sydney Olympics 'the best ever' and that was due not only to the spirit of goodwill that characterised the whole enterprise, but also the care that had been taken over preparations. A contingent of 5000 international journalists (for example) found themselves accommodated together in a well-appointed, high-tech media village at Lidcombe, about twenty kilometres west of the city. Comfortable accommodation was provided in a mixture of old and new buildings and the supernatural must have been far from the minds of the keyed-up commentators as they settled in and set up to report on their respective nation's participation in the games. If they had known the history of the old building however, they might have given a casual thought to ghosts, for it was the former Lidcombe Hospital and reputedly haunted by many disturbed spirits.

A Japanese sports writer sent by a Tokyo-based magazine discovered he was not alone in his room one night when a hazy, female figure dressed in a hospital nightgown appeared suddenly at the foot of his bed. 'She had a friendly, concerned expression on her face and I did not feel at all frightened by her presence, although I knew instinctively that she was not a living person,' he told colleagues the next day, most of whom dismissed his story as a dream or the result of jet lag. With the spectacular opening ceremony to report on and the start of competition, the sports writer put the whole episode out of his mind and had almost forgotten it when he went to visit his aged parents in the town of Kamaishi on the east coast of Honshü in March 2011.

'My parents lived in a house near the harbour,' he recalls, 'and when the tsunami struck we had no warning. A giant wall of debris with cars, boats, parts of other buildings and the bodies of people and animals came roaring down the street. It reached my parents' house in seconds. The sound was indescribable. I could see my mother screaming, but could not hear her. I put my arms around my parents just as everything around us disintegrated. I remember being lifted off my feet and then everything went black.

'Some hours must have passed before I came to. I found myself sitting on the sharp edge of a piece of concrete that might once have been a building or part of a bridge, sticking out of a swirling sea of watery mud. It was deathly quiet. I was not sure whether I was alive or dead and I couldn't work out where I was. Kamaishi as I knew it was unrecognisable; I could see nothing familiar at all. I couldn't even tell where the land ended and the sea began. Then the strangest thing happened. I suddenly realised I was not alone on my small concrete island. There was a woman sitting beside me and when she turned her face I could see she was European. For a moment I didn't recognise her, although she was smiling at me as though she knew me. Then, as you would say in English, "the penny dropped". It was the figure I had seen in Sydney eleven years earlier dressed as I had seen it then and suddenly I felt at peace and safe. The lady kept me company for many hours. We didn't speak; there didn't seem to be anything to say. I tried to move a couple of times but she put her hand on my shoulder. As night came lights appeared in the distance. It was a team of rescuers with powerful torches and they had spotted me. The lights blinded me momentarily and when I turned to look at my companion she was gone. I was alone again and about to be rescued. I had survived by some miracle and the intervention of a *yūrei* — a kindly spirit — from 8000 kilometres away in Sydney.'

The protagonist in this story can be found at his desk in Tokyo or out on assignment any day of the week. He has not shared his experiences with many others and would only allow his story to be published here if his name was withheld. And can he explain what happened in Australia in 2000 and in Japan in 2011? To that question he simply shakes his head and says that some things are best left unexplained. He's probably right.

16.
Romeo and Juliet in the Jungle

> *If a man is killed before his life span is completed, his vital spirit is not yet exhausted and may survive for a while as a ghost.*
>
> **Chu Hsi (Chinese philosopher, 5th Century AD)**

We tend to think of multiculturalism as an invention of the last century when migrants from war-torn Europe and later Asia and the Middle East flocked to our shores seeking new lives and new opportunities but, in fact, Australia has been 'multicultural' since the arrival of the first white men more than two centuries ago. Convicts transported here were mostly British but the free settlers that followed came from right across Europe and the gold rushes of the mid-nineteenth century attracted prospectors from all corners of the globe, including tens of thousands of industrious Chinese. The benefits of multiculturalism are evident all around us today and, sadly, so are the racism and the intolerance that gave rise to the following story.

The principal characters in this sensational tale were a nineteen-year-old youth with a Chinese father and an Anglo-Saxon mother, and a sixteen-year-old girl, daughter of an Aboriginal mother and a Spanish father, all of whom lived in Cooktown, Queensland, in the late 1870s. Like Romeo and Juliet these two were star-crossed lovers whose parents forbade them to marry on racial and religious grounds. The Spanish father swore he would strangle his daughter rather than see her marry a 'heathen Chinaman' and the Anglo-Saxon mother threatened to disown her son if he married 'a papist black gin'. Tempers flared, nerves frayed, unretractable words were spoken and arguments raged in both families through long, hot, tropical nights.

In desperation the youngsters decided to run away together. They probably planned to walk the 150 kilometres through rugged mountains and dense rainforest to the Palmer River where a gold rush was then in progress and where they might disappear and make a new life together.

As soon as their absence was discovered the girl's father (a store keeper) went to the police and charged the young man with abduction. The police sent out search parties and after a couple of weeks the runaways were brought back to Cooktown. Several sympathetic local residents testified to the young man's good character and previous good behaviour and the charge against him was dropped, but one aspect of the case baffled the police. When the young man was searched he was found to be carrying gold sovereigns and small nuggets of gold worth several hundred pounds. It was known that neither family had ever possessed such riches and no one in the region had reported the theft of sovereigns or nuggets in recent weeks.

At first the young man was reluctant to explain how he had come by this treasure but, when he realised he would be charged with stealing if he did not, he told a remarkable story. The girl corroborated every word and the police, unable to disprove the story, accepted it and recorded it in their official files. The press picked up the tale and it was reported in newspapers as far afield as Shanghai, St Petersburg and New York.

The young man told how he and his girlfriend set out from Cooktown, avoiding the main tracks, living off the land and supplementing their meagre diet with damper made from a small bag of flour the girl had stolen from her father's stock. One afternoon they wandered into Limestone: a little shanty town about 100 kilometres south-west of Cooktown near the headwaters of the Palmer River. Limestone had grown up around a goldfield that had since run out. The prospectors and townspeople had drifted away and the town was completely deserted. There were a few huts with doors and windows standing open, a one-room hotel and a cemetery in which stood a tiny Chinese joss house, all rapidly disappearing under the encroaching jungle.

The boy and girl explored the joss house. Its walls, once gaily painted red and yellow, were cracked and peeling; a faint smell of incense lingered inside and scraps of paper with Chinese characters inscribed on them hung from the ceiling. The young man noticed a glazed porcelain urn about the size of a teapot and used for storing ashes of the dead standing amid the dust and leaves on the floor, apparently forgotten when the building was abandoned. He knew the purpose of such urns but gave it an irreverent kick anyway.

In an overgrown garden they found some dry little oranges on a stunted tree and had these for their supper, then bedded down for the night in one of the disused huts. The night was hot and sultry. Fruit bats squabbled in the forest canopy and swarms of mosquitoes plagued them, but eventually the couple fell asleep in each other's arms.

In the middle of the night something woke the young man. He looked towards the doorway of the hut and to his amazement saw the vaguely outlined figure of a man standing there. At first he thought it was a policeman or a black tracker and that the authorities had caught up with them but, as he watched, the figure became clearer and he could make out its face and clothing, both of which were Oriental. The figure began to glow with an unearthly light and stared back at the terrified youth with smouldering eyes. It then raised one of its arms and made a beckoning movement three times — then vanished.

The young man woke his sleeping companion and told her what he had seen. She tried to convince him he had been dreaming and went back to sleep, but he sat up watching the door until dawn came and the sun dispelled his fear. As soon as the girl woke up the young couple made ready to leave, but just as they emerged from the hut they heard the sound of approaching horses. They hurried back into the hut and watched as a gang of prospectors travelling down from the goldfields came riding up. They were a tough and rowdy lot and one of them fired off a shot to see if the sound raised anyone in the town. When no one appeared they laughed and dismounted outside the little hotel. The young couple watched as the men went inside and tore the place apart in the hope of finding some forgotten grog, then settled themselves down on the verandah of the hotel to rest. They remained there most of the day, smoking, swapping yarns, cussing, swearing and sleeping. Finally, in the late afternoon, they remounted and rode away, oblivious to the two pairs of eyes that had been watching them, nervously, all day.

It was then too late for the young couple to leave on foot so they decided, reluctantly, to spend another night in the hut. For several hours all was quiet then, at around midnight, the oriental spectre appeared again in the doorway, bathed in a bright, golden light. Both the lovers were awake and they clung to each other in terror as the figure loomed over them. Both could see its sunken face and hollowed eye sockets and the dry skin stretched over its cheekbones. Dangling from its otherwise shaven head was one long pigtail that glistened in the moonlight like a fat black snake. A high-collared jacket in blue (secured with wooden buttons) and baggy trousers hung from its body as if there was barely enough inside to fill them. Spindly ankles were encased in white stockings and feet in blue slippers; bony wrists extended from the jacket sleeves and attached to them were spider-like hands with long curved nails the colour of ivory. As on the previous night the spectre's eyes shone with a strange yellow light — like the glow of sunlight through a piece of amber, the young man later described it. No pupils were visible and no eyelids descended to break the unrelenting stare that was focused on the terrified lovers.

The ghost began to beckon again, more earnestly this time, and seemed intent on making the couple follow it. Trembling from head to toe and clasping each other's hands the boy and girl obeyed, following the glowing figure down the street to the cemetery. The ghost kept looking over its shoulder to make sure the couple was there; its glistening pigtail swaying back and forth with each twist of its head. Its gait was unsteady and stumbling and although its feet seemed to be touching the ground they raised no dust and left no imprints.

When it reached the joss house the ghost entered and beckoned to the couple to follow. The bright light that emanated from the figure lit up the interior of the little building and the smell of incense was now so strong it filled the couple's nostrils. The ghost moved about as if searching for something, then stopped beside the overturned urn. As its reluctant companions watched, the ghost rose slowly off the ground, its rising causing a breeze which stirred the dry leaves on the floor and set the scraps of paper on the ceiling fluttering. The figure came to rest over the urn, hovering about a metre off the ground. It turned its gaze back onto the young couple and as they watched its scowl dissolved away and was replaced by an expression of deep sorrow — 'like the thing had suddenly remembered some terrible injustice' the girl later described the change.

The glow faded from the ghost's eyes and its whole figure drooped, looking no longer threatening but shrunken, helpless and pathetic. The girl felt the ghost's pain and instinctively reached a hand out towards it, offering human comfort, but the ghost drew back. For a moment it seemed inclined to linger but then with one final sorrowing glance at the couple it disappeared, suddenly and completely, just as it had the night before, plunging the little joss house back into total darkness.

The stunned young couple came to their senses and ran as fast as they could back to the relative safety of the hut, jamming the broken door across the entrance. They sat huddled together for the rest of the night, trying to comfort each other with hugs and hollow words and waiting to flee at first light.

The sun again dispelled the young man's fears and he persuaded the girl to go with him to take one last look at the joss house before they departed. His curiosity had been roused and he wanted to look more closely at the urn. When they reached the joss house everything was just as it had been the day before — the dust and leaves undisturbed, the incense smell once more very faint, the scraps of paper hanging limply in the morning heat and the urn lying exactly where the young man had kicked it over.

The young man picked up the urn and read aloud the inscription engraved on its base in Chinese characters: 'Within this humble vessel lie the ashes of a Son of the Celestial Kingdom, Fen Cheng Loo'. Instinctively both boy and girl knew they were now numbered among the late Mr Fen's acquaintances.

'Please put it down and come away,' the girl begged her companion, but the boy was annoyed with Mr Fen's ghost for showing him up as a coward in front of his sweetheart, so he removed the stopper and upended the urn. Instantly his hand was covered in fine white ash. The wind caught some of it and blew it in his face. Horrified, he dropped the urn, which hit the hard ground with a loud crash and shattered. Both boy and girl gasped and stared in amazement. The urn had had a false bottom and among the shards of pottery a fortune in gold sovereigns and small gold nuggets lay shining in the sunlight.

17.
Australia's Most Famous Haunted House

They say that shadows of deceased ghosts
Do haunt the houses and the graves about,
Of such whose life's lamp went untimely out,
Delighting still in their forsaken hosts.

Joshua Sylvester (English poet, 1563–1618)

What was it that made a woman faint with terror, a fearless youth run screaming across windswept paddocks on a bleak winter night, a child hysterical with fear, two people fall down with fright and an office bearer of the National Trust of Australia unwilling to discuss her experience of 'unspeakable horrors'? Was it one of the ghostly figures, or the bloodstained floorboards that no amount of scrubbing would clean, or the invisible, icy hands that gripped the throats of unsuspecting victims who ventured into the building known as Australia Most Haunted House?

Bungaribee was a stately homestead on a small rise overlooking the Great Western Highway at Eastern Creek, about forty kilometres west of Sydney. It was a graceful, white, two-storey building surrounded by wide, flagstoned verandahs. An elegant, cedar-panelled circular drawing room surmounted by a squat tower overlooked sweeping lawns. Wisteria and oleander bloomed in the gardens and tall pine trees cast cool shade. Bungaribee had been the hub of local society in its heyday and the echoes of music and laughter, the rustle of crinolines and the flash of scarlet uniforms lingered in its quiet recesses and gilt mirrors — and yet all was not what it seemed. There was an all-pervading sense of sadness about the house that seemed to come from the bricks and mortar, as though the building itself was grieving for past sorrows, and a sinister feeling that caught innocent visitors unawares and sent shivers down their spines.

Bungaribee was built by Major John Campbell, who arrived in Sydney in 1821 with his wife Annabella and their thirteen children. Campbell acquired a number of small properties in the Eastern Creek area and consolidated them into one large estate. For so numerous a family Campbell also needed a large house. The site he chose was significant in local Aboriginal lore; some claimed it was sacred land and should not be profaned by the construction of a white man's humpy. It had also been the site of a great battle between warring tribes. The Aborigines called it *Bun-garri-bee*, meaning burial place of a great chief, and that was the name Campbell adopted for his estate.

An unusually large convict workforce was assigned to Major Campbell and construction began on the house in 1824, using bricks baked on the property. A story that the bricks were imported as ship's ballast from England and hauled in handcarts drawn by pairs of female convicts all the way from Circular Quay was invented; however, there was more than usual unrest among the convicts at Bungaribee. On at least two occasions they broke out and escaped *en masse* to the bush. A number died during the construction of the house and at least one was murdered.

Campbell borrowed heavily to build his house and stock his estate and was under constant pressure from his creditors. He sought aid from the Reverend Samuel Marsden, who declined to make him a gift of newly imported merino sheep, and from John Macarthur (a distant relative), who reluctantly advanced him 800 pounds as a mortgage against the property. As the house was nearing completion in 1826, Annabella Campbell became ill and died. The last section of the house, the round drawing room and tower, were begun the following year, but brought Campbell little joy. He scratched his leg, the wound turned septic, and less than a year after the death of his wife, Major Campbell was laid to rest beside her in St John's churchyard, Parramatta.

Bungaribee was put up for auction and bought by Thomas Icely, who began what became the long tradition of using the property as a horse stud. Some of the most successful racehorses of the period came from Icely's stables, but within two years he had departed and a new owner, the prosperous Sydney butcher Charles Smith was in residence. Smith was followed in quick succession by four more owners, including the ill-fated speculator Benjamin Boyd — the seventh owner in less than twenty years.

Why, you might ask, did such an attractive, well-situated and commodious property change hands so often? True, there were droughts, floods and financial crises to plague owners but there was also an ever-growing catalogue of personal tragedies surrounding the house that brought them anguish and sorrow. After the deaths of the convicts then the Campbells, the house's next victim was an army officer who, legend has it, lost a duel then shot himself in one of the small rooms in the round tower. When found, his body lay in an enormous pool of blood. In 1837 Charles Smith's brother Benjamin (a strong and healthy man) dropped dead near the gates of Bungaribee and then the body of one Major Frederick Hovenden was discovered in the grounds. Hovenden had apparently been fleeing his creditors and sought refuge at Bungaribee. Beside his body lay his cap and scratched on it were the words *died of hunger*.

From the 1860s onwards the house entered a period of stability — at least as far as occupancy was concerned — but if the Cleve family, the Bouldens and the Waters remained longer than their predecessors they did so at a great price. Strange events were beginning to happen, centred on the circular drawing room and its tower. There were three small rooms in the tower, reached by a circular staircase. In the room where the officer had shot himself the massive bloodstain reappeared on the floor. Time and again reluctant housemaids were sent to the room with bucket and brush to clean the floor but the stain simply reappeared the next day. Strange sounds, scratching, scraping and muffled screams could be heard in the tower along with the sound of clanking chains at night.

One family left their seventeen-year-old son in charge of the house while they went on a short trip. The lad was sturdy and game and decided to spend his first night alone in the house in one of the tower rooms. Around midnight he awoke in panic. Powerful, cold, clammy hands were clasped around his neck, squeezing the breath from his body. The young man could see nothing but fought his invisible assailant desperately. Eventually he broke free, ran down the stairs and out of the house, screaming in terror. He did not stop running until he reached the centre of a large open paddock, where he was found the next morning by farm workers, cramped and shivering.

Some years later a boy of five was put to bed in one of the tower rooms. In the middle of the night his parents were woken by terrible screaming. When they rushed to their son they found the little boy crouched on his pillow, hysterical with fear. His eyes were glassy and he stared into an apparently empty corner. 'Don't let him touch me!' the child screamed. 'Don't let him come near me!'

Two women had similar experiences. One was grasped on the arm by cold, invisible fingers as she climbed the stairs and the other felt frigid, clutching hands at her throat. The second collapsed and was found wrapped in a tablecloth, gibbering insensibly. Did the murderous spirit hands belong to the officer who suicided in the tower, or to one of the other unfortunates who died at Bungaribee? At least two possible culprits were seen — in ghostly form.

Early last century a young woman and her male companion attended one of the many fashionable balls held at Bungaribee. The circular drawing room was used for dancing and refreshments served in the next room. The young couple were the last to leave the drawing room when supper was announced. As they moved towards the door the young woman drew her companion's attention to a strange woman dressed in white, who was peering in through the French windows. The woman seemed to be crying; alternately rubbing her eyes and clawing at the glass with splayed fingers as if trying to gain entry to the room. The couple reacted as anyone would and moved towards the door, assuming the woman was in trouble, but then stopped in their tracks when they realised that they could see the verandah posts *through* the figure. The young woman screamed and her companion shouted for help, but by the time the other guests returned to the tower room the woman in white had vanished.

In 1957 a letter appeared in the *Sydney Morning Herald* from a Mr Sydney McKeon, who wrote:

> *Some fifty years ago I was employed by Robert Boulden who leased Bungaribee House and lands. The family had previously resided at Bungaribee but had moved away because of ghostly manifestations in the house. Mrs Boulden*

(a strict Christian) told me that night after night the family had seen an old man — or so he appeared to be by his bent body — in convict garb and wearing leg-irons slowly ascending the stairs to the tower room, where he would vanish. Again, when members of the family were returning home late at night, this same old lag would be sitting upon one of the gateposts. The horses would refuse to go through the gateway and the family had to drive to another entrance. On other occasions, on arriving home late, the family saw the tower rooms, which were unoccupied, illuminated by a strange glow.

When interviewed by a journalist at about the same time, Annie Forsyth Wyatt, Vice President of the National Trust of Australia, who lived near Bungaribee, admitted that she had seen the bloodstains in the tower and other 'unspeakable things' that she could not bring herself to recount.

Other visitors to the house were less reluctant to share their experiences. While wandering the grounds one hot summer night, a male guest from New Zealand claimed to have witnessed a ghostly re-enactment of the murder of the convict. 'I heard a scuffling sound and angry grunts coming from behind a large clump of pampas grass and thinking it was a person or an animal in distress I hurried over,' he recalled. 'To my amazement I found two men there: one lying on the ground, the other with his knee on the prone man's chest. The second man held a brick in his hand and as I watched he struck the other man's forehead with the brick. I shouted "Stop!" but neither figure seemed to hear me. The murderer raised the brick to strike again, so I reached out to grab his hand, but at the moment my hand should have come into contact with his, the whole ghastly spectacle simply vanished.

I lost my balance at that point and fell to the ground, landing where the figures had been just a moment before. Dirt-covered and deeply shocked I returned to the house and told my host what I had seen. I tried to describe every detail, but felt at the time there was something I had forgotten. Weeks later and hundreds of miles away I remembered. Both men had been wearing heavy iron fetters and chains on their ankles.'

Another visitor to the house told of her terrifying encounter with the white lady on the verandah outside the tower room. 'It was late afternoon,' she said. 'I was sitting on the verandah reading when all of a sudden a cold wind swept over me. I shivered, and thinking it was just the evening coming on, decided to go indoors. As I rose from my chair my book slid off my lap and fell onto the flagstones. I stooped down to pick it up and while I was bent over a pair of feet in white satin slippers suddenly appeared beside the book and just inches from my hand. I got such a surprise I fell back onto the chair and when I looked up there was a tall, slender woman dressed all in white standing over me. She had a pleading expression on her face and I could see tears rolling down her cheeks. I remember holding the book out in front of me like a shield and mumbling "What do you want?" but no sound came from the figure. Instinctively I knew she was not real — not a living person — and my fears were confirmed when her features started to melt like wax. Although the air was still, her white gown billowed out towards me and I shrank back, then she slowly faded away ... and I started breathing again.'

Stories like these about Bungaribee were numerous and when the building began to deteriorate with age and neglect its derelict appearance added to its reputation. Around 1910 the land was subdivided and sold off as small farms. In 1926 a Mr Charles Hopkins bought the house and spent a great deal of money restoring it. Among the unexpected finds during the restoration was what looked like a tomb covered by a large slab of stone in the garden, but even offers of extra pay could not induce Hopkins's workmen to open it. For a short period the house enjoyed a revival, but when Hopkins departed it was left unoccupied. The roof leaked, the windows and doors swung open in the wind. Rats, snakes and pigeons took up residence in its mouldering rooms. The garden became overgrown and the graceful, sweeping carriageway disappeared under a sea of weeds. By the early 1950s the once elegant house was in complete ruin. Thieves had removed anything of value and vandals had smashed the rest. Most of the roof was gone, leaving the shell of the building wide open to the elements.

In 1956 the Commonwealth Government bought what remained of the land as the site for the Overseas Telecommunications Commission's radio transmitting station. The facility required a wide belt of open land around the transmitter and the decision was made to demolish what remained of the historic old house. If such a decision was made today it would raise a storm of protest, but in the 1950s the community was largely indifferent to issues of heritage and conservation. Those who knew the house and its reputation were probably glad to see it go. Fortunately the man chosen to deliver the *coup de grâce* to the 130-year-old building, a Rooty Hill builder named John Lawson, had a passionate interest in history. Lawson dismantled the ruins carefully, preserving many of the old building materials and meticulously recording the antique building methods.

Lawson discovered that the round tower was supported by two hollow columns, which stood the full height of the building. Inside these were the bones of hundreds of possums who had fallen in and been unable to escape. He attributed the scratching and screaming sounds heard in the tower to these animals and the bloodstains to their urine. He may have been right but nothing Lawson turned up could explain the ghostly figures seen by so many people. The legends and stories persisted long after the building disappeared; and to this day senior citizens of the district still speak with awe about old Bungaribee — Australia's most famous haunted house.

18.
The Ghost of Mount Victoria Pass

You'd call the man a senseless fool,
A blockhead or an ass,
Who'd dare say he saw the ghost
Of Mount Victoria Pass;
But I believe the ghost is there,
For, if my eyes are right,
I saw it once upon a ne'er-
To-be-forgotten night.
The lonely moon was over all
And she was shining well,
At angles from the sandstone wall
The shifting moonbeams fell.
In short, the shifting moonbeams beamed
The air was still as death,
Save when the listening silence seemed
To speak beneath its breath.
The tangled bushes were not stirred
Because there was no wind
But now and then I thought I heard
A startling noise behind
Then Johnny Jones began to quake;
His face was like the dead
'Don't look behind, for heaven's sake!
The ghost is there!' he said.
He stared ahead — his eyes were fixed;
He whipped the horses like mad.
'You fool!' I cried, 'you're only mixed;
A drop too much you've had.
I'll never see a ghost, I swear,

But I will find the cause.'
I turned to see if it was there,
And sure enough it was!

From *The Ghost at the Second Bridge*, Henry Lawson (Australian writer and poet, 1867–1922)

The spectacular Blue Mountains of New South Wales have been a popular playground for holidaymakers and day trippers for over a century, but their rugged beauty was not always appreciated. To early colonists the mountains formed a seemingly impenetrable barrier to the expansion of the settlement; and it was not until 1813, twenty-five years after the colony was founded, that a primitive road was hacked through the dense bush and rugged sandstone ridges, opening the western plains to acquisition and development.

Convicts laboured and lost their lives building that road, moving thousands of tonnes of rock with picks and shovels and constructing stone bridges as strong and dependable today as they were nearly 200 years ago. The steepest section of the road wound up and over Mount York, but the danger of accident was so great that an alternate route (only slightly less precipitous) was opened and Victoria Pass came into being in 1832. Modern travellers speeding along the smooth black ribbon that is the Great Western Highway give little thought to the perils, physical and otherwise, that lurked at Victoria Pass. In earlier times it was quite a feat to climb to the top and descend the other side without mishap or delay and, if travelling at night, there was the added risk of encountering the Ghost of Victoria Pass, which haunted the second bridge on the eastern side.

Travellers reported that their horses would become restless as they approached the bridge, then the ghostly and ghastly figure of a young woman would suddenly appear in front of them. As suddenly as she appeared the spectre would then disappear, leaving witnesses anxious to put as much distance as possible between themselves and the scene of their harrowing experience.

History can put a name to this ghost. She was born Caroline James, and at the time of her death she was Mrs William Collits. Caroline came from a shady and unstable family. Her father ran a sly grog shop on the land where the old Woodford Academy now stands in the village of Woodford and her drunken mother had hanged herself there. Despite this unsavoury background Caroline married into a respectable family: the Collitses, proprietors of the inn at Hartley Vale. Unfortunately for Caroline, the Collits who took a fancy to her was the black sheep of the family, William, described by his father as 'a spendthrift idiot'. William Collits and Caroline James were married in 1840, but their marriage was anything but blissful. Caroline's younger sister was married to a thug named John Walsh, who was Caroline's as well as her sister's lover before and after their marriage. When her new husband turned out to be a poor substitute for Walsh, Caroline left him and moved in with her accommodating sister and brother-in-law in a *ménage à trois*.

There was talk of reconciliation between Caroline and William in the New Year of 1842. They met, along with Walsh, for a drink in Joseph Jagger's tavern near Hartley, but soon after leaving the tavern Walsh attacked William. Caroline came to her husband's aid by holding Walsh's arms and screaming to William to run for his life — which he unhesitatingly did.

The next morning a postman delivering mail came upon the battered body of Caroline Collits beside the road on Victoria Pass. Her skull had been smashed with a large stone which lay, stained with her blood, nearby. John Walsh was arrested for her murder but pleaded innocence, accusing not William Collits as you might expect, but Joseph Jagger, the tavern keeper, of committing the crime. The jury at Walsh's trial did not believe him. He was convicted and hanged.

William Collits remarried seven months after Caroline's murder and lived a long and happy life. His family achieved posthumous fame in the 1930s when they and their inn became the subject (with much alteration of fact) of the first successful musical comedy entirely written and produced in Australia on an Australian subject —*Collits' Inn*, starring Gladys Moncrieff and George Wallace. Needless to say, the black sheep's branch of the family and this gruesome episode do not figure in the plot.

Poor Caroline achieved fame of an entirely different kind — destined to spend an eternity of cold and windy nights haunting the bridge at Victoria Pass, spooking horses and terrifying travellers. There were numerous hair-raising accounts of encounters with her ghost including this one from two youths driving a cart over the pass near midnight one night.

The youths reported that as they approached the bridge their horse became so skittish that one of them had to climb down and the lead the animal. The youths assumed it was a night bird or another animal that had spooked the horse but as they drew closer to the bridge they saw what the horse had already seen or sensed — a tall, slim, female figure dressed in a black gown of some shiny material that glowed darkly in the moonlight. The figure was standing beside the stone parapet of the bridge looking down into the gully below.

The youths assumed it was a living person and the one leading the horse called out: 'You're out late, miss. Are you all right?' At first the figure seemed not to hear, then it turned slowly towards the youths and their horse and cart, keeping its head tilted downwards and its features in shadow. When the figure moved, the horse stopped in its tracks and no amount of encouragement or tugging would make it step onto the bridge.

The youth sitting on the cart called out. 'Would ya mind steppin' off the bridge for a moment, missus? It's our horse, ya see, she's scared —'

The youth never finished his sentence. The words froze in his mouth as Caroline's ghost raised its head to show its face and stared directly at the group. 'I never seen nothin' so *bloody* frightenin' before or since,' he later said. 'A soon as we saw 'er face, we knew she weren't 'uman. 'Er eyes shone like a tiger's ... there were sparks of fire in 'em and shooting out of 'em. She raised one arm 'igh in the air then t'other and her 'air streamed out in the breeze like seaweed in shallows. Then the worst part 'appened. The thing's mouth slowly opened and a soft moanin' noise came from inside the black 'ole. It got louder and louder until it seemed like it was all around us and *inside* us; and it changed from a moan to a terrible 'owl. You know they talk in the Bible about demons howlin'? Well I reckon that's what that were ... a demon howlin'! It sounded like no 'uman or animal I ever 'eard.'

The terrifying sound was too much for the horse. Using today's vernacular we might say it 'freaked out' at that point and, unable to turn around, reared in the shafts of the cart. The youth on the driver's seat had to hang on for dear life as the animal bolted, carrying the cart with it. The other youth grabbed the tailboard as it passed and clambered aboard. Horse, cart and passengers careered across the bridge — over the ghost, through it or under it — and on down the road for several hundred metres before the youth in the driver's seat managed to bring the horse under control.

'What in the 'ell *was* that?' one youth asked the other.

'I dunno, but I 'ope I never see it again. It ain't *followin'* us, is it?' his companion asked.

The first youth mustered his courage, turned and looked back. 'It's *still there* ... on the bridge,' he reported. 'Go mate! Just *go*!' he shouted, his voice quaking.

The youth on the driver's seat flicked the reins and the horse picked up speed again. They didn't stop till they reached their home town, Blackheath, five kilometres further down the range; horse and humans all lathered in sweat.

Some comfort from her tormented afterlife may have come to Caroline in the 1880s when Henry Lawson came to live in the nearby village of Mount Victoria: the young poet wrote a sixteen-verse poem about her, entitled 'The Ghost at the Second Bridge', quoted in part at the beginning of this story and reminiscent of the youths' experiences. The poem gave Caroline a permanent place in Australian literature, but it was small recompense for the ills done to her in life.

Some say that Caroline Collits put a curse on the village of Mount Victoria, but its current prosperity belies that. No one has seen the Ghost of Victoria Pass for many years, which is hardly surprising. The road has been upgraded and widened so many times that the old bridges are barely visible; and if Caroline was still inclined to put in an appearance on the roadside at night, dressed from head to toe in black, it's doubtful if the occupants of the cars hurtling by would even notice her.

19.
The Ghost in the Machine

There are two gates of sleep, one of which it is held is
made of horn and by it easy egress is given to real ghosts.
The other shining, fashioned of gleaming white ivory,
but the shades send deceptive visions that way to the light.
Virgil (Roman poet, 70BC–19BC)

Most doctors (like other practitioners of the sciences) are sceptical about things supernatural. An exception is Dr Chloe Hill — and, no, that's not the good doctor's real name. As her remarkable story unfolds you will understand why a pseudonym had to be used to preserve her anonymity and her reputation.

Chloe is currently doing her internship at a Sydney public hospital and hopes to set up in private practice in a year or two, but her story begins when she was still a student in the autumn of 2010. The school of medicine Chloe attended offered dissection of human cadavers as an elective component in the medical degree course and Chloe, like most of her fellow students, opted for it, believing that exposure to a real body would be more beneficial than studying plastic models or computerised images.

The cadaver allotted to Chloe to work on was that of a middle-aged man who had bequeathed his body to medical science. The man was overweight and had succumbed to a massive heart attack, so the external parts of his body were untouched, but large flaps of fatty tissue had to be divided and clamped back before Chloe could begin work on his internal organs.

Chloe worked quickly and deftly, all the while trying not to let her gaze wander onto the cadaver's face. A short, thick, grey-streaked beard that looked more like steel wool than human hair framed the lower part of the face in sharp contrast to the upper part which was hairless — no eyelashes, no eyebrows and a smooth, shiny scalp. This curious arrangement made the cadaver's head look as if it was attached to its body upside down. That might have struck your average medical student as comical, but a twisted mouth and tiny, pig-like eyes gave the face a sinister cast, as though cruelty in life somehow lingered on in death.

After removing all the cadaver's abdominal organs and laying them out on stainless steel trays, Chloe reached for her laptop and began making detailed notes of her observations. Apart from the cadaver's face, which continued to trouble her, Chloe found the whole exercise exhilarating and engrossing. The professor of anatomy who was supervising came by and questioned Chloe about the condition of the cadaver's heart, praising the acute observations she had made about it. Time passed quickly and in what seemed much less than the four hours the clock on the wall of the dissecting room indicated, Chloe was removing her surgical gown and mask and cleaning herself up in the scrubbing room.

That evening Chloe's boyfriend Reece took her to a Thai restaurant for dinner. During the meal Chloe regaled Reece with all the details of her morning's anatomical adventure. Now Reece was not a medical student (he was studying architecture), but he knew Chloe well and appreciated how passionate she was about medicine. He put up with all the gory details while he tried to enjoy his roast duck in red curry sauce and his jasmine-scented custard, but when it came to responses the most he could manage was an occasional, unconvincing 'wow' or a half-hearted 'terrific'. Reece was a patient and trusted friend and although neither he nor Chloe knew it then those qualities were about to be tested.

A week later Chloe discovered she had a minor problem with her laptop. A tiny spot of bright light (no bigger than a pin head) appeared in the centre of the screen. Chloe thought nothing of it the first time the spot appeared, reminding herself that the machine was getting old. If the spot didn't go away, Chloe decided she would drop her laptop off at the local computer repair shop to have it checked, then thought no more about it.

Chloe had noticed the spot of light on a Friday and did not switch her computer on again until the following Monday morning. When she did the spot was still there and she fancied it was a little brighter than she remembered. It was annoying, but nothing more. That night when she checked her emails the spot was definitely brighter and also a little larger; and to her surprise Chloe found that it remained on the screen after she switched the laptop off. Thinking there must be some leakage of power from the battery, Chloe made the decision to call into the repair shop the next day.

Before she left home the next morning Chloe checked that the spot was still there and it was, but when she reached the computer repair shop and opened the laptop to show the technician, the spot was gone. 'Prob'ly just a glitch in the wiring that's fixed itself,' the technician said. When Chloe reached home she opened the laptop again and the spot was back, glowing brighter than ever in the centre of the empty black screen. It also appeared to be larger again, as if it was growing a little in size each time Chloe looked at it. It was now about the size of a match head and large enough for Chloe to discern that it was not round but oval and slightly elongated, like an egg lying on its side.

Chloe had a lecture that day and she took her laptop into the lecture theatre, but it would be fair to say that she did not hear most of the talk. When she opened the laptop, the elongated, glowing shape was now about two centimetres long and Chloe found herself absorbed in trying to work out whether the shape had any recognisable form. As the lecture came to an end and Chloe closed the laptop she concluded it did not and that the thoughts of planets, glow-worms and jelly fish that had flashed through her mind were all fanciful.

Reece came around that evening and Chloe told him about the annoying fault in her laptop. 'Give us a look,' suggested Reece. When Chloe lifted the lid of the laptop she gasped. The glowing spot was now about four centimetres in length and a centimetre in height and its shape instantly triggered an alarming memory. Reece was mystified when his girlfriend slammed the lid down and announced firmly, '*No*, I don't want to look at it any more ... let's go out and get a coffee.'

Reece sensed Chloe's distress and over two cappuccinos tried to reassure her with: 'Don't let it get to you, love ... it's only a machine'. But Chloe knew that sitting on her coffee table in the lounge room of her flat was something much more than a few circuit boards, a collection of wires and a plastic case.

Later that evening after Reece had gone home Chloe summoned up the courage to open the laptop. The glowing shape had grown larger again and Chloe could now make out the shape of the cadaver she had dissected ten days earlier, laying in profile on its dissecting table, half covered by a grey cloth as she had first seen it. There was no mistaking the shape: the cadaver's belly rose like a smooth mound in the centre, its feet stuck up at one end and its bald, bearded head made another bump at the other end. Chloe stared at the image in disbelief and with fear rising inside her. Again she slammed the laptop closed and before she went to bed she locked it away in a drawer.

For the next two days Chloe could not bring herself to unlock the drawer but the longer she delayed the more morbidly curious she became. Finally, near lunchtime on the third day, when bright sunlight was streaming into her flat and the noise of birds, cars and people going about their business in the street drifted in through the windows, she unlocked the drawer and carefully took out the laptop. Chloe placed it in the centre of her kitchen table and gingerly opened it. A second later she began to tremble uncontrollably. The ghost of the cadaver (for that most assuredly was what had entered Chloe's computer) was now quite clear and filling about a third of the screen. Its head was turned towards her, the face carrying a hideous scowl and those pig-like eyes wide open and staring back at Chloe.

Now most of us might have smashed the laptop at that point or taken it somewhere and burned it, but Chloe lacked the resolve to do either. She locked the laptop away again and tried to forget its existence, but curiosity inevitably got the better of her. The next time she looked the ghost had 'grown' again in size and had raised itself up on one elbow. Its free hand was extended towards Chloe and those awful eyes were still staring directly at her.

A week later when she looked again, she found the ghost had begun to rise from its table and now had the grey sheet secured around its belly. The head and the hand were halfway across the black void between ghost and victim and reaching out towards her. A day later it was closer again — almost filling the screen — and Chloe could see the individual hairs on the ghost's chin, its bloodshot eyes and the blackened fingernails on its outstretched hand.

On what would prove to be the last time Chloe looked at her ghostly tormenter, it was so close its face alone filled the screen. Chloe realised that the ghost's next step would be to leave the screen and to materialise in front of her. The whole experience had been terrifying, but that prospect did not bear thinking about.

Chloe slammed the lid, grabbed the computer and ran from her flat. With the computer held firmly under her right arm she ran the two kilometres that separates her flat from Reece's. People stared as Chloe careered along quiet suburban footpaths. Two individuals asked if she was OK as she rushed by, but Chloe didn't stop to reply. All the while she was praying that Reece would be home when she reached his flat.

He was and responded immediately to Chloe's pounding on his front door. 'What's wrong, babe?' he asked. 'You look *awful*.' Chloe was panting and between gasps for breath she asked Reece if he would get his car out and drive her somewhere. '*Any*where,' he said and five minutes later Reece, Chloe and the laptop were speeding along Oxford Street then Old South Head Road, heading for The Gap.

'Why are we going to The Gap?' Reece asked. He was growing increasingly concerned about Chloe's state of mind and her insistence that they drive to Sydney's most notorious spot for suicides alarmed him.

Chloe had thrown the laptop onto the back seat of Reece's car and she now pointed over her shoulder to it. 'We're going to get rid of that *thing*,' she explained and a shiver coursed through her body when she spoke the final word. 'I want to see it smash into a *million* pieces and be swallowed up by the sea!'

Reece concluded that he must trust Chloe and pressed her no further, concentrating on his driving and fulfilling Chloe's insistent pleas to go faster.

The car screeched to a halt in the car park in Military Road at The Gap and Chloe reached into the back for the laptop, but it had shifted along the seat during the journey and she couldn't reach it. Reece reached over and took hold of it. 'Don't open it!' screamed Chloe and Reece assured her he would not.

Reece carried the laptop once the couple had abandoned the car, leaving the doors open. They raced along the cliff-top paths towards the highest point, startling lazy lizards sunning on rocks and making gulls squawk indignantly and take flight. Finally they stopped at the railing of an observation ledge, both breathless and windblown.

Stretching as far as the eye could see was the vast blue Pacific Ocean. To their left rose picturesque North Head across the entrance to Sydney Harbour and to the right the spectacular coastline stretched away towards Bondi Beach. 100 metres below them, at the foot of a perpendicular cliff, the sea boiled and roared as it crashed onto jagged rocks.

Chloe took the laptop from Reece. She held it in both hands, raised her arms above her head and hurled it out into the windy void beyond the railing. Reece and Chloe clung to the railing so tight their knuckles turned white as they watched the laptop falling and tumbling over and over as distance made it grow smaller and smaller. Finally it struck a jagged rock at the base of the cliff and shattered into 'a million pieces'. A huge, foam-capped wave rolled over the rock and swept away what remained of the laptop and, Chloe hoped, its ghostly occupant. At that moment a sound that resembled an immense sigh resounded through the jagged rifts in the cliff and swept up and over the two tiny figures on the cliff top — a combination of wind, waves, the cries of seabirds and perhaps another element that had once been human.

One day if you are unlucky enough to need the services of the accident and emergency department of the hospital where Chloe is now an intern, you may encounter her, but you will be unlikely to realise it is she as she tends to you with calm professionalism and gentle skills — and that's exactly how Chloe would like it to remain.

20.
Ball, Chain and Whip

Do I believe in ghosts? No, but I am afraid of them.

Marquise du Deffand (French aristocrat, 1697–1780)

Australia was colonised by the British to provide a dumping ground for murderers, thieves, rapists and rebels, but if the villains who arrived in chains were an unsavoury lot, those put in charge of them were often not much better. The power-drunkenness of such men (liberally spiced with sadism and bestiality) created monsters and their convict charges were easy prey. Not surprisingly many a brutal overseer or superintendent of convicts met a sticky end and their enraged ghosts refuse to depart, still seeking retribution 200 or so years later.

One particularly nasty example is said to reside at Hyde Park Barracks in Macquarie Street, Sydney — once home to 900 convicts and arguably Sydney's most haunted building. Reports of the ghosts of emaciated convicts in convict garb, female figures in filmy white robes, clanking chains, ghostly footsteps and strange lights have been reported from this building for the past sixty years, but the phenomenon that upsets witnesses most is the ghost of a former superintendent. This evil spectre materialises in the doorway of what was once his office; and all agree he is not a pretty sight and the sounds he makes are far from pretty.

'I was leaving the building one night at about six o'clock when I remembered that I had not switched a photocopier off,' one former employee recalls. 'Only the security lights were on, but because it was summer there was plenty of soft light coming in through the windows. I was walking back to the office when I heard a noise behind me. I turned thinking another colleague was working back or a security guard was on his rounds, but what I saw stopped me in my tracks and made me scream — the first and only time I have *ever* screamed involuntarily in my life.

'In a pool of bluish light like a spotlight stood a giant of a man dressed in old-fashioned clothes — a greasy white shirt with a red bandana knotted around the neck, tight black pants, heavy boots and a maroon jacket. He had a large belly that hung over the top of his pants and tufts of wiry, grey hair poked through gaps in his shirtfront. He was completely bald and his face was red and veiny with bulbous lips and bulging eyes. He was leering at me and I could see spittle dribbling from his mouth.

'I knew without doubt that I was face-to-face with a ghost. It seemed solid but parts of it were fuzzy and moved in and out of focus. I held my briefcase up in front of me and yelled "Leave me alone!", then I backed away and the thing followed me. Then it spoke and I can still hear its gruff voice and its hollow-sounding tone as clearly as if I had heard it yesterday: "'Ello, m'dear," the spectre said. "You come t' keep me company?" "No!" I shouted back. The creature's expression changed. What had been half a smile turned into an evil scowl. "Ain't I good enough for ya ... ya stinkin' whore? You'll feel me fist if ya don't gimme a kiss!"

'At that point I ran. I didn't look behind me to see if the thing was following but I could hear it shouting abuse at me. Never in my life have I heard such *awful* language. I didn't stop running until I reached St James's Church across the road. I don't know what led me there — shock, fear, a cry for God's help? Who knows? I pushed on one of the old doors and it swung open. I stumbled into the church and slumped down on the nearest pew. I sat in that peaceful, comforting House of God for almost an hour until I had calmed down enough to go home. And you know, after that I *never* stayed in the barracks alone — day or night.'

A few years ago an organisation called the Centre for Metaphysical Studies conducted a survey of supernatural events at the barracks and members of that group reported being confronted by the same nasty spectre and also being given one of its foul-mouthed tongue-lashings.

Just how this obnoxious spectre came to meet his death is unclear. Witnesses have never commented on any life-threatening injuries visible on his face or figure, but visible (and horrible) they most certainly are on the one in our next story: another convict-keeper whose haunt lies about fifty kilometres west of Macquarie Street.

The old Great Western Road between Parramatta and Penrith is rich in ghost stories. According to an article in the *Nepean Times*, ghosts would sit upon the top rail of the fences that lined the road 'like swallows on a telegraph wire' and the most ghoulish of them all was to be found at Quarry Hill, near where the University of Western Sydney now stands.

Quarry Hill gets its name for the obvious reason — there was once a quarry there where hundreds of convicts toiled and many died, gouging thousands of tonnes of stone from the hillside with picks, shovels and bare hands to pave the roads of an expanding colony.

The gruesome saga of this ghost begins at the quarry face in the winter of 1838. A young convict, unfit for such hard labour, collapsed one day and the overseer had him carried a short distance away. The young man regained consciousness to find his face pressed against the rough bark of a gum tree, his shirt ripped down and coarse ropes binding him to the tree trunk. By turning his head slightly he could see the fate that awaited him. The overseer was limbering up his right arm and in his hand he gripped a vicious-looking cat-o'-nine-tails. The first lash drove the breath from the young convict and a searing pain the like of which he had never experienced before shot through his whole body. Fifty hard lashes were rained down on him and by the time the overseer desisted there was little flesh left on the young man's back.

The swooning and delirious convict was carried to a local infirmary where rum was poured on his wounds and later salt rubbed into them to aid healing. After a month of excruciating and unremitting pain, a surgeon pronounced him fit to return to work at the quarry.

The convict's back (which had been soft and white) was now tough like leather and so was his resolve to avenge himself on the overseer. He waited two days for the right moment. While the overseer's attention was diverted he crept up behind him, raised his pick and swung it with every ounce of strength he could muster. The overseer never knew what hit him — the sharp point of the pick entered his head at the base of the skull and ended up poking out of his forehead.

The convict paid for his moment of sweet revenge with his own life — strung up by the neck then buried in an unmarked grave, but it was not his ghost that was soon being reported by travellers on the Great Western Road. It was the overseer's and a more terrible sight, witnesses said, could hardly be imagined.

The ghost appeared near the entrance to the quarry, sometimes by moonlight, sometimes in lightning flashes on stormy nights. It was covered from head to toe in fine dust. In its hand it carried the blood-soaked pick that had taken its life and from a huge cavity in the ghost's forehead rivulets of dark blood streamed over its face, neck and chest.

Coachmen cracked their whips and raced their horses past the spot while mothers covered their children's eyes and closed their own for fear of seeing the grisly sight. Travellers on foot prepared themselves with tots of rum and ran as fast as their legs could carry them to the next inn. Plenty saw the ghost and many who did not (including those who closed their eyes) imagined they did.

Stories of the ghost of Quarry Hill persisted for fifty years and more. One night in 1880 an employee from Fleurs, a large estate near today's St Marys, was sent to Penrith to fetch a doctor. When the man approached Quarry Hill his horse took fright and his dog began to howl. Only by blindfolding and leading the horse and carrying the trembling dog was the man able to pass. Well into the last century old-timers still spoke in whispers about the Quarry Hill ghost and travellers (unaware of the stories) commented on the unaccountable feeling of dread that overtook them on that stretch of the busy road.

It is impossible to put names to either the ghost at Hyde Park Barracks or the one at Quarry Hill, but a third colleague of theirs is the most famous of the many ghosts who haunt the picturesque village of Richmond in Tasmania and he can be named. A few biographical details about him also survive.

George Grover was convicted of stealing at Winchester in the south of England in 1825 and transported to Tasmania where he served seven years before obtaining the post of flagellator (official flogger) at Richmond. When repairs were required to the stone bridge spanning the Coal River alongside the village, Grover was also put in charge of the convict work force.

Chained convicts quarried large blocks of stone at nearby Butchers Hill, then carried them in handcarts to the bridge. The stout and sadistic flagellator rode on top, cracking his whip like an Ancient Egyptian slave driver and inflicting as much pain and misery as he could on his long-suffering charges.

Grover's reign of terror came to an end one foggy day in March 1832 when he fell or was pushed off Richmond Bridge. One version of the event has the convicts turning on him and beating him to death with their manacled fists before hurling him off the bridge, but a report in the *Hobart Town Courier* says he fell or was pushed from the bridge parapet 'where he had lain himself down while drunk'. Someone wrote in large, bold lettering across his convict record: *Murdered March 1832* as if to say 'thank goodness'.

There have been claims ever since that whenever a heavy fog envelops Richmond, Grover's angry ghost can be seen stalking the bridge, searching for his killers and lusting for revenge. Some claim to have seen him trying to clamber up the slimy sides of the bridge from the rocks nine metres below. One witness — a mild-mannered young curate who was a stranger to the district and knew nothing about Grover or his ghost — had to be hospitalised after his encounter with the spectre.

The curate was crossing the bridge one evening when he heard a strange scratching sound and cries for help coming from under the bridge. The curate was short-sighted and when he peered over the parapet on the northern side of the bridge all he could see was mist swirling over the surface of the river. Then, when he turned to check the other side, a pair of large, hairy hands suddenly appeared, gripping the parapet. Thinking someone was clinging on for life the young curate rushed forwards. Below the hands was a pair of brawny wrists and these the curate grabbed in his own slim, white hands. 'Hang on,' the curate said, 'I will try to pull you up.'

The curate was not a strong man and he doubted he had the strength to be a Good Samaritan, but he was determined to give it his best shot. He prayed for divine assistance, took a deep breath then tugged. To his amazement the figure offered no resistance; it rose quite effortlessly. In less than a second the figure's face was level with the curate's, but it was not a normal face; anything but. The curate later described it as the face of a demon from hell — 'living, yet not living'. The eyes were alive and fixed on the curate with an evil, mocking gaze; the rest of the face was a bloody mass of whiskers and battered flesh.

The curate let go of the spectre's wrists and ran for his life. He looked back just once and the spectre was still there, floating beside the parapet, and from its bruised and broken lips came a cackle of demonic laughter. The curate ran to a house at the end of the bridge and pounded on the door before collapsing on the doorstep. Later he was admitted to a hospital in Hobart and it was many weeks before he recovered his senses.

Richmond Bridge is not the only place in the village that Grover's unsightly spectre is said to appear. A figure, believed to be him, has also put in occasional appearance in the flogging yard at Richmond Gaol, where he plied his bloody trade as flagellator. One small boy who visited the gaol with his grandmother a few years ago became visibly distressed when they entered the flogging yard. When asked what the matter was, the child pointed at an empty space and denounced 'the horrible man with the bloody face' that only he could see and who was terrifying him.

George Grover and his two nasty colleagues in New South Wales all began life at the bottom of the social ladder and none climbed up it very far, but our fourth and final convict-keeper came of more distinguished stock. Captain Patrick Logan, commandant of the penal settlement at Moreton Bay (Brisbane) from 1825 to 1830 could trace his ancestors back to the time of the Crusades. He was a distinguished soldier, a capable administrator and a far-sighted visionary. Unfortunately he was also ruthless and just as merciless to his charges as the others.

Captain Logan's cruelty earned him the title 'The Fell Tyrant'* and made him the subject of one of Australia's best-known folk songs, *Moreton Bay*, which describes the horrific plight of convicts under his rule. Misconduct earned them up to 300 lashes and many died strapped to the flogging frame. Logan was feared and despised by the convicts and the final verse of *Moreton Bay* rejoices at his violent death.

The Captain was also a courageous explorer who made many journeys sometimes alone, into the interior, surveying and mapping the wild terrain. It was while returning from one of these excursions, riding alone along a bush track in what is now South Brisbane, that Logan met a ghost. The Captain spotted a man in convict uniform a few yards in front of him and, thinking it was an escapee from the settlement, hailed him and ordered him to stop.

Logan expected the figure to run but to his surprise it approached him, reached out a sinewy arm and grabbed one of his stirrups. Logan's horse took fright and reared. The Captain lashed out with his riding crop but the blow passed straight through the shadowy figure. He spurred his horse to a gallop but the ghost clung on, floating effortlessly beside the terrified

---

* 'Fell' is an old-fashioned adjective meaning terrible, fierce and destructive.

horse and rider. It was not until they were nearing the south bank of the Brisbane River that the ghost suddenly let go and disappeared.

Logan's fear may seem out of character for a ruthless man with an inquiring mind, but something else had unsettled him: Captain Logan had recognised the ghost. It was a convict called Stimson, who had absconded, been recaptured at the very spot where he appeared, and died while being flogged on the Captain's orders exactly one month earlier.

Logan met his own death on another expedition. He set out with his batman and five trusted convicts on 9 November 1830, to map a creek west of the outpost at Limestone Hills (Ipswich). The party was stalked for most of its journey and attacked twice by hostile Aborigines but, despite this apparent danger, Logan went off on his own on 17 October, planning to rejoin the party at a rendezvous at dusk. When he found he could not reach the spot before nightfall, Logan built a rough shelter and settled down for the night. In the early hours of the morning of the eighteenth he was attacked and killed by Aborigines or — according to some historians — by convicts.

At noon that day a party of prisoners working on the river bank at the Moreton Bay settlement spotted Captain Logan on horseback on the far side of the river, waving to them. None had any doubts about who it was. Two of them downed tools and hastily launched the punt that was used to ferry people across the river and rowed over to pick up their commandant. When they arrived on the south bank (the spot where Stimson's ghost had disappeared and the Queensland Performing Arts Complex now stands) there was no sign of Logan. He and his horse had vanished into thin air.

At that time the Fell Tyrant's battered body was growing cold in a shallow grave in the bush seventy kilometres inland.

21.
The Rabbi, the Bishop and the Pearl

'I am the Ghost of Christmas Past.'

'Long past?' inquired Scrooge: observant of its dwarvish stature.

'No. Your past.'

***A Christmas Carol*, Charles Dickens**
(English novelist, 1812–1870)

On 12 March 1912 a severe cyclone was bearing down on the small town of Port Hedland on the north coast of Western Australia. In port that day was the 3726-tonne passenger steamer *Koombana*, pride of the Adelaide Steamship Company's fleet, scheduled to depart for Broome 500 kilometres to the north. The captain decided it would be safer to put to sea and weather the storm in deep water. The *Koombana* steamed straight into the path of the cyclone. It was never seen again and has gone down in history as the worst civilian shipping disaster in Western Australian waters. Not one of the 138 people on board survived.

Among the victims was a man named Abraham Davis, well known in Port Hedland and Broome as a successful pearl buyer (and no relation to the author, as far as I know). This was the heyday of pearling on the Western Australian coast and the rough shanty town of Broome was the pearling capital of the world. Pearls of unprecedented size, quality and lustre and tonnes of precious pearl shell were being harvested from the Timor Sea. The dangerous work was done by Japanese and

Filipino divers but the profits were made by men like Davis, some honest, others shady and most somewhere in between.

Davis had first come to Broome as manager of his brother-in-law Mark Rubin's pearling empire, comprising several ships, dozens of divers (kitted out in the company's distinctive livery when above water), an impressive office in Dampier Terrace and agents trading the company's wares as far afield as London. When his brother-in-law over-extended himself and went broke in 1908, Davis took over what remained of the enterprise and also the Rubin family home in Hamersley Street.

By local standards this building (described as a 'bungalow') was palatial, with polished wooden floors and wide verandahs. Davis employed a team of Japanese craftsmen to further enhance it by installing ornate moulded ceilings and expansive bay windows. He also retained the most remarkable feature of the house — a German-made pipe organ that dominated an enclosed verandah on one side of the house; it had been his sister's pride and joy.

The Rubins and Davis were Jewish and after the departure of his kin, Abraham Davis became the unofficial rabbi for the Jewish community in Broome and the covered verandah (complete with organ) became their makeshift synagogue. It was said that the strains of the organ, the cantillations of the *chazzan* and the responses of the congregation could be heard wafting across Roebuck Bay every *Shabbat* — strange and incongruous sounds in a place well-accustomed to incongruities.

In 1910 Davis transferred his business to Port Hedland but retained ownership of the bungalow in Broome. At the time of his death he also owned a large stock of pearls, including the famous (or infamous) 'Rosea', an exquisite, pink-hued gem the size of a marble and valued at almost 20,000 pounds.

The Rosea had been wrested from the sea in 1905 and passed through many hands, leaving a trail of treachery and death in its wake, before Davis acquired it. Some believed the pearl was cursed and possessed black powers that would bring bad luck and death to all who touched it. It had (believers claimed) already accounted for a drowned diver, a murdered buyer, the lives of the buyer's murderers (who had been hanged for their crime) and the suicide of a subsequent owner. The popular writer Ion Idriess eventually used the Rosea pearl's turbulent history as the basis for his novel *Forty Fathoms Deep.*

When Davis's death on the *Koombana* was reported many people blamed the curse and asked the question: what has become of the ill-fated pearl? It was not among his stock or his personal effects in Port Hedland, which meant that Davis had either been carrying it when he boarded the *Koombana* (in which case it had returned to the bottom of the sea) or he had hidden it somewhere. As the pearl had been bought in Broome, people speculated that it might be hidden in or around Davis's bungalow and the strange events that followed seemed to support that theory.

In 1914 the bungalow was bought by the Anglican Church as a residence for the first Bishop of North West Australia, the Right Reverend Gerard Trower. Bishop Trower moved into what was thereafter known as the Bishop's Palace a few months before the outbreak of World War One. Gerard Trower was an energetic, practical administrator with a fine mind and a zealous faith. He had previously been Bishop of Likoma in Nyasaland (Malawi), where he had built schools, hospitals, a theological college and a fine cathedral. No doubt his superiors hoped he would do the same in his new diocese. The Bishop wrote that the house in Broome, comfortable though it was, was of little use to him, his territory being so large and priests so few that he spent most of his time travelling. However, when he was in residence he sometimes had a quite unexpected, late-night visitor.

Soon after he moved into the pearl buyer's former home, the Bishop was awakened one night by a strange light and an unaccountable breeze stirring the curtains in his bedroom. As he watched, mystified, a hazy figure surrounded by an aura of soft light entered the room — not through the door but through a solid wall. The Bishop thought he might be experiencing some divine revelation — the visit of an angel perhaps, to give him guidance or call him, prematurely, to his Maker — but as the figure became clearer he realised that it was a middle-aged, heavily bearded man with flabby folds of flesh the colour of bruises under his eyes, wearing the robes and prayer shawl of a Jewish rabbi.

The spectre (according to the Bishop) addressed him in perfect English and introduced himself as Abraham Davis, the former owner of the house. The Bishop asked what he wanted but the spectre gave no answer, preferring to make light conversation about the house, the weather and anything but his reason for being there. The Bishop and the Rabbi chatted amicably for ten minutes, then the latter began to look furtively around the room, slowly faded, and finally vanished, leaving the Anglican cleric rubbing his eyes in astonishment.

Davis's ghost reappeared to Bishop Trower several times, always apologising for its intrusion but clearly bent on some mysterious purpose. As the Bishop later recalled: 'Finally, on our fourth or fifth encounter, I quizzed my spectral visitor directly on the purpose of its visits. "Are you in need of something, sir?" I asked. The spectre screwed up its face into an obsequious smile, stroked its beard with one pale and heavily-ringed hand and replied: "It is such a fine night, my friend. Does one need a reason to be abroad on such a night?" I was determined to pin the spectre down so I pressed on. "I get the impression that you have a quest ... that you are searching for something lost," I said. The spectre bowed its head and replied: "I seek only what all men seek ... wisdom and serenity."'

Visitors to the palace also reported seeing the Rabbi wandering the garden at dusk when the Bishop was away, a substantial figure that appeared to be flesh and blood until it passed uninterrupted through thorny bushes and effortlessly through solid obstacles. Observers all commented on its rabbinical robes and its beard, which was variously reported as neat and black or long and grey. Others reported that the spectre seemed to be afflicted with a limp. None seem to have been particularly alarmed or agitated by its presence.

Despite the assumption that ghosts need no sustenance, the ghost of Rabbi Davis seems to have retained a keen interest in food. The Bishop's housekeeper reported it appearing suddenly one evening in her kitchen and inspecting the food she was cooking. 'I had a nice leg o' mutton simmering away on the stove with a pot of potatoes and another of broad beans,' she said. 'I watched him bend over the stove and cast a suspicious eye over the contents of the pots. I think he was checking to see if the food was kosher, and disappointed to find it was not.' On another memorable afternoon, the ghost was seen mingling with guests at a garden party hosted by the bishop; not speaking, but bestowing ecumenical smiles on everyone and, some say, stealing a plate of buttered scones!

What was it that made the ghost of the dead pearl buyer return to his bungalow so many times? Was he simply curious to see his old house and to meet the Christian priest who entertained gentiles in his former synagogue, or was he searching for the Rosea pearl? When news of the Bishop's other-worldly visitor spread most people chose to believe the latter.

Bishop Trower departed in 1927; and if his successors ever saw the ghost they never admitted it. The building became sleeping quarters for the staff of a nearby hotel, then operated as a cheap boarding house for some years. Eventually it fell into ruin, but the legend that the ghost of Rabbi Davis haunted its crumbling walls persisted until it was finally demolished in 1980.

As far as I know the Rosea pearl has never turned up. Perhaps it lies on the seabed in the wreck of the *Koombana* (believed to be in deep water midway between Port Hedland and Broome), or maybe it's still buried where the Bishop's Palace stood, waiting for some fortunate (or unfortunate) person to stumble upon it.

22. Crimes of Passion

Of all ghosts, the ghosts of our old loves are the worst.

The Memoirs of Sherlock Holmes,
Sir Arthur Conan Doyle (Scottish mystery writer, 1859–1930)

Unlike those in most other state capitals, Perth's daintily odd Government House is on the edge of the central business district and overshadowed by tower blocks, but of the thousands of people who pass its gates each day few know the story of the cold-blooded murder that once occurred there and the ghostly legacy it left behind.

Beside the main block of Government House stands a ballroom, designed in 1899 by the father of Australian composer Percy Grainger. In former times this large, airy room was the centre of the city's social life. Charity balls were regularly held there and it was at one of these that the murder took place.

Imagine, if you will, the packed interior on an August night in 1925, decked out with long ropes of flowers and lit with ever-changing pastel-coloured lights. The dance floor is filled with smart young couples, some in fancy dress, the rest in chic gowns and tuxedos, strutting and gliding to the music of a jazz band. Silvery laughter, clapping and cigarette smoke fill the air and the cares of the world seem far away.

Suddenly, among the dancers, a pretty young dark-haired woman in an electric-blue dress raises her arm. As if in slow motion, a lace handkerchief slips from her hand and flutters to the floor, revealing a small black pistol. One deafening shot rings out and a man in a tuxedo clutches his forehead. Blood begins to spurt as he falls like a stone to the floor.

Audrey Jacobs was an independent young woman used to getting what she wanted, and what she wanted was Cyril Gidley, handsome young marine engineer and notorious womaniser. They had been lovers until Cyril tired of her and moved on to fresh conquests. According to evidence at Audrey's trial the two had met unexpectedly at the ball. Audrey had then gone home to fetch her gun and visited St Mary's Cathedral on the way back before exacting a terrible revenge on her ex-lover.

Due in part to the persuasive powers of Arthur 'Ginger' Hayes, her defence council, Audrey Jacobs was acquitted at her trial and walked free to loud cheering from the public gallery, but what really saved her was the absence of one key witness, the man standing closest to the shooting, who had disappeared in the commotion. That witness kept his identity secret for forty-six years until he published his autobiography — it was Claude Kingston, J. C. Williamson's celebrity concert manager, who had decided he could not afford to get entangled in the affair and wondered for the rest of his life whether his testimony might have altered the outcome of Audrey Jacobs's trial.

If Cyril Gidley's killer had been punished perhaps his ghost would not haunt the scene of the crime. Soft footsteps, thought by some to be a woman's and by others to be those of a man wearing dancing pumps, have been heard pacing the ballroom at Government House. Gidley was an Englishman and also an anti-Royalist and that may account for a flurry of ghostly activity in 1977 when Prince Charles was due to attend a ball there to celebrate the Queen's Silver Jubilee.

Organisers complained that furniture carefully set in place to observe royal protocols was mysteriously moved around and crockery and glassware in the supper room rearranged at night. A portrait of the Queen was tilted to an odd angle and potted plants placed in buckets ready to be installed the next day were found dry and wilted.

The official explanation was 'wind' and it was pointed out that the building had a reputation for being 'draughty', but the real culprit was spotted by a security guard at dusk on the evening before the ball. A young man dressed in a tuxedo and fitting the description of Cyril Gidley at the time of his death was spotted leaning on the railing of one of the balconies, casually smoking a cigarette.

The security guard shouted a challenge and reached for his high-powered torch. The figure turned and looked down, but when the torch beam reached the spot where it had stood it was gone. The security guard rushed upstairs to find the balcony empty. Only the faint smell of cigarette smoke lingering in the air reassured him his eyes had not been playing tricks on his brain.

There were also reports of a female ghost being seen in the ballroom, but as Cyril Gidley's is the only recorded death in the building her origin is a mystery. Gidley was by all accounts a solidly built man who, even in spectral form, would be unlikely to be mistaken for a female. Could it be Audrey Jacobs? Well, after her trial she married an American and went to live first in South Africa then in the United States. Her death, presumably in the United States, went unnoticed.

A jealous lover was also responsible for a female ghost who haunted the grounds of Coolgardie Hospital a generation earlier. By all accounts Elizabeth Gold was an attractive young woman — attractive enough to turn the head of Captain Charles de Garburgh Gold, a distinguished soldier twenty-six years her senior. Captain Gold was the scion of a renowned British military family and a widower with two grown-up children. His great-grandfather died at Bunkers Hill during the American War of Independence; his grandfather fought at Waterloo; and his father commanded the British troops in New Zealand at the outbreak of the Maori Wars. Captain Gold had had his charger shot out from under him, been wounded twice and awarded the Medal of Abyssinia.

Elizabeth and Captain Gold were married and somehow ended up in Coolgardie in 1896. He was by then retired from the army and may have gone there to watch over mining investments. Shortly after his fifty-seventh birthday, in May the following year, Gold suffered a ruptured appendix and was admitted to Coolgardie Hospital, where he died of peritonitis.

After the Captain's death, Elizabeth Gold moved into a house in Hunter Street where she became very friendly with her neighbours, Mr and Mrs Kenneth Snodgrass. The father of five children, Snodgrass was a respected accountant who served on the boards of several public institutions, and Mrs Snodgrass's friendship was a great comfort to the young widow.

Elizabeth was just thirty-two and found herself at a loose end. She conceived the noble idea of devoting the rest of her life to nursing. Whether the idea originated from her husband's short stay in hospital or whether nursing was an old, unfulfilled ambition is unknown but, for whatever reason, she set off for Perth and nurses' training college.

In less than a year she was back, employed as a probationary nurse at Coolgardie Hospital. Among the other trainee nurses was one of the Snodgrasses' daughters and the hospital matron was Kenneth Snodgrass's cousin. Elizabeth picked up her friendship with her neighbours where it had left off, but

Mrs Snodgrass was now spending long periods in Melbourne. In her absence the relationship between Elizabeth and Kenneth Snodgrass developed into far more than friendship. They became lovers.

Snodgrass was fifty-five, about the same age Captain Gold had been when he and Elizabeth married. A routine developed. Once a week Snodgrass would tell his children he was popping over to see Mrs Gold but, as well as making love to her, he would interrogate her about other men. Snodgrass was that most dangerous of lovers — the jealous kind.

About a year after the Captain's death it was announced that a charity ball in aid of the hospital was to be held in the local hall. Elizabeth informed Snodgrass that, like all the nurses who worked there, she was expected to attend. He could not appear in public with her and the thought of Elizabeth dancing with other men infuriated him. Snodgrass demanded she make some excuse not to go. Elizabeth refused point blank; she was going. Snodgrass badgered her for days but she would not be swayed.

The day before the ball Kenneth Snodgrass borrowed a revolver from a friend. He needed it, he said, to shoot some feral cats that were annoying his hens. Mrs Snodgrass arrived back from Melbourne the next day. Snodgrass made some excuse to leave the house that evening and waited for Elizabeth on the path behind the hospital, where he knew she would pass on her way to the ball.

At dusk, while the sky glowed lemon and purple shadows descended over the dusty bush, she appeared — a vision of loveliness in an elegant white ballgown. Snodgrass stepped out in front of her, brandishing the revolver. He begged her to change her mind and go home but she refused. The mixture of hatred and pity on her beautiful face enraged him. He raised the gun and fired. The bullet hit Elizabeth in the breast. She staggered then recovered and began to run across a tennis court towards the hospital. She managed only a few frantic steps before he fired again. The second bullet struck her in the head and she fell. A huge patch of blood spread across the white fabric of her gown and dripped from her head onto the tennis court.

Snodgrass stood over Elizabeth's lifeless body, the smoking revolver still in his hand. Suddenly anger and passion were replaced with horror as he realised what he had done and to whom. He raised the gun again, held the end of the barrel under his chin and squeezed the trigger. The dead lovers were found lying side by side on the fault line of the tennis court.

Elizabeth Gold was buried the next day. Clouds had gathered during the night and the short service at the graveside was held under a grey and threatening sky. Just a few of the other nurses from the hospital attended. The rest of the community had grasped the truth of the situation as soon as news of the double slaying had broken. Within hours Nurse Gold had been posthumously demoted from respectable widow to Jezebel. One of the nurses placed a small cross of wild, yellow everlasting daisies on the coffin as it was lowered into the ground, then a sudden heavy rain shower washed the sand from the clergyman's hand as he was about to sprinkle it on the lid.

Snodgrass's family paid for an elaborate headstone and a wrought-iron fence around his grave. Elizabeth's remained unmarked for three quarters of a century, then a former president of the Coolgardie Council, the late Jack Tree, paid for a simple plaque to be added. Both headstone and plaque carry the same date of death: 31 May 1898.

The respectable citizens of Coolgardie might have preferred to forget Elizabeth Gold, but the lady herself gave them no opportunity. Quite soon after her murder reports began to come in of people seeing her ghost: a wraith-like figure in a flowing white gown floating across the tennis court behind the hospital. A cook and several nurses claimed to have seen her. The cook told how she had been taking some scraps up to a rubbish bin near the tennis court one evening when she saw 'a vague white shape, like a girl in an evening dress'. She dropped the scraps and fled. One of the nurses described the figure as appearing to be dancing — or playing tennis.

Another nurse claimed to have had a close encounter with the ghost and later told the press: 'I knew nothing about Nurse Gold or her story when I went to work at the hospital in the 1920s and I did not believe in ghosts. At the time I also thought people who claimed to see ghosts were nutters ... but I've changed my mind about that. I came off duty one evening at about six o'clock and I ducked out the back entrance planning to take a short cut past the tennis court to get back to my lodgings ... I had a date with a nice young man that night.

'On the path beside the court I saw a movement behind some bushes and I called out "Is there anyone there?" thinking someone might have been waiting to leap out at me. A woman came around from behind the bushes and walked towards me. She had long, dark hair and she was wearing an old-fashioned pearly white evening gown. My first reaction was to think to myself how beautiful she was and I was envious of her pale almost translucent skin — a rare sight in that scorching hot part of the country.

'"Hello," I said or something like that. The woman kept walking towards me and I got the sudden and quite alarming impression that although she was looking at me she couldn't *see* me. I stepped off the path and she passed right by me ... just a few feet away. I heard the swish of her gown on the ground and I could see she wore white satin evening slippers. Without realising what I was doing I reached out to touch her dress. My hand passed straight through the fabric and I felt nothing. Then, three or four yards down the path, she just vanished. One moment she was there; the next she was gone. I didn't stop shaking till I got to my lodgings and the next day when I commenced my shift I told the nurse I was replacing what I had seen, expecting her to tell me I was a fool. "Oh, that's Lizzie Gold ... she's a ghost," the other nurse said quite matter-of-factly. "Most of us have seen her."'

Hospital authorities always debunked reports of Nurse Gold's ghost, suggesting witnesses must have seen bed linen flapping on the hospital laundry's clothesline. The cook was especially vocal in refuting this. She said she was quite capable of recognising a bed sheet and was adamant that the ghost existed.

Eventually the tennis court was ripped up and the area remained strewn with rubble for many years, but the sightings continued. Jack Tree was quoted as saying the apparition only appears on 31 May, the anniversary of the murder–suicide, but admitted he hadn't seen it himself. He went on to say: 'When the hospital was operating the authorities wouldn't allow people on the grounds at night but now it's closed there's nothing to stop anybody going there on May thirty-first, any year, to see for themselves.'

If any reader thinks that sounds like an invitation they can't refuse, don't be put off by the locals when you arrive in Coolgardie. When asked by strangers about their most famous ghost, like as not they'll reply with a quip something like: 'Listen, mate. The only way you'll find gold in this town is to dig for it!'

23.
Phantom Steeds

My Lady hath a sable coach
With horses two and four
My Lady hath a gaunt blood-hound
That goeth on before.
My Lady's coach hath nodding plumes,
The driver hath no head,
My Lady is as ashen white
As one that is long dead.

Sabine Baring-Gould (English novelist and poet, 1834–1924)

In Baring-Gould's famous poem 'my lady's coach' is black and somehow we know her horses must be black too. Australia has its own pair of spectral black steeds, but rather than being harnessed side by side to a sable coach, their haunts are separated by about 200 kilometres.

One is said to appear in the courtyard of the Royal Oak Inn (one of Australia's oldest pubs, now called the Mean Fiddler) on Windsor Road at Rouse Hill west of Sydney. The story goes that on one tragic night in the nineteenth century a magnificent black stallion kicked a groom to death in the stables behind the inn. The animal was destroyed and its carcass buried but, from time to time, its ghost has made spectacular appearances, whinnying and snorting, pawing the ground with its hooves, rearing on its hind legs and flicking its ebony-black mane and tail in the moonlight. There have also been reports of its victim appearing, his head showing the marks where the animal's hooves clove his skull.

One witness reported hearing the noises the spectral horse makes, going outside to investigate and being confronted by it. 'There was bright moonlight casting deep shadows across the courtyard and at first I thought the big patch of black in front of me *was* a shadow. Then the thing snorted and reared up. I could see its coat shining in the moonlight and its eyes bulging and glowing like black coals. I saw its raised hooves held above my head then coming down to strike me. I threw myself off to one side. I must have hit my head on a barrel. I was dazed momentarily and when I regained my senses I struggled to my feet expecting to have to ward off another attack from the creature — but it was *gone* and there was no sign or sound to show it had ever been there. I have fought in battles and seen many terrible things in my time,' the witness concluded, 'but *nothing* that scared me half as much as that ghostly creature.'

John Seath, who held the licence of the inn until 1910, is said to have encountered the ghost of the groom in the stables one night and claimed it was so horrible to look at he could not bring himself to describe it. Ironically, Seath himself is now said to haunt the old inn. Legend has it that he buried a fortune in coins and banknotes in its grounds and died suddenly before disclosing the whereabouts of his fortune to his next of kin. Seath's ghost, locals will tell you, has now joined the spectral horse and the ghost of the groom and wanders the inn, frustrated and angry that his treasure is lost.

'The Black Horse of Sutton' is one of Australia's best-known ghost stories and a staple of the folklore of southern New South Wales. It tells of a Sutton farmer who rode into Goulburn one day to arrange a land deal. As he was nearing home on the return journey his dogs ran out to meet him, startling his mare and causing her to rear. The farmer was thrown to the ground and killed. Meanwhile, the farmer's wife was sitting on the verandah of their farmhouse unaware of the tragedy and waiting patiently for her husband's return. In the still of evening she heard the sound of galloping hooves in the distance. Relieved, she got up and walked to the verandah rail ready to greet her husband.

Suddenly, out of the lengthening shadows came a glistening black stallion, riderless and galloping at a furious pace. It crossed the patch of lawn in front of the house without hesitating, hooves digging, sending chunks of earth flying through the air. The creature headed straight for the house and the verandah where the shocked farmer's wife stood transfixed. The stallion made no attempt to slow, stop or turn. Then, at the moment it should have crashed into the verandah rail, it vanished, just a metre from the terrified farmer's wife.

The stallion had disappeared, but the sound of its galloping hooves continued, muffled for a few moments then loud again at the rear of the house. The spectre — for, as the farmer's wife had come to realise, this was no flesh and blood creature — had apparently passed right through the walls of the house before galloping off into the hills behind.

The distraught wife took this strange and totally unexpected experience as an omen and raised the alarm. A search was made for her husband and his body was found a kilometre or so down the road. The meddlesome dogs were whimpering and fussing over it while the farmer's mare grazed quietly nearby.

This was the first tragedy to strike the family and the first time the black stallion appeared but it was not the last of either. When the widow's eldest son was killed at the Boer War the phantom steed made another appearance; and again, when the youngest son was killed in an accident, the four-legged banshee returned.

Old-timers will stake their lives on the authenticity of this story, but if you ask the family's name or the exact location of the farm no one remembers. A bit of modern detective work reveals that there was a family name Ryan who owned a farm at Mulligan's Flat near Sutton whose history fits at least some of the details in the story. William Ryan was killed in the way described in the story returning from a trip, not to Goulburn, but to Queanbeyan, way back in 1857; and his youngest son did die in an accident, but there is no record of another son being killed in the Boer War. So is the story fact or fiction? Well, probably a bit of both. But we shouldn't let that detract from a damn good yarn and I for one would love to see that magnificent black stallion pass straight through a house! Wouldn't you?

Both of the above spectral steeds seem to have been magnificent animals, but without the slender grace of the racehorses who feature in our next three stories, all set in Victoria.

Many famous racehorses were bred at historic Bundoora Park on the outskirts of Melbourne; and two of the most famous, Wallace (first colt of the legendary Melbourne Cup winner Carbine) and Shadow King, who ran in six Melbourne Cups without winning any, are buried near the present-day museum.

It is claimed that ghostly hooves can be heard near the horses' graves and that they are made by the ghost of a mare named Lurline, who was shot by careless rabbiters over a century ago. Believers in the invisible, four-legged phantom suggest Lurline comes galloping down to investigate when she sees anyone near the graves of her famous stablemates. The phantom hoof beats are said to be so realistic that those who hear them expect to see a horse appear at any moment — but none ever does.

Another story (this time from Ballarat) features a winner of the Melbourne Cup — though it is not the horse whose ghost figures here, but its frustrated owner. During the gold rush era, Walter Craig built and operated Craig's Royal Hotel, one of Ballarat's most imposing pubs. The hostelry earned the title 'royal' after it played host to Prince Albert, Duke of Edinburgh and it continues in that tradition today as one of the state's finest boutique hotels.

So wealthy did the hotel make Mr Craig that he was able to indulge his passion for racehorses. One of these, Nimblefoot, was entered into the 1870 Melbourne Cup and, a few nights before the race, Craig had a dream in which his horse won the coveted cup. But, as he explained, there was an odd feature to the dream — the jockey riding Nimblefoot was wearing a black armband. Walter Craig died a couple of days later. Nimblefoot won the Cup and Jimmy Day, the jockey, rode wearing a black armband in memory of the late owner.

Over the years there have been reports of Walter Craig's ghost discreetly wandering the hotel. Perhaps he's searching for the 1280 pounds prize money his horse earned by winning the Cup. One witness described it as 'a portly ghost with a bushy beard' — not frightening but disturbing because of its forlorn expression and the long, sorrowing sighs it emits and which echo along the empty corridors of the building.

Legendary Australian jockey 'Darby' Munro, who rode three Melbourne Cup winners, attributed his first success as a jockey to a ghostly mare and a ghostly jockey; and his remarkable story makes a fitting end to our horses' tales. Munro — known to his admirers as 'the Demon Darb' — was just fourteen when he won his first race at a country meeting in Victoria. Years later he confided to well-known race commentator Bill Collins that he had had some supernatural assistance to get over the line that day.

'It was a fair size field for a country meeting,' Munro told Collins, 'about a dozen horses, as I recall. I got a good start and settled in nicely in third place on the inside. I made my move about midway through the race and overtook first one then the other leading horse, but my mount was tiring. He was a good little horse and he struggled on, but about 100 yards from the finish the rest of the field was fast catching us. Then another horse suddenly loomed up on the outside and shot straight past us! The new leader was a pretty rough-looking nag, but it was going like hell. The jockey wore purple and green colours and I swear he gave me a wink as they passed.

'Now I was only a kid at the time and there would have been no shame in coming in second, but I saw red when the bastard winked at me. My horse must have been pretty pissed off, too, so when I gave him a cut on the rump he shot forwards and caught up with the cheeky bugger.

'While all this was happening I was trying to remember who the horse and the jockey were, because I couldn't recall seeing them in the field, at the marshalling point or on the starting line. Anyhow, my little mount tried to hang on to the finish, but in the last few yards the other horse put on a spurt and crossed the line about half a length ahead of us.

'I was cursing and swearing and sobbing because it seemed I'd come within half a length of having my first win, but then all hell broke loose. Everyone started cheering and people came rushing up to me. The horse's owner and trainer and the chief steward shook my hand and congratulated me on *winning* the race. I opened my mouth to argue, looked around to locate the horse I thought had really won, found there was no sign of it or a jockey in green and purple and closed my mouth again very sharpish.

'You know, to this day, I have no explanation for what happened all those years ago. I asked a couple of people I knew well if they had seen the other horse and rider and they looked at me as though I'd gone crackers. I've wondered if some old horse and jockey long dead had reappeared on the track at that moment just to spur me on. Maybe the wink was a deliberate challenge. If so, I'm bloody grateful! My win that day was really the start of my career.' As an afterthought, Darby added: 'You know, Bill, when I die I wouldn't mind being a ghost on a good mount and maybe dropping in on a few big races.'

'The Demon Darb' died in 1966 and the Darby Munro Stakes is run annually by the Sydney Turf Club in his memory. If ever you have the privilege of watching this race, I suggest you count the horses and riders *very* carefully.

24.
Banished Spirits: the Ghosts of Port Arthur

> *Ghosts are the souls of men who met with a violent death, hanged, beheaded, impaled or departed this life in such a way.*
>
> **Lucian (Greek satirist, 2nd Century AD)**

The tragic slaying of thirty-five innocent people by a crazed gunman at Port Arthur in 1996 and the devastation caused to historic buildings there by a tidal surge just a few months ago are still fresh in the minds of Australians and yet, when history replaces memory, these events will come to be seen as single chapters in the long saga of cruelty and hardship that is the history of the old penal settlement. That Port Arthur is the haunt of many ghosts should surprise no one.

What is surprising is that the most haunted places in the complex are not the sombre prison buildings but the innocent-looking parsonage and the comfortable former residences of the commandant and the medical officer where families lived, for the most part happily and well, amid all the misery and deprivation that surrounded them.

Rumours of ghosts at the Port Arthur parsonage go back to the middle of the nineteenth century, when the Reverend George Eastman, a man of enormous girth, died in an upstairs bedroom. His empty coffin was manoeuvred up the narrow stairs but, when filled, it was found to be too heavy to be brought out the same way. A rope was rigged to lower the coffin from the bedroom window to the ground, but halfway down the rope snapped, the coffin fell and the bloated corpse of the late, lamented clergyman tumbled into the garden. For many years after that people reported smelling putrefying flesh, hearing moaning or morbid screams and seeing strange lights inside the parsonage. Some claimed Reverend Eastman's corpse reappeared from time to time, spread-eagled in the garden where it had, so ingloriously, landed.

The photographer and journalist George Gruncell published an account of other strange events at the parsonage in the 1870s. Gruncell told of a doctor finding all the windows of the parsonage ablaze with light one night and deciding to call in to welcome home Reverend Hayward (one of Eastman's successors) and his family, who had been absent for some weeks. Reverend Hayward answered the door but said that his wife and children had not yet returned. The embarrassed doctor explained that he had assumed all the lights had been Mrs Hayward 'putting things in order'. 'Lights?' asked the puzzled cleric. 'What lights?' Hayward and a servant had been alone in the kitchen at the back of the house and the only light burning was there. Others had also seen the bright lights and the phenomenon was the talk of the settlement the next day.

The Haywards themselves discovered light streaming from under the door of the minister's upstairs study one night soon after. The door was closed and the room apparently empty. When they peered through the keyhole the couple were amazed to see the whole room brightly illuminated but when they opened the door all was in darkness. A sceptical judge visiting the house soon after witnessed the same phenomenon, but a careful investigation of every object in the room by the minister, the judge and the doctor failed to find any explanation.

Later the sister of the Catholic chaplain at Port Arthur slept in a ground-floor bedroom at the parsonage while her brother was away and woke, screaming, one night, terrified by a loud banging sound that seemed to come from the floor and walls all around her. In the same room a few months later a housemaid fainted and when Reverend Hayward brought her round (by boxing her ears) she told of seeing a horrible, spectral figure at the window with a knife in its hand, poised to strike some invisible victim. Gruncell himself stayed at the parsonage and heard ghostly footsteps at night when all the living occupants of the house were in bed. He also observed Reverend Hayward's distress when the minister was walking down the stairs one evening and a cold, clammy hand came to rest over his own on the banister rail. Also, in company with Mrs Hayward, Gruncell found a lighted candle in a locked room early one morning before anyone else had risen.

What the Haywards believed to be the cause of all this mischief finally appeared (as a filmy, white figure) one night to Mrs Hayward's mother, a formidable lady whose husband had once been commandant at Port Arthur. Thinking it was a burglar and fearing attack, the old lady lay still in bed and watched the figure strike a match then glide silently across her room and out the door. When recounting her experience the sharp-witted matron did not comment on the size of the spectre (or Gruncell didn't report it), which effectively eliminates Eastman's ghost as the intruder.

The same strange, bright lights have been seen by staff and visitors to the Port Arthur parsonage in recent years and the mysterious banging heard by a house attendant. The same attendant (who, until then, had not believed in ghosts) also listened in horror one day to the stairs in the parsonage creaking loudly — first the bottom step, then the second, then the third and so on, until whatever invisible thing it was that was climbing reached the top. Objects, including a heavy vase filled with flowers, have also been mysteriously moved about inside the parsonage at night, long after it has been locked up and the burglar alarms set.

In the early 1980s when three builders were staying in the much-haunted house renovating it, one of them reported seeing a ghost — the first recorded sighting since Mrs Hayward's mother's 'filmy, white figure' of more than 100 years before. As the builder was entering his room one night he caught sight of a woman dressed in old-fashioned clothes. Instantly the temperature in the room dropped and the curtains billowed, although the windows were firmly closed. Seconds later the figure vanished and everything returned to normal. Another of the builders woke in the middle of the night with the sensation that he was being attacked. It felt, he said, as if someone was sitting on his chest and driving the breath from his lungs. At the same time each of the builders heard the oft-reported banging noises. The work the three were carrying out well might have upset the spirits in the old house — they were removing the second floor where much of the ghostly activity had occurred over the years and reducing the building to its original, single storey.

The Port Arthur church, now in ruins, stands a few metres from the parsonage. When foundations for the church were being dug in 1853 two convicts, William Riley and Joseph Shuttleworth, got into an argument. Riley killed Shuttleworth with a blow from a pickaxe and was hanged for the crime. The following year another convict fell to his death from the roof of the almost completed building after another argument. It was popularly believed that these two violent deaths were the reason the church was never consecrated — which is untrue. It was never consecrated to one denomination because it served all denominations. Less easy to explain is the fact that ivy, which grew in profusion on every other part of the building, would never grow on the bloodied spot where the second convict landed.

The church also figured in a strange occurrence a few years back when a large party of tourists were assembled there at 10.45 pm on a clear, starry night. Suddenly the whole church was lit by a brilliant flash of light that illuminated every side and every corner. It was not lightning and was far brighter than any camera flash could produce.

The medical officer's residence, which housed a succession of doctors and their families, is also reputed to be haunted. When it was used as a hotel in the 1920s a lady guest was wakened in the middle of the night by a tiny girl dressed in an old-fashioned nightgown, tapping on the outside of her bedroom window — metres above the ground — and attendants in recent times have heard children's laughter coming from empty, upstairs rooms. A lady dressed in pearly grey is also said to haunt the medical officer's residence. According to a former resident this ghost was often seen drifting down a passageway in the house and terrified at least three housekeepers, who resigned in quick succession. The same resident claimed he was awakened one night by the grey lady standing at the foot of his bed, snorting loudly. He assumed she was displeased at his presence and he was not overjoyed at hers. He switched on the light and shouted: 'Go away! Get out now! Get out of here!' and claims she did, never to return.

Strange noises (moans, footsteps, etc.) have been heard in the former commandant's residence for more than a century. Like the medical officer's residence this gracious old house, with its charming English gardens overlooking the bay, was turned into a hotel in the 1880s. Ghostly activity seems to have peaked in the last twenty years, since it, too, was restored to its original condition. Stories, and spirits, are numerous.

The ghost of Commandant Charles O'Hara Booth, the house's most famous occupant, is said to stand at the window of the room in which he slept, keeping a watchful eye on the settlement and silently weeping; and the ghost of a former nanny (dismissed after one of her charges met with an accident) has been seen in a wooden rocking chair in the nanny's room at the end of the house. This room and the innocuous-looking, spindly old chair are the subject of many stories. An attendant found the chair gently rocking by itself one Christmas Eve morning and on the same day another year voices were heard in the apparently empty room. Attempts by visitors to take photographs inside the nanny's room sometimes produce quite unexpected results: cameras jam; flashes fail to work; and when someone does manage to take a photograph, faint, shapeless, blurs usually appear on the screen.

The gate to the commandant's residence has been opened by unseen hands in full view of a group of tourists and many visitors' wristwatches stop at the moment they enter the building. A male attendant, claimed that, when alone in the house one day, he was grabbed on the bottom by an invisible assailant; and a spectral male figure with its head twisted to one side (like a hanging victim) has been seen at least twice in the hallway. Bells installed in the nineteenth century to summon servants occasionally ring when the house is empty; and a phantom coach and horses has been heard (and on one occasion seen) by groups visiting the cottage at night. One visitor started a sketch of the commandant's residence while visiting Port Arthur but did not have time to complete it. Some days later and many kilometres away the amateur artist got the sketch out to finish it from memory and found to her amazement that a female figure in period costume had been neatly and mysteriously drawn in the foreground.

A ghostly legacy seems also to have been left from the time when the house was the Carnarvon Hotel. A group of archaeologists sleeping there during restoration in 1983 had several terrifying experiences. One female heard footsteps in the night climbing the stairs and entering the room she slept in. No figure appeared but a soft groan echoed through the dark house before the footsteps returned the way they had come. Another of the archaeologists was awakened in the night by the hand and face of an elderly woman (no body or arms) looking over his bed then floating up towards the ceiling and fading away. A different female member of the party claimed to have seen a vision on the ceiling of a room where they were all playing cards one night. She saw, she said a woman being chased by a man. Her description of the woman tallied with her colleague's memory of the face he had seen; and later both recognised her in an old photograph they were shown of the former manageress of the Carnarvon Hotel.

Beside the commandant's residence stands the old powder magazine surmounted by an impressive watch tower. A reliable witness claims that he was grabbed on the arm by an invisible hand when walking nearby and on one memorable morning the sound of a ghostly bugle was heard playing Reveille from the empty tower. Directly behind the watch tower stands Tower Cottage, the former married officers' quarters. Two people who slept there at different times in recent years either dreamed identical dreams or saw the same apparition — a soldier in a red uniform leaning over the bed looking down at them.

Directly across the bay from the commandant's residence stands Jetty Cottage at the end of the commandant's jetty. The ghost of a young man, possibly Private Robert Young, who drowned near the jetty aged just twenty in 1840, is said to haunt that area. According to the account of a woman who, staying at Jetty Cottage a few years back, woke in fright to find the ghost in her room, he has straight black hair and wears a ruffled, white shirt. Another guest at another time saw the same figure sitting on the front steps of the cottage and on the jetty on two consecutive nights. This second guest also claimed to have heard a woman screaming at exactly 10.30 o'clock each night. Others too have heard the pitiful screams that resound through the lonely cottage and float across the water.

There are many other stories of ghostly activity at Port Arthur, not all confined to these comfortable houses and cottages. The multi-storeyed penitentiary, built in 1848 and now a roofless shell, seems blessedly free of ghosts at the moment but the smaller Model or Separate Prison, where inmates were kept in solitary confinement and required to wear masks to hide their features, echoes, it is said, to the screams of a fourteen-year-old prisoner who was confined in the condemned cell for two weeks awaiting execution. Another convict, William Carter, committed suicide in his cell in the Model Prison by hanging himself with the straps of his hammock. Tourists visiting this particular cell often experience unaccountable feelings of anxiety and depression long before they are told the story of Carter's suicide. Then there are the dark cells where prisoners were inhumanely imprisoned for long periods in total darkness and total silence. Is it coincidence that light bulbs in one of these cells continuously blow, just as visitors enter?

Many prisoners arrived at Port Arthur insane and many more became so after a spell in the punishment cells of the Model Prison. To cater for these unfortunates an asylum was built. This quaint building with its three-tiered tower became a museum and the rear portion was converted into a staff tea room. Two women working at the museum had a strange experience one day when a door slammed shut, trapping them in a small room. Try though they might, the heavy door would not budge. Their calls for help attracted two visitors walking by. The man tried to open the door from the outside but it seemed to be stuck fast. His wife half jokingly said, 'Let me try,' and applied her slender hand to it. The door swung open effortlessly. It had never jammed before and has never jammed since. Two other employees seated at a table in the staff tea room one day watched in amazement as a heavy ashtray glided across a flat bench top and had to be grabbed to stop it falling to the floor.

But of all the creepy places in this ghost-ridden location, the creepiest is not a building but an uninhabited island about a kilometre off shore — the 'Isle of the Dead'. This small, windswept outcrop served as the settlement's cemetery from 1830 to 1877. 1,769 prisoners were buried there in mass graves and 180 free people in individual plots. One of the last resident convict gravediggers consigned to this lonely place, Mark Jeffrey, a tall Irishman with a short temper, is the subject of a macabre story. Jeffrey (who was serving a life sentence for manslaughter) lived in a small hut on the island, grew a few vegetables and kept a few chickens. On Saturday night each week he was picked up by boat and brought to the mainland to attend church on the Sabbath, then returned on Monday morning. The authorities were glad to get rid of this hothead for most of the week and not at all pleased when they spotted a signal fire burning early one mid-week morning. When a detachment of guards rowed across to investigate they found Jeffrey in a wild, agitated state, begging to be taken off the island. He told how, on the previous night, his hut had been shaken and rocked by some invisible force then a fiery red glow had lit the walls and the surrounding ground. Jeffrey had scrambled from his bed thinking a fire had broken out but was confronted, not by a natural phenomenon, but by the devil himself, eyes smouldering, horns erect, encircled in sulphurous smoke. The guards and the medical officer who examined Jeffrey at the settlement concluded his mind had become 'unhinged by crime and suffering' and did not force him to return to the island.

The Isle of the Dead can be visited today and even on the brightest, sunniest days there is an oppressive atmosphere there, far stronger than one feels in any conventional graveyard. The chances of encountering His Satanic Majesty are pretty remote but, with almost 2,000 bodies buried below ground, a few spirits would not be out of place.

25.
Ghostly Gourmands

He was eaten of worms and gave up the ghost

The Bible, Acts 12:23

Given that we can safely assume ghosts don't need to eat, it's amazing how many of their stories involve food. That staple of human existence — flour — is the common ingredient in our first two; the second as sad as the first is shocking.

The cruelty with which many of our ancestors treated Aborigines should be a constant source of shame to white Australians today. The lives of the Indigenous people of this continent were held to be of so little value that the murder of hundreds mattered less to a station owner than the death of a favourite dog.

As late as the 1920s there were reports of 'pesky' Aborigines being disposed of with gifts of flour liberally laced with arsenic. This barbarous practice had been common for a century and just occasionally backfired on the perpetrators.

There is a story of a station owner in the Mullewa region of Western Australia who left a sack of poisoned flour lying about that his wife used by mistake to bake two loaves of bread. That evening a group of Aborigines on walkabout came to the back door of the homestead asking for food. The station owner's wife wanted to give them one of the freshly baked loaves but her husband wouldn't hear of it. 'Waste o' good bread,' he grumbled as he tucked into a slice himself. It took about fifteen minutes for the poison to take effect and another four hours, during which the station owner writhed in agony, for death to claim him.

Ever since (the story goes) the ghost of the poisoned poisoner has haunted the station bemoaning his fate and scaring the wits out of every Aborigine it encounters. 'He's a *horrible* sight, that's for sure,' one witness reported. 'His skin's bluey-grey and his eyes are all blood-shot, and ya know, when he opens his mouth t' yell at yer all that comes out is this long, pitiful moan ... like a dingo howlin'. You'd feel sorry for the poor bloke if you didn't know what he did t' them blackfellas ... and if he weren't so *bloody* terrifyin'. I seen him twice when I was a kid and I can tell ya, I didn't hang around long neither time!'

Flour also produced a much more likeable and less frightening spectre which haunts a large pocket of vine-infested grassland known as Munro Plains, a few kilometres west of Tully in far north Queensland. Settler Colin Munro established a farm there in 1852 and built a substantial homestead for his young family. He also employed an Englishman named Dick Grosvenor as tutor to his children. Grosvenor was a gentle giant weighing 140 kilograms, well educated and softly spoken, who admitted, proudly, to being eighty years old. The Munro children adored the old man and would sit for hours on his ample knees, stroking his waist-length beard while he told them tales of his travels and explained the mysteries of the world to them.

One day while the family was away Dick went to get a dish of flour from the 90-kilogram bag kept in the homestead storehouse. While reaching in the old man overbalanced and fell headfirst into the bag. He was unable to regain his footing and within minutes had smothered in the flour.

Old Dick Grosvenor was sorely missed by the Munro family but they were not deprived of his company for long. He reappeared as one of the fattest ghost ever seen in Australia, his head, whiskers and clothing covered in flour, smiling benignly and waving a ghostly white hand at the children.

Around 1908 the family left to take up another property near Mission Beach but the ghost stayed on at Munro Plains. Soon there was no one left who remembered him or could put a name to him. Later residents in the area, who occasionally saw him wandering about dejectedly, referred to him simply as 'the sad old cove with the long, white whiskers'.

Also from Queensland comes a gruesome ghost story set in a Brisbane butcher's shop. The shop stood behind the Brisbane Arcade in Adelaide Street, facing the present King George Square. It was there during World War Two and for many years after, but it is gone today. The shop was L-shaped, the meat being prepared in one part and the customers served in the other.

The story goes that the butcher and an apprentice got into an argument one day. A meat cleaver was thrown and the apprentice died. Subsequent owners of the shop, their staff and customers would occasionally hear the sound of the men arguing and struggling, then terrible screams coming from the back of the shop. A former customer told the *Courier Mail* years later that the sounds she heard there one afternoon were the most terrifying and disturbing she had ever heard in her life.

'I started going there to buy sausages; they made good sausages they did, with plenty of meat in them — not like the rubbish you get today — and my hubby loved them. Anyhow, I went in there one day just on closing time. It was a stinking hot afternoon I remember and I said to the lady behind the counter I'd just have a pound because they might go off in the heat. She went round the corner to get my sausages and as soon as she moved out of sight, there was this terrible, blood-curdling scream that echoed off the tiled walls, followed by a shocking gurgling noise. I was the only customer in the shop and I hadn't seen anyone else behind the counter, so I didn't know what to do. I called out "Are you all right?" I got no reply, so I put down my shopping bag and stepped behind the counter, expecting to see the woman lying dead or some bloke attacking her. But the woman was just standing there with my pound of sausages in her hand. She was white-faced and trembling, but there was no one with her. When she saw me she pulled herself together and said, "Oh, you mustn't come back here ... this area is for staff only."

'I said: "I heard you scream. I thought you were in trouble." She replied, "No I'm all right, thank you. It wasn't me who screamed." I could tell something was going on so I pressed the point. "Look," I said, "I was only a few feet away and I heard you *scream* and then a horrible gurgling noise!" At that the woman turned even paler and I thought she was going to faint. My sausages slid from her hand and landed in the sawdust on the floor. There was a chair for customers out front so I insisted she sat down there. She seemed terribly relieved to be on the *outside* of the counter. When I put my hand on her arm to comfort her I could feel her trembling and she started to cry. "I just can't take it any more," she said. "I've worked here for just over a year and that's the third time I've heard those awful noises. It's just horrible ... and there's *no one* there. It's the ghosts ... I know it is!"

'Between sobs the woman told me the story of the butcher murdering his apprentice and I advised her to find another job. I don't know whether she took my advice or not, but I told my hubby if he wanted any more of their sausages he'd have to go and get them himself.'

The glutinous, yellow lining of a cow's stomach known as 'tripe' was a staple in butchers' shops until about fifty years ago and is on the menu for our next story. Served piping hot with lashings of onion, tripe was a dish relished by our forefathers, although it has now gone right out of fashion and its passing seems to have caused little regret.

One such forefather was a stevedore who lived at Cottesloe near Fremantle. His great delight was to come home from the Fremantle wharves to a plate piled high with freshly steamed tripe and fried onions. The pungent smell of the food would fill the house while the stevedore filled his stomach.

Pain, warning of a heart-attack, was mistaken for indigestion one night and the offal-guzzling gourmand departed this life unexpectedly. His disconsolate widow stayed on in the house for the rest of her life, but could not bring herself to cook tripe and onions ever again. That did not stop the unmistakeable smell of that dish from returning to the dining room about once a week at dinner time for the next twenty years!

Tripe was a food that children had to be 'encouraged' to eat and one of the many ghosts stories from the historic Rocks area of Sydney concerns a man who made encouraging his children to eat a mission. Louis Garel lived in Harrington Street in The Rocks in the late nineteenth century and the story goes that he would pace around his dining-room table at meal times with a stern look on his face and his hands clasped behind his back admonishing his large brood with his favourite saying: 'Eat up and grow strong!'

When Mr Garel's mortal life ended they carried his body out of the house in a coffin but his spirit remained. His ghost was regularly seen by family and visitors to the house, gliding around the dining table and up and down the stairs, stern expression still on his face and hands still firmly clasped behind his back. Observers swore that the faint, hollow sounds that came from the ghost's lips were the words: 'Eat up and grow strong.'

Like private dining rooms, public restaurants seem to be among the most popular haunts for ghosts and a couple of Australia's most famous have resident spooks their owners have been proud to acknowledge. One such restaurant is Oatlands House at Dundas in Sydney's west. Oatlands House has a long and colourful history. It was built in the 1830s by Percy Simpson, former officer in the Royal Corsican Rangers and one-time governor of the Greek island of Paxos. In Australia he (like many men of his class) pursued two careers — civil servant and pastoralist. At different times he was superintendent of the Great Northern Road, a police magistrate and a crown lands commissioner — all the while building a rural empire at Oatlands.

The next owner was also a politician–pastoralist, James Brindley Bettington. The last of his line to own Oatlands House died in 1915. Today Oatlands House is an award-winning function centre and, although the cuisine is *nouvelle* and the service up-to-date, one timeless link with the past is said to remain — a ghost called Rebecca.

According to local stories Rebecca was a beautiful young woman who was jilted on her wedding day. Occasionally since then her ghost is reported to have appeared in the upper storey of the house or in the garden, magnificently dressed in an old-fashioned satin wedding dress and searching for her errant bridegroom.

The owner in the 1990s, celebrated restaurateur Oskar Nemme, reported that his staff were reluctant to go upstairs on their own and some who had worked at Oatlands House for twenty years and more claimed to have seen this sad, romantic spectre many times. But it is not only staff who have seen her, according to Mr Nemme. A woman sitting in a car outside the restaurant one day (who knew nothing about the ghost) came running inside, pale and trembling, with a remarkable story to tell.

She accosted the first staff member she encountered and with a trembling voice posed two questions: 'Where is the bride?' and 'Is she all right?' The staff member (a waitress) could see the woman was in distress and shepherded her to a chair. 'What bride would that be, madame?' the puzzled waitress asked.

'The bride who just *arrived*, of course,' the woman replied and when she saw the doubtful expression on the waitress's face she became impatient. 'The *one* who walked through the bougainvillea ... she came in through the same door I did, just a moment ago!'

Now the waitress knew there was no wedding reception booked for their establishment that afternoon, no bride was expected and the only person to enter the restaurant in the previous fifteen minutes had been the confused woman herself. The waitress began to wonder if the woman was drunk or mentally unstable and called to a colleague to summon the manager.

After being given a glass of water and reassurances that no one was trying to trick her and that she was not the victim of some conspiracy or cruel practical joke, the woman calmed down and was able to relate exactly what she had seen.

She had driven into the car park intending to have lunch in the restaurant, she said, but before she got out of her car she noticed a young woman in a long white satin bridal gown striding across the car park. Thinking it odd a bride should be arriving alone and on foot the woman watched her head towards the building. In the bride's path was a huge, purple bougainvillea in full flower, but rather than stepping around it, the bride headed straight towards the thorny bush. The woman watching felt a cold shiver pass through her body, thinking the bride must have been daydreaming and was about to destroy her gown and possibly injure herself badly.

'I jumped out of my car and called out to her to be careful of the thorns, but she didn't seem to hear me. She kept walking and went straight *through* the bougainvillea ... as if it wasn't there!'

No one knows what Rebecca's surname was. Perhaps she was one of Simpson's numerous offspring, or perhaps she was a Bettington. Whoever she was she certainly is a benign and harmless spirit — 'A very friendly ghost' is how Oskar Nemme described her — who only *very* occasionally alarms.

Cleveland, on the shores of Moreton Bay near Brisbane, also has a famous haunted restaurant. This pleasant suburb almost became the capital of the State of Queensland. Many people believed it a much better site for a state capital than the flood-prone and insect-infested former penal colony on the Brisbane River. Among Cleveland's strongest supporters was Francis Bigge, late of the Royal Navy, parliamentarian and grazier, who built a residence there in 1853. Later the house was leased by the State Government as a police residence and court house. It stands today in yet another guise: as the award-winning Olde Courthouse Restaurant, complete (it is proudly claimed) with its own resident ghost.

Stories of the Cleveland Courthouse ghost — a middle-aged woman in a long gown, her dark hair gathered in two tight buns over her ears — have circulated for generations. No one knows for sure who she is, but most people believe it is Francis Bigge's wife, Elizabeth. Mrs Bigge actually died back home in England (she hanged herself, legend has it), so if it is she, her spirit must have decided to return to the scene of one of the happier periods in her life.

This spectre is normally well behaved, content to amuse itself tapping staff and diners on the shoulders or blowing gently in their ears, but it has been known to lose its temper on rare occasions. Crockery and ornaments have occasionally taken flight, seemingly on their own, and crashed into broken shards. Light switches have been turned on and off by her unseen hands, sometimes at embarrassing moments. Taps are also a favourite prop for this meddlesome spook. Carefully turned off they suddenly appear to turn themselves on; and turned on (to fill a sink, for example) they will be found moments later firmly turned *off*. Valuable pictures have also become dislodged from walls and crashed to the floor — curiously without the frames ever breaking or the glass shattering.

No doubt out of consideration for the restaurant's fine reputation and its patrons, 'Elizabeth', as everyone calls the ghost, usually behaves herself during trading hours and confines her rare destructive acts to when only staff are about to witness them.

One former employee explained that no one is really frightened of the ghost. 'I guess we've all got used to her ... and she is a *great* excuse for anything that goes wrong in the kitchen or the dining room. I always liked to think of her as one of the team; someone who was just as proud of the place as we are ... and who got a bit annoyed when we didn't quite meet *her* standards.'

So, dear readers, next time you tuck into fresh bread, succulent sausages (or even sizzling tripe) don't be surprised if there's an uninvited guest at your table; and when you treat yourself to a meal at a famous restaurant check the bill of fare for phantoms.

26.
Spirits You Can't Drink

> *You want to know whether I believe in ghosts? Of course I don't. If you'd known as many of them as I have you wouldn't believe in them either!*
>
> **Don Marquis (American journalist, 1878–1937)**

Like restaurants, hotels seem to be among the favourite haunts of ghosts the world over. Here are a collection of spooky tales from some of Australia's most famous haunted hostelries, featuring gory ghosts, sad ghosts — and a phantom pussy.

The Coach and Horses Inn, formerly known as the Clarkfield Hotel, near Sunbury, north-west of Melbourne, has been in the news many times — not for its historical significance, its architectural charm or its good service, but for the numerous ghosts that reputedly dwell there. The old bluestone pub was built in 1857 as a stopping point for Cobb & Co. coaches on the run to Bendigo, and its two oldest ghosts belong to the gold-rush era. Legend tells of an Irish seaman named Patrick Reagan who jumped ship in Melbourne and made his way to the goldfields where he 'struck it rich'. Unfortunately, while stopping at the Clarkfield Hotel on his way back to Melbourne, Reagan was set upon by a group of dishonest police troopers who shot him and stole his gold. A medium from Penola in South Australia visiting the Clarkfield Hotel in the 1980s claimed that she had a vision of a fierce gun battle behind the hotel, with Reagan exchanging shots with the troopers and trying to flee down the hotel steps. In later years Reagan's ghost became a familiar sight around the hotel, usually seen racing down the stairs, clutching a bullet wound to its chest and with blood seeping through its spectral fingers.

The ghost of a Chinese miner who was involved in a fight and later hanged in the hotel is also, reputedly, still hovering about. Then there's the ghost of the intellectually disabled girl aged about eleven who appears in a taffeta dress. She, it is said, disturbed her parents during a violent argument in one of the hotel bedrooms and was killed by her father, who then threw her body down a well. Her ghost has been reported many times — a forlorn, wasted spectre draped in a tattered, lilac coloured nightgown — and a group of psychic investigators boasted of having recorded her sobbing and pleading on audio tape. It is also believed that the ghosts of both her parents have appeared in the room where the murder took place at different times and beside the well, which was filled in some years ago. The mother's ghost has been described as wild-eyed and the father's as grim and stony-faced.

With such a fraternity of ghosts in residence it is not surprising that there are many reports of sightings and ghostly encounters. In 1983 a cocky newspaper reporter spent a night alone in the stables behind the hotel in the hope of catching a ghost to write about. He didn't, but when walking past the infamous well the next morning he commented that the old pump mounted above the well was useless if it didn't work. The pump, he claimed, promptly came to life and started producing a steady stream of fresh water. When a plumber inspected it a few hours later the pump was found to be dry and completely seized up with rust.

When the owners at that time, Don and Judy Busner, sold up they thought it only right to warn their successors that the hotel was haunted and that they had often been kept awake at night by strange noises, glasses smashing in the back bar and pictures in the murder room flying through the air. The new owners, Frank and Sharon Nelson, were sceptical but on the third night after they took over they heard strange noises downstairs at around 3 am. Frank got up and went to investigate. He stopped halfway down the stairs when hit by a blast of icy cold air, then he was struck from behind by some invisible force. He fell down several stairs and fractured his ankle. Was he, one wonders, bowled over by Patrick Reagan's wounded ghost on one of its headlong flights? A few days later while he lay convalescing with his lower leg in plaster, Frank cried out in pain. The same force, or something similar, was twisting his broken ankle inside the plaster cast!

A relative of the Nelsons who slept in the murder room one night claimed that the air turned cold in there as well and that something tried to strangle her in the middle of the night. Staff also saw near-human forms on the stairs and in the murder room. Chef Ian Ross was reported as saying he heard the door of the murder room bang one night so got up to investigate. He found the door wide open then watched a bright, glowing figure walk across the room towards the fireplace and back again. Ross was, he said, too frightened to move or cry out. His successor, Nick Tsantalis, told *The Age* he had a permanent sensation of being followed wherever he went in the hotel and had found the kitchen filled with fine mist one morning. Something heavy that he could not see also pinned him to his bed one night, he said, and for several nights afterwards Tsantalis slept in his car.

Frank Nelson was confronted by a hideous face staring out at him when he was cleaning the outside of a window one day. It was not, he swore, his own reflection and when he tried to open the window it would not budge. Minutes before it had opened smoothly and did again after the apparition vanished.

News of strange events occurring at the old hotel spread and the press began to take an interest, but what began as good publicity soon developed into a media circus. Psychics, mediums, amateur ghost hunters and legions of thrill seekers also converged on the hotel, demanding to be allowed to camp in the murder room and on the stairs. Eventually it became too much for the Nelsons and they departed

Their successors, Steve and Deborah Dudley, had an equally torrid time. They suffered every imaginable mishap. Equipment failed, including three washing machines in as many days. In a short time the Dudleys also departed in despair.

The next owner employed a couple to manage the hotel while he set about restoring it. Within a year or two the grand old building was back to pristine condition, tastefully redecorated with period-style wallpaper and fabrics and furnished with antiques. But did the ghosts approve? Well, if so, they didn't let up on their campaign of terror. The manager's wife was reported in 1991 as saying that she refused to go downstairs at night time because of the ghosts; and their four-year-old daughter went through a long period where she woke every night distressed and crying out: 'I can't sleep with that *thing* in the corner!' The parents could see nothing, but the child's fear was genuine and heartrending. Nor could they see what caused a friend, who slept in another room, to call out for help in the middle of the night claiming (like Tsantalis) that something or someone was sitting on his chest.

If reports on the internet can be relied upon, it seems that ghostly encounters continue to occur in the old building to this day. Now called The Coach and Horses Inn it really is a very charming pub, the sort of interesting and appealing-looking place that it is hard to drive past. Those who do stop will be rewarded with good fare and good service and maybe (if they're very lucky) a glimpse of one of the legendary ghosts.

A ghost of mild disposition resides in a hotel in the Barossa Valley town of Lyndoch. 'Rob the Projectionist' (as the locals call this apparition) always appears in the same spot — a corner of the comfortable private bar of the old Lyndoch Hotel.

Rob was popular in his lifetime. Every Saturday he travelled up from Adelaide with two feature films (on giant reels stored in steel cases), booked into his favourite room in the hotel then showed the films that night in the Lyndoch Institute. Rob seemed to get as much pleasure out of this arrangement as the entertainment-starved locals, until his wife died and he began to lose interest in movies and life. One Saturday he forgot to bring the films. He bungled the program many times and people stopped coming. Finally, on a Saturday night after he had shown films to an almost empty house, Rob committed suicide in 'his' hotel room. He was found the next morning clutching a photograph of his wife. The note he left simply said: *Sorry, there'll be no pictures next Saturday*.

Most people thought that was the last they'd see of Rob but that was not to be. His ghost began to appear on Saturday nights in his hotel room, much to the alarm of other guests sleeping there and the despair of the publican. When challenged the ghost always made the same reply: 'I always have this room ... every Saturday night I show pictures up here.' When new owners renovated the hotel they demolished some of the guest rooms including the one Rob haunted and turned the area into a private bar. Rob, however, isn't moving. His old room may now be part of the bar but, it is said, he still appears there — a forlorn figure in grey shirt and slacks —

lingering among the drinkers. The bar staff sometimes ask, half jokingly: 'What will you have Rob?' and inevitably get the same reply: 'I always have this room ... every Saturday night I show pictures up here.'

The old Mahogany Inn at Mahogany Creek east of Perth is also reputedly haunted and like the Coach and Horses it sports a collection of spirits. The ghosts of Mary Gregory and her stepsister Fanny Byfield (young daughters of the original licensee) have been reported as appearing in the window of an attic where they both died, fifteen months apart, in 1867 and 68. More recently this inseparable pair has been seen by an employee in one of the modern accommodation units that were built over their graves. The frightened woman reported coming upon the two little ghosts sitting on a bed; she then watched them float out of the room.

'They were sweet little girls, both dressed in cream-coloured dresses trimmed with lace,' she told a friend. 'One had long, pale reddish hair and the other had shorter brown hair. They were speaking to each other and they laughed together, but I couldn't hear *any* sound at all. It was a bit like watching a silent movie except it was in colour and the girls were so close I could have reached out and touched them, but of course I was too scared to do that. I was fascinated by their feet. They both wore button-up boots that went halfway up to their knees. When they got up their legs weren't moving and their feet weren't touching the ground ... they just "floated" across the room and out the door. I still find it hard to believe that I saw them ... but then I'm sure that they couldn't see me. They belonged to a different time when I didn't exist, so to them I guess *I* wasn't there. It was spooky, but somehow I felt privileged; as though I had been given a special gift.'

Another harmless spectre has been reported as materialising (rarely but regularly) in a particular corner of the inn's original tap room. Tradition says this is a wizened old man who sits in a favourite chair, smoking a blackened pipe. His identity and reason for being there remain mysterious.

The rattle of chains and unearthly cries have also been reported from the cellar of the Mahogany Inn on nights when the moon is waning. The popular theory is that they are made by the ghost of James Peacock, a convict who disappeared mysteriously from the inn in the 1850s; and an old dead tree in the garden is said to be the haunt of yet another ghost — this one a man convicted of murder. His name was Malcolm and he was hanged from the tree although many believed him innocent. The tree promptly died and Malcolm's supporters took that as a sign that a miscarriage of justice had been committed. Malcolm's ghost (the story goes) has wandered around the tree on moon-bright nights ever since, seeking retribution. His face is reported to wear a permanent scowl, his eyes bulge and his neck is disfigured by a livid mark where the noose choked off his life.

Over the years animals have added credibility to the Mahogany Inn ghost stories. Before the graves of the little girls were covered over neighbours wondered why their little dog trotted off in the direction of the inn at a certain time every night. One night they followed and found the little creature standing beside the graves, wagging its tail and excitedly communicating with something their eyes could not see.

The owner of the inn in the 1980s could never get *his* dog to enter the tap room. The animal wandered happily everywhere else but nothing would entice it to enter the domain of the old man's ghost. A spectral cat also appeared one night in the dining room. Doors and windows were all firmly closed when a waitress reported that a large tabby cat with distinctive markings was roaming around the tables. When the owner went to investigate the room was still sealed but the cat was gone. He was not surprised. The waitress's description of the markings matched those of his own cat, run over and flattened by a semi-trailer on the highway years before.

27.
Spectral Spare Parts

All heart they live, all head, all eye, all ear,
All intellect, all sense, and as they please
They limb themselves, and colour, shape, or size,
Assume, as likes them best, condense or rare.

***Paradise Lost*, John Milton (English poet, 1608–1674)**

There's only one thing more terrifying than seeing a ghost and that's seeing a *part* of one. Many of Australia's best ghost stories, such as 'The Ghosts in the Glen', feature disembodied faces, hands and other body parts — and so do these macabre tales.

An oversized and disembodied face was witnessed by a group of five surveyors sent to the Coxs River near the present town of Wallerawang 120 or so years ago. On arrival the party decided to camp in an old house on the river bank while they carried out their work. The foreman described the house as convict-built, uninhabited and fast falling into ruin. A boundary rider from a nearby property joined the company around their campfire the first night and warned them that the old house was haunted. He described how a down-on-his-luck shearer had hanged himself from a river oak nearby, how a schoolmaster had disposed of himself the same way inside the house and how the wife of the former owner had been murdered by a swagman. The stories were good campfire entertainment but not enough to dissuade the surveyors from sleeping in the house — something they soon regretted.

After bedding down they heard a loud thud and all the doors in the house flew open. They lit a candle and searched about but could find nothing. They closed all the doors and returned to their blankets. Moments later a horrible gurgling sound, like someone being strangled, was heard and the doors sprung open again.

On the second night moaning was heard and some loose boards one of the party was sleeping on began to shake violently. Next a pool of light appeared on the ceiling and in it a face slowly took form. 'It was the most frightening and at the same time strangest thing I have ever seen,' one of surveyors later reported. 'It was about four times the size of a normal face and exactly like an image in a mirror except there was no mirror. And there was no head behind the face, no throat, no neck and no body supporting it. It was like a big mask, except that it was "alive" — not living, mind you, but *alive*. The skin was the colour of putty and the features were those of a woman but distorted by terrible pain or inconsolable grief. The eyes were opened very wide, but the pupils were milky like a blind person's and the same horrible gurgling sound we had heard the night before was coming from the thing's mouth.' The surveyors lay on their blankets staring up at the frightful image, too afraid to move. After a few minutes it and the sound faded until both disappeared, but all the carefully fastened doors stood open again.

On the third night a loud crash like glass smashing was heard, the doors flew open again and then a tall, female figure with the face seen the previous night appeared in the moonlight just outside the front door. The figure glided into the room where the men lay and stopped in their midst, looming menacingly over them.

'The thing seemed to tower over us and raised its arms above us like a bird about to take flight or an animal about to attack its prey,' our witness reported. 'At that moment I knew what a mouse must feel like when it's been spotted by an eagle. Anyhow, my mate Joey, who was sleeping nearest to the door, was the first to move. He leapt up and threw himself out the doorway. I went next, although my legs were shaking, and the others followed, all of us diving to escape then stumbling out into the clearing in front of the house.'

The surveyors spent the rest of that night huddled together around the embers of their campfire. When the sun came up the next morning they cautiously entered the house to retrieve their belongings. They did not find (as they had expected) any broken glass but, although none of them was injured, the room they had slept in was spattered with fresh blood. There was a dark pool where the figure had stood and the clear imprints of their own feet where they had unknowingly stepped in the blood in their flight to escape.

The surveyors hastily packed up, completed their work and set off on their return journey to Sydney, relieved to leave the old house to its ghostly tenant. 'I'm the first to admit,' our observer concluded, 'that I was absolutely terrified by the ghostly figure, but with hindsight I'd have to say there was a strange sort of comfort in seeing that the face belonged to a body. Neither figure nor face was human, but somehow the disembodied face seemed least so. I can recall every detail of it and the sound it made to this day and I'm sure I will take the memory of it to my grave.'

One could forgive the surveyors if they consoled themselves with a few stiff drinks after their ghostly experience, but the colourful character who is the subject of our next story turned drinking into a full time occupation. 'Black Sandy' Cameron is fondly remembered among the many residents of Scottish descent in the Penola district of South Australia. He was one of the Camerons who ran Penola station, where the poet Adam Lindsay Gordon worked as a horse breaker.

Black Sandy got his name, people say, from the bushy black beard he wore — but he seems also to have been the black sheep of the clan. He lived almost entirely on a diet of good Highland whisky and his family feared he would drink himself to death. When business took them away for a few days the family contrived to prevent this by getting a nimble Aborigine to carry Black Sandy's whisky barrel to the top of a tall gum tree and tie it there with a stout rope.

A sober and very angry Black Sandy discovered the trick and went after the Aborigine but he, wisely, had gone bush. Sandy stood beneath the tree and studied his problem carefully. At age sixty-seven, portly and none too steady on his feet, he dared not risk climbing the tree himself but he desperately needed a wee dram.

The solution suddenly came to him. He went into the homestead and got his gun and a large dish. One bullet carefully aimed at the barrel produced a very satisfying stream of whisky. The dish quickly filled and Black Sandy began to drink. Unable to countenance wasting a drop of the precious amber liquid he kept drinking. Eventually the cask was empty and Black Sandy was full. When his family returned they found him lying under the tree, stone dead. To add to their grief they also found the large diamond ring he invariably wore missing from his cold, stiff, right hand.

The Camerons were not deprived of Black Sandy's company for very long, however, for he soon reappeared in ghostly form. *No*, that's an exaggeration — the only part of Black Sandy that reappeared was his right hand. That lonesome limb is said to materialise occasionally to this day at old Penola station, clutching door handles, rattling cups and prying corks from whisky bottles — and, to the chagrin of Black Sandy's heirs, *it wears the diamond ring.*

A much less pleasant story comes from Bookham, on the Hume Highway west of Yass. Bookham is the sort of little town motorists speed through without noticing, but it does have two fascinating ghost stories linked to one of Australia's best-known and grisliest murders, each story seasoned with a surfeit of dismembered ghostly body parts.

A little Irishman named William Munday, who had a very big chip on his shoulder, went on a murdering rampage one autumn night 144 years ago at Conroy's Gap near Bookham, killing his employer, John Conroy, Mrs Conroy and three male shepherds. Munday used a sharpened shear blade to stab his victims then chopped them up with an axe and piled the pieces, in his own words, 'ready for burning'. It took just one week from the murders and Munday's arrest for ghost stories to germinate. The *Yass Courier* reported:

Since the murder it would appear that some persons have temporarily taken up their abode in Conroy's house and on the first night of their sleeping there a hand described as heavy as that of a human creature passed over their bodies while they laid in bed. On the second night a figure dressed in black was seen in the room where the murders were perpetrated.

From that time until well into the last century there were stories of strange noises being heard and dismembered bits of bodies materialising around the district.

One swagman who camped near Conroy's Gap came staggering into Bookham one day claiming he had woken up to find a bloodied human leg sharing his bedroll and a bloodied human hand had overturned his billy, scalding the swaggie's arm.

'I puts me 'and down inside me bedroll I did, this morning just as the sun was comin' up, and I feels somethin' soft and wet beside me. I thought a possum or some other little *animal* had climbed in t' keep warm, but when I pulled me 'and out it were all covered in blood. Then I *really* panicked. I tossed back me blanket and jumped up like a friggin' kangaroo and there, *lying in me bed*, was this loose leg! It were all mangled and bloody at the thigh, the skin was greyie-white and the toenails, they was black. I got such a fright I must'a passed out. I came to when the sun was well up and I scrambled onto me 'ands and knees. Me bedroll was lying a few feet away and it was empty — no leg and not a drop o' blood.'

The swagman then told how he had convinced himself that the whole experience had been a bad dream and tried to put it out of his mind. But that delusion lasted only until he had built up his campfire and put his billy on to boil. 'I was feeling a might shaky and desperate for a cup o' tea. I leaned over me billy to see if it were starting to boil an' I noticed what looked like a burned bit of wood lying on the edge of me fire. I didn't remember seeing it afore, so I poked at it with the stick I was gonna use to lift me billy ... and the bloody thing moved! I don't mean it just fell over; it actually *moved*, first one way and then t' other. I poked it again and this time it rose up from the ashes and I could see it was *an 'and* — a 'uman 'and, just like yours or mine — except there were nothin' above the wrist and it was all burned crisp like bacon. I must'a screamed and the thing took a swipe at me billy. Next thing I know me arm's burning an' dripping with boilin' water and the '*orrible* thing's disappeared!'

Most of the good folk of Bookham who listened to his tale were prepared to believe the swagman, even without the evidence of his scalded arm; too many of them had seen or heard about the ghostly goings on at Conroy's Gap to doubt him.

I guess the swagman might have been lucky in one sense. If it had been the ghost in the old house on the Coxs River (which a murdering member of his brotherhood was responsible for) instead of one at Conroy's Gap he might not have lived to tell his tale.

The second story that may or may not be related to William Munday's murdering rampage concerns the ghosts of two young women, seen in daylight and darkness along the banks of Stoney Creek near Conroy's Gap. One appears in elaborate mid-nineteenth-century dress, the other in the simpler style of a later period. There have been reports of sightings of this ghostly pair for a century and more and there are at least two theories about who the women might have been. Hearsay has it that when William Munday was in police custody he made the statement: 'I didn't like killing Sissie; she had been kind to me.' Sissie? There was no 'Sissie' (or Elizabeth) at Conroy's Gap when the murders took place and if Munday had a sister she was back in Ireland. Was she perhaps an earlier victim and is she perhaps the older of the two ghosts?

The second and more widely credited explanation concerns two young Melbourne women carrying a small fortune in jewellery who disappeared when a Cobb & Co. coach they were travelling in broke an axle at Conroy's Gap. The driver told the women to stay inside the coach while he rode into Yass for help. When he returned a few hours later the women were gone. One female skeleton and a gold ring (hooked on a twig) were later found in what became known as Dead Woman's Gully.

Whoever they were in life it seems these ghostly damsels are in no hurry to leave. As recently as 1994 workmen at the

Bogo Stone Quarry at Conroy's Gap reported seeing a young woman dressed in a long white dress standing near a gate; she suddenly took fright, scrambled up an embankment and vanished. Then in 2007 a public servant inspecting the site for a proposed wind farm at Conroy's Gap claimed to have seen the same figure on a hillside — but only its head, torso and dress. Where its legs and feet should have been was nothing but thin air!

Before we leave stories of ghostly spare parts here's a final one recounted in a national magazine in July 1979. The correspondent wrote that she and her family had recently moved into an old house in the northern New South Wales town of Casino. At around midnight on the third night the woman's mother got out of bed to go to the bathroom. There was bright moonlight so the mother didn't bother to switch any lights on. As she went to open the bathroom door a shadowy black-skinned hand appeared on the door handle and opened the door for her — just a hand, ending at the wrist.

Badly shaken the mother returned to her bed but was unable to sleep. She got up again and this time headed for the kitchen via the lounge room. Halfway there a sudden gust of hurricane-force wind hurled her backwards through the still open bathroom door. When she regained her feet the terrified woman ran to the kitchen and searched for the light switch. The wind followed her and she could feel the solitary hand trying to drag her back to its lair.

The correspondent ended her account there. If the angry spirit (presumably Aboriginal) that manifested itself that night thirty-two years ago has ever reappeared no one has reported it. I, for one, sincerely hope it and all the other dismembered bits described in these stories never do!

28.
The Bugler's Ghost

When the night wind howls in the chimney cowls,
and the bat in the moonlight flies,
And inky clouds, like funeral shrouds,
sail over the midnight skies —
When the footpads quail at the night bird's wail,
and black dogs bay at the moon,
Then is the spectres' holiday —
the dead of the night's high-noon!
As the sob of the breeze sweeps over the trees,
and the mists lie low on the fen,
From grey tombstones are gathered the bones
that once were women and men,
And away they go, with a mop and a mow,
to the revel that ends too soon,
For the cockcrow limits our holiday —
the dead of the night's high-noon!
And then each ghost with his ladye-toast
to their churchyard beds take flight,
With a kiss, perhaps, on her lantern chaps,
and a grisly grim 'good-night';
Till the welcome knell of the midnight bell
rings forth its jolliest tune,
And ushers our next high holiday —
the dead of the night's high-noon!

***Ruddigore*, Gilbert and Sullivan**
(writer and composer of comic operas)

There's an old story still told around the Castlereagh area of outer Sydney about the Bugler's Ghost. While no one can vouch for its authenticity, its charm is undeniable and the principal named characters were real people.

Until well into the nineteenth century the Hawkesbury–Nepean river system formed the frontier of white settlement in the colony of New South Wales and, at what is now Emu Plains on the west bank of the Nepean, stood a stockade — a meagre bastion of British military might, protecting the settlement from the perils of the wild mountains beyond. Later this became the barracks for a detachment of troops assigned to guard the convicts working on the road over the Blue Mountains. Nothing is left of the complex today, but it is commemorated by Barracks and Stockade Streets and some of its probably reluctant occupants are recalled in this old story.

Off-duty soldiers from the barracks would row across the river to enjoy the delights of Penrith (a couple of inns and a bawdy house or two) and return to quarters, rather worse for wear, late at night. One night a small boat overloaded with a group of these revellers returning to their quarters hit a floating log in the river. The boat almost capsized and three of the occupants were thrown into the water, including the company's bugler who was as we might say today 'legless'. There was much yelling and thrashing about as the men in the boat tried to drag their comrades back on aboard. Two were rescued spluttering foul water but alive. The bugler was less lucky. When found he was floating face downwards and when dragged aboard he was quite dead.

The wet and bedraggled party rowed back to the eastern bank and carried the bugler's body to the Penrith courthouse, where a doctor was roused from his nearby bed. Yawning uncontrollably, the doctor pronounced the bugler dead and suggested that as the weather was hot, he should be buried forthwith. 'Can't have him going *orf* now, lads,' the physician advised (between yawns). 'He already has a *very* peculiar pong about him from the river and very soon, I promise you, he'll stink worse than that little fish we pulled out of his drawers!'

By this time most of the damp soldiers were tired of hanging about and decided to return to their barracks. Only two of his erstwhile comrades volunteered to bury the unfortunate bugler. They commandeered a farmer's horse and cart and loaded the body onto the tray then drove ten kilometres to the nearest cemetery at Castlereagh.

On arrival the pair roused the Anglican minister of Castlereagh, Henry Fulton, from his bed. Now Fulton was a fiery Irish patriot and no admirer of the military and he was not best pleased to be troubled on a hot summer's night by two redcoats smelling of grog and bearing the remains of a third in a cart. Muttering words no one would expect to hear from a clergyman's lips, Fulton sent one of his sons to rouse the local grave digger. That worthy then set to work by lamplight to gouge out a shallow grave in the hard, dry soil of the cemetery with pick and shovel. By the time all was prepared it was after midnight and the bugler was laid to rest by moonlight attended by his two remaining friends, the sleepy grave digger and the crotchety parson.

Thereafter, the story goes, the bugler, angry at being deserted by the rest of his comrades, would rise from his grave at around nine each night, dance a jig and play his bugle. The people of Castlereagh lived in fear of this awesome sight and none would venture near the cemetery after dark. Not many claimed to have actually seen the ghost, but everyone had heard his bugle. It was described as an eerie sound like a bugle being played a long way away and the few who claimed a glimpse of the ghost swore he wore his military uniform and that his red coat glowed, his pipe-clayed belt glistened and his polished buttons glinted in the pale moonlight.

A few witnesses also told of being able to smell the strong, sweet odour of rum wafting across the graveyard when the ghostly music started and one Castlereagh matron (of impeccable character) claimed the ghost had made a 'most unseemly' proposition to her as she passed the graveyard on her way home from a prayer meeting one night.

Reverend Fulton's son, John, determined to lay the ghost and prove these stories were figments of over-fertile (or over-fuelled) imaginations. He went to the house of a friend who lived near the cemetery and asked him to join him in a vigil to catch the ghost. The friend refused, saying he had heard the spooky bugle and nothing would induce him to enter the cemetery at night. Young Fulton then asked the grave digger if his two sons (both big, burly lads like their father) would accompany him, but they too claimed to have heard the mysterious music and would have no part in the venture. So Fulton set out alone, carrying an unlighted lantern, a tinderbox, a roast beef sandwich, a stone jar of beer — and a long coil of rope, with which he presumably expected to catch someone pretending to be the ghost.

The young man arrived at the cemetery at around eight o'clock in the evening and positioned himself behind a tall gravestone just a few metres from the bugler's plot. There was a cool breeze blowing from the north-east that set trees bordering the graveyard shivering and whispering. The moon was rising and its light cast deep shadows around the gravestones and made dew on the grass glow with an eerie phosphorescence. It was, one might say, a perfect night for ghost hunting and while he tucked into his sandwich and his beer, young Fulton felt an exhilarating cocktail of excitement, anticipation and trepidation coursing through his veins.

On the stroke of nine the sound began: a soft, wavering trumpeting that floated over the graveyard and made young Fulton sit up and brace himself. He peeped over the headstone and focused his gaze on the bugler's grave — but of a dancing ghost or any other visible form there was no sign. Fulton also sniffed the air but found no trace of rum. He climbed to his feet, emerged from his hiding place and listened more closely, then burst into raucous laughter — laughter that echoed across the graveyard and sent startled night birds flapping into the sky.

John Fulton enjoyed telling the story of the Bugler's Ghost for the rest of his life, not least because he believed he had 'laid' it. The sound, he would explain, did not come from the bugler's grave but came floating in on the breeze, carried over the waters of the Chain of Ponds Creek from Windsor, where the Windsor Town Band practised twice a week, commencing at 9 pm.

Now, readers who know the area might argue that fifteen-odd kilometres is a long distance for sound to carry, but John Fulton was convinced his theory was correct. Most of the good people of Castlereagh, however, continued to avoid the cemetery at night.

29.
'Do You Have That in Grey?'

There is a ghost that eats handkerchiefs.
It keeps you company on all your travels.
Christian Morgenstern (German poet, 1871–1914)

If someone conducted one of those 'Top 10' surveys on the colour of ghosts' clothing, then grey would undoubtedly be the first colour on the list. It seems to be far and away the most fashionable shade for lady ghosts, in the form of grey crinolines, grey uniforms, grey dresses and grey habits. And why is that? Well, historians might suggest that the colour has links with death and mourning, but I suspect it's simply vanity — choosing a shade to match the wearer's complexion! Jokes aside, the dozen or more 'grey' ladies who feature in Australian ghosts stories (including the couple we've already met) have little else in common. They range from kind nurses to cruel harridans and from gracious women who are ladies to a gracious lady who was not a woman at all.

The Mater Misericordiae Hospital at Crows Nest in Sydney is reputedly haunted by a grey-habited nun, the ghost of a nursing sister who died during the devastating influenza epidemic of 1919. This ghost appears more often to patients than staff according to a nurse who trained there in the 1960s. Often, she is on record as saying, nurses would go to help patients only to be told: 'It's OK, nurse, the nun did it.' There was, the nurse claimed, a policy not to alarm patients by denying the existence of the nun or referring to her as a ghost.

The most hair-raising experience the nurse herself had with the grey nun was on a night when a patient died. The occupant of the next bed was awake and said to her: 'I knew she'd died, nurse: the nun came, said a prayer and turned the oxygen off.' Sure enough the oxygen had been turned off, the hose neatly coiled and the cylinder set aside.

Another ghostly, grey-habited nun is said to dispense comforting words and good counsel to patients in the alcoholics ward at St Vincent's Hospital in the inner Sydney suburb of Darlinghurst. Many a distressed dipsomaniac in Ward 14 has commended the hospital on having such a caring and compassionate team member. And, before the reader suggests the sympathetic sister might be a symptom of the patients' condition, I hasten to add that many doctors and nurses have seen her too.

The medical superintendent of St Vincent's spoke publicly about their grey nun in *The Bulletin* in 1980 and said that his staff were reluctant to talk to strangers about her, considering that their relationship with her was something special and private. Some years later one staff member, Sister Catherine O'Carrigan, broke ranks and told *The Australian* that there was 'very much a sense of security' when the ghostly grey nun was about.

Stories about this gentle spectre abound. She is supposed to have fallen to her death down a stairwell many years ago or been the victim of some unresolved crime. Since then her ghost has resided in a lift well and made itself useful around the ward, chatting to patients and dispensing blessings.

One particularly interesting feature of this ghost's appearance is that her feet are not visible. Black stockings protrude from under her habit and disappear into the floor.

Hospital records give a possible explanation for this: the floor of Ward 14 is now a few centimetres higher than it was in the grey nun's time. She, it seems, still walks on the old level.

A motley mansion with a motley history at Bothwell, Tasmania, is said to be haunted by yet another of these ghostly grey females, but this time her occupation is a mystery. Inverhall, as the house was originally named, was built by the first Australian-born commissioned officer in the British Army, Captain D'Arcy Wentworth, brother of the politician William Charles Wentworth. Captain Wentworth sold out to a testy magistrate who renamed the house 'Schawfield' after himself and went bankrupt enlarging it to accommodate himself, his long-suffering wife, their one son and their seven daughters — Sarah, Anne, Susan, Isabella, Janet, Elizabeth and Henrietta.

When Magistrate Schaw and his brood departed the house became Bothwell Academy 'for the sons and daughters of gentlefolk', where knowledge and discipline were meted out in equal measure. Later, as Wentworth House (the name it bears today), the house had several owners before becoming an Anglican rectory.

The unidentified grey ghost's favourite haunt is the unusual cantilevered staircase that rises steeply from the entrance hall at Wentworth House. The spectre is described as a tall, slim, elegant young woman wrapped in a long grey cloak with a cascade of reddish-brown hair falling over the collar. Her face has been described as pale and unblemished, framing an upturned nose and a pair of large, hazel-coloured eyes with very long lashes. Witnesses claim that she appears at the top of the stairs at night and seems oblivious to their presence and to whatever may be happening around her. The spectre pauses at the upper landing, gathers up the folds of her cloak then floats effortlessly down the stairs. When it reaches the entrance hall the heavy front door (whether bolted or not) will swing silently open, allowing the apparition to glide, noiselessly, out into the night.

This grey lady was also spotted in the yard one day by a tenant chopping wood. Unsure whether she was human or phantom he asked her what she wanted. In reply she simply disappeared; and a bishop staying at Wentworth House when it was a rectory mistook her for a chambermaid after she appeared suddenly behind him reflected in his shaving mirror. 'Yes, yes. I'll be down in a moment,' the lathered cleric snapped impatiently. Later he complained to his host about the maid's intrusion on his ablutions. 'So you've seen our ghost,' said his host calmly. 'We see her all the time.'

No one has been able to work out just who this spectre was before death claimed her, but there has been much speculation that she might have been one of the magistrate's daughters, at least five of whom he managed to marry off before he quit Tasmania. So it's reasonable to suggest her surname might once have been Schaw — but her given name? Well, maybe it was Sarah, or maybe Anne ... or Susan, or Isabella, or Janet, or Elizabeth, or Henrietta.

The town of Roma in Queensland also has a 'grey lady' ghost but, unlike the anonymous one at Bothwell, Roma's can be identified and her strange story, before and after her death, is well documented. Jim Lalor, owner of Gubberamunda station, which bordered the town, gave a couple named Bonnor permission to build a weatherboard cottage on his land behind the Roma Hospital. Bonnor was a bush carpenter who worked for Lalor, but it was his wife who interested the local gossips. When she came into town Mrs Bonnor always wore the same severe, grey dress with an old grey shawl wrapped tightly around her shoulders. Her face was expressionless and if anyone spoke to her in the street she ignored them. One day the Bonnors disappeared without explanation to Lalor or anyone else. There was food in their cottage and Mrs Bonnor's large grey cat was still there.

The cottage remained empty for a while then a saddler named Johnson rented it and moved in with his family. The cat slunk away into the bush. One of Johnson's daughters, Matilda ('Tilly'), became seriously ill and had an operation at the hospital. She came home swathed in bandages and was put to bed. Next morning she was agitated and told her mother that 'the lady in grey' had visited her during the night. The figure had stood at the foot of her bed and told her, in a persuasive voice, that the way for her to get well was to remove all her bandages. Mrs Johnson told Tilly she must have been dreaming, but later in the day the horrified mother found her daughter lying unconscious on her blood-soaked bed. The girl had ripped off all her bandages. Before the doctor arrived, Tilly died. The death certificate, curiously, shows the cause of death as pneumonia, which either puts paid to the story or more likely was a convenient way of sparing the distressed parents a public inquiry.

At the time of Tilly's tragic death, her elder sister was being courted by a local chemist. On leaving the Johnsons' house one evening the young man felt a sudden urge to look back. There, standing in the moonlight beside the cottage door, was 'the lady in grey', her eyes glaring at him. The young man did not hang about. He bolted for his life — straight into a barbed wire fence. Five minutes later he staggered, trembling and bleeding, into the hospital. That was the last straw for the Johnson family. They moved out of the cottage and Mrs Bonnor's grey cat moved back in.

The last of these grey lady ghosts is undoubtedly the most intriguing of them all. Its haunt is a ninety-year-old house in Ozone Avenue, Mount Martha on the Mornington Peninsula outside Melbourne. This ghost appears in an empire-line grey satin gown trimmed with silken tassels and wearing a grey veil over its face. So, what's so intriguing about that? Well, the ghost's identity is known and, in life, he was an Englishman named Herbert Dyce Murphy.

'H. D. M.' as he was known to his chums, was quite a character. After graduating from Oxford University, he joined British Intelligence and carried out spying missions in Europe disguised as a woman — and if you are curious regarding how successful his disguise was, I suggest a visit to the National Gallery of Victoria. There hangs a painting called *The Arbour* by E. Phillips Fox and the shapely young lady with auburn hair dressed in white in the centre of the painting is believed to be Murphy.

In 1911 'H.D.M.' was considered manly enough to accompany Sir Douglas Mawson on his expedition to the Antarctic and in 1923 he returned to Australia and built the house in Mount Martha for himself using his own hand-made bricks. In 1920 'H.D.M.' signed on as ice master to the Norwegian whaling fleet, piloting the mother ship through ice floes in the North Sea and Arctic Ocean for three months every year. This might be described as Murphy's last great adventure, but it was a long one, continuing for a remarkable forty-five years and ending only in 1965 when the fleet's insurers discovered that the man they entrusted the safety of their ships to was in his eighty-sixth year.

In his final years Murphy was considered a great raconteur but often stretched the truth about his exploits — although the truth was so remarkable it hardly needed any embroidery. As well as being immortalised in paint, Murphy is also immortalised in words. He was the inspiration for the central character 'Eddie' in Patrick White's great novel, *The Twyborn Affair*.

And the ghost in Ozone Avenue? Well, later owners of the house claimed to have seen him/her in their living room sitting quietly in an armchair, shapely and smooth legs modestly crossed and with a cigarette held in a long ivory holder emitting wisps of odourless smoke. Ash has also been seen to drop from the cigarette, scattering and drifting like a flight of tiny grey moths, but when the carpet is later checked no trace of it has ever been found.

Neighbours also report the ghost as a familiar sight in the house's garden. Outdoors it moves with a cat's insolent elegance, grey gown shimmering in the moonlight, tassels swaying gently and face demurely concealed behind its grey veil. Occasionally the spectre will stop, reach out a slender hand to shake dewdrops from a cobweb or draw a flower to its face to savour the fragrance, before blending into the grey shadows.

30.
The Ghosts of Yarralumla

> *Whenever I take up a newspaper and read it, I fancy I see ghosts creeping between the lines. There must be ghosts all over the world. They must be as countless as grains of the sands, it seems to me.*
>
> *And we are so miserably afraid of the light, all of us.*
>
> **from *Ghosts*, Henrik Ibsen (Norwegian playwright, 1828–1906)**

Those familiar with the much-publicised story of the Aboriginal ghost at Yarralumla may be surprised at the use of the plural in the above title, but, like all good mysteries, the reason will be revealed in time. Meanwhile, let me say that those who claim there is only one ghost in the governor general's residence are quite right — but it's not the much publicised one.

Yarralumla already had a long history as a grazing property when the Federal Government acquired it in 1913, eventually converting it into the official residence of the governor general of Australia. It was just before the last private owner, Frederick Campbell, left Yarralumla that a document was discovered that gave rise to the story of the Aboriginal ghost. A visitor to the house was being shown over a stone vault in the garden that had formerly contained the remains of an earlier owner, Colonel John Gibbes, when he discovered a dusty and cobweb-covered manuscript that was immediately delivered to his host. The handwritten, unsigned document read:

In 1826 a large diamond was stolen from James Cobbity, on an obscure station in Queensland. The theft was traced to one of the convicts who ran away, probably to New South Wales. The convict was captured in 1858, but the diamond could not be traced, neither would the convict (name unknown) give any information, in spite of frequent floggings.

During 1842 he left a statement to a groom, and a map of the hiding place of the hidden diamond. The groom, for a minor offence, was sent to Berrima Gaol. He was clever with horses and one day, when left to his duties, cleverly plaited a rope of straw and then escaped by throwing it over a wall, where it caught an iron bar. Passing it over, he swung himself down and escaped. He and his family lived out west for several years, according to Rev. James Hassall who, seeing him living honestly did not think it necessary to inform against him. I have no reason to think he tried to sell the diamond. Probably ownership of a thing so valuable would bring suspicion and lead to rearrest.

After his death his son took possession of the jewel and, with a trusty blackfellow, set off for Sydney. After leaving Cooma for Queanbeyan they met with, it was ascertained, a bushranging gang. The blackfellow and his companion were separated, and finally the former was captured and searched, to no avail, for he had swallowed the jewel.

The gang in anger shot him. He was buried in a piece of land belonging to Colonel Gibbes, and later Mr Campbell. I believe the diamond to be among his bones. It is of great value. My hand is enfeebled with age, or I should describe the troubles through which I have passed. My life has been wasted, my money expended, I die almost destitute, and in sight of my goal.

I believe the grave to be under the large deodar tree. Buried by blacks, it would be in a round hole. Believe and receive a fortune. Scoff and leave the jewel in its hiding place.

Written near Yarralumla, 1881.

Frederick Campbell, it is said, accepted the authenticity of the document. The references to Gibbes and himself and to 'the large deodar tree' were probably the convincing factors. There was, and still is, a magnificent deodar (Himalayan Cedar) in the garden of Yarralumla. Fortunately, Campbell did not see fit to uproot the now 180-year-old tree, diamond or no diamond, and none of the vice-regal occupants have either.

This story gave rise to reports that the ghost of the Aborigine stalked the gardens of Yarralumla on moonlit nights and had been seen digging around the roots of the deodar tree. In none of the published versions of this story was anyone ever quoted as having seen the ghost first hand and in light of evidence that surfaced many years later that is not surprising.

In 1984 Sergeant Bill Wittle, a loyal and popular guard at Government House from 1939 to 1962, published a chatty little book filled with anecdotes about his vice-regal employers and regal visitors to Yarralumla. In one chapter Wittle describes how a woman presented herself at the front gate one day in 1942 asking if it would be possible to see over her former home. The wife of the incumbent governor general agreed and Sergeant Wittle minded the children she had brought with her while the lady visited the house. Although she signed her name (according to Wittle) 'Mrs Little', she was the former Kate Campbell, daughter of Frederick Campbell.

On her return to the gate Sergeant Wittle asked the visitor if she could throw any light on the story of the ghost and the diamond. She laughed and agreed to let Sergeant Wittle in on a little secret. It was she, she said, aided by a school friend staying at Yarralumla during the school holidays, who had written the document that gave rise to the ghost story. She had taken a sheet of heavy parchment notepaper from her father's study, composed and written the story on it then disguised it with dust and cobwebs to appear old. She and her friend had placed it in the vault and it was they, she added, who took the visitor down there so he could find it.

Ghost story exploded? Well, nothing is ever that simple in the natural or supernatural world. History shows that Frederick Campbell did have a daughter named Kate but her married name was Newman, not Little. The visitors' book for 1942 does carry the signature of a 'Mrs Little' but not a 'Mrs Newman'. Another former security guard, Bert Sheedy, claimed that he too met the former Miss Campbell on her visit and laughed over the ghost hoax, but he claims it was in 1952, not 1942!

A letter to the editor of the Sydney Morning Herald, published 3 August 1945, corroborates the two men's stories. It read, in part:

> *In the past few years I have occasionally read allusions to a story of a diamond under the old deodar tree beside Yarralumla House. Hitherto I have ventured no public comment but when, on reading another book mentioning the story, bringing in my mother's name, I felt an urge to give the facts as I know them.*

The writer then went on to explain the same sequence of events described by Sergeant Wittle. The letter was signed 'Kate Newman'. So the Ghost of Yarralumla is finally and firmly laid to rest — well one of them, anyhow.

* * *

The *Canberra News* of 27 August 1970 carried a feature article quoting Sir Murray Tyrrell, private secretary to a succession of governors general from 1947 to 1973, about his encounter with a ghost at Yarralumla seven years before. Sir Murray told how, in February 1963, preparations were under way for a visit by the Queen and the Duke of Edinburgh. Sir Murray left his office one day and was walking towards his cottage in the grounds when a flustered official approached him and asked if he had seen a strange person entering the front door of Government House. Sir Murray said he had not, but the official was insistent that he had.

Now security was not of such paramount importance as it is these days, but had been stepped up for the royal visit, so the prospect of a stranger lurking in the house at that or any other time was cause for concern. Sir Murray decided to check out the report himself and entered the front door of Government House. As his eyes grew accustomed to the change in light, Sir Murray spotted the strange, hazy figure slowly and deliberately climbing the stairs from the foyer to the first floor.

Sir Murray shouted but the figure took no notice. The middle-aged private secretary then bounded like a man half his age up the stairs in pursuit, but when he reached the first floor landing the figure had vanished. He searched every room in the vicinity but could find no trace of the intruder.

Mystified and alarmed, Sir Murray summoned one of the security guards who were patrolling the grounds with guard dogs and hastily explained what he had seen. The security man and his dog began to mount the stairs, several at a time, then suddenly the animal stopped and would proceed no further. No order or coaxing would get the dog to move. It stood statue-like, halfway up, and bared its teeth at its handler in a display of uncooperativeness that was quite unlike the normally faithful and fearless creature.

Sir Murray Tyrrell always stood by his account of the events of that day and never found a rational explanation for them. As neither Sir Murray nor the other official who first saw it mention the colour of the ghost's skin it is reasonable to assume it was white and they did describe it as male.

There is an old story about a man having died or been murdered near the old Yarralumla homestead (demolished in 1881 to make way for the present building), but a descendent of Colonel Gibbes who takes an interest in his family's history informed me a few years ago that as far as he knows the only male to have died at 'old' Yarralumla was the Colonel himself. So perhaps it was his shade that was observed in 1963. Perhaps the old Colonel decided he was duty bound to put in an appearance when the monarch was due and maybe *he* is the real Ghost of Yarralumla.

31.
'Atten-shun! Pre-sent Ghosts!'

Ghosts are souls not fully cleansed from the visible, material world;
still retaining some part in it and therefore visible
Plato (Greek philosopher, 4th Century BC)

'I saw it *with my own eyes*!'

I like that expression, so often used by witnesses to ghostly appearances; and I've always wondered how (at least before the age of corneal transplants) anyone could see anything with somebody *else's* eyes. It was used recently to add authenticity to the claim of a sighting of a ghost at Sydney's Victoria Barracks, but in this case it was unnecessary for many others have seen the same apparition.

No building in Australia evokes the essence of queen and country or British military might better than this expansive and impressive old sandstone complex. For visitors it is like stepping back a couple of centuries and if one closes one's eyes it's easy to see red-coated soldiers marching and gold-braided officers riding on the dusty parade ground, with elegantly dressed *mem-sahibs* watching from the shady verandahs. One can almost hear the clatter of hooves, the swish of carriage wheels, the rumble of field guns, the crack of muskets and the eerie echo of bugles long gone. But imagination is not required to see one figure from the barracks' past — only your presence in the right place at the right time and a spot of good luck.

For more than 100 years people working or visiting the barracks and passers-by on Oxford Street have spotted a spectral figure on the upper level balcony of the Officers' Quarters. Accounts differ but some details are common to all reports — the figure is female, tall, young and slender and dressed in a pink gown — high-necked, tight-waisted and expanding out to a full, flowing skirt. One observer described the colour of the fabric as like that last blush of colour as a sunset fades.

The figure usually has one slender hand resting on the balcony railing and its eyes seem to be gazing into the far distance — over the parade ground and down what would have been (when this spectre was flesh and blood) the sandy track leading to the city. In the words of one witness the spectre 'looks ever so sad; as if she's waiting for someone to return to her'.

No one can put a name to this ladylike ghost. Perhaps in life she was the wife of one of the lieutenant colonels who commanded at the barracks, or the sister, daughter or mistress of some officer who marched away and never came back. Just occasionally, it seems, her sadness is dispelled. She is reported as slowly turning her head towards observers and giving them a wan smile; and one witness (a man walking up Oxford Street on a sunny spring afternoon) noticed her watching him, waved and received a gentle wave in return.

Such brief encounters aside, the ghost who has become known simply as 'the lady on the balcony' is elusive. Efforts to get close to it always fail. Witnesses at ground level see it and the inquisitive (or foolhardy) dash up the stairs to try to corner it, but on arrival the balcony is always empty and occupants of the upper level deny having seen anything at all.

* * *

This gentle spirit is just one of many that inhabit Victoria Barracks and not, as you might expect after so many sightings, the most famous. That distinction belongs to the ghost of Private Charles Crowley, formerly of the Eleventh Regiment — the 'North Devonshires' — the first British regiment to occupy the barracks.

'Charlie', as he was known to his comrades (and still is to his victims), shot dead the popular Sergeant Pearson after an argument at the barracks in 1853. Charlie fled but was captured just a few kilometres away in Leichhardt and locked away in the barracks prison to await court martial. Remorse or fear drove Charlie to hang himself and in doing so he escaped one punishment only to be condemned to another. According to the reports of eyewitnesses his ghost has remained in and around the barracks prison ever since.

In the 1960s and 70s Warrant Officer Bert White and his family lived in the old Provost Sergeant's quarters above the prison cells. W.O. White described Charlie's ghost as young, tall, wearing an old army greatcoat and able to glide through walls. The Whites believed that Charlie watched over them and Mrs White told how on one occasion a piece of falling masonry stopped in mid-air while she snatched one of her children to safety.

'It was the strangest thing I've ever seen,' Mrs White recounted. 'This big lump of sandstone — it was part of the lintel over a window — just *stopped*, frozen in mid-air, about six feet off the ground. I grabbed our youngest and we both toppled backwards onto the gravel. Then the piece of stone continued its fall, crashing with a horrifying *crunch* into the gravel.'

Another time Mrs White claimed she received a psychic message from Charlie when she was shopping in Oxford Street. The message told her to return home immediately. When she got to their quarters she found the children had been playing with matches and had lit a fire endangering themselves and the building.

Charlie's altruistic antics have sometimes backfired on the recipients. During the years of the Great Depression when the Royal Military College occupied the barracks at least one cadet had reason to resent Charlie's interference. This young man was accused of cheating at his passing-out examinations and when asked to account for how he (*not* the brightest student in his class) managed to answer every question correctly, he told a story that only got him into worse trouble.

The cadet told how he had gone to bed early to get a good night's sleep before his exams, but had been awakened in the middle of the night by a scratching sound and a faint light that filled his room. 'I rolled over in bed and found this joker sitting at my table with his back to me. He had my pencil box open and he was writing, using the fountain pen my mum gave me for my sixteenth birthday.'

The cadet sat up in bed and was about to challenge the intruder when he realised that he could see *through* the strange figure and that the light was coming *from* it. 'It was a human figure — a man — but he looked like he was made of thick, smoky glass; the kind you can just see through but which distorts shapes behind it. I could make out the calendar on the wall behind the figure, but all the letters and numbers were blurred. And there was this "halo" of light around him; a soft, shimmering band of yellow that cast a warm glow over the room *and* over me. The light made the white sheet covering my legs look mustard-coloured and the skin on my hands and arms looked jaundiced.'

The cadet was too frightened to speak or cry out and watched in stunned silence until 'Charlie' (for this surely was his ghost), finished scribbling, folded the paper he had been writing on, put away the pen and placed the pencil box over the paper to serve as a paperweight. The ghost turned its head and smiled at the cadet, showing discoloured teeth with many gaps, then slowly faded away. With it went the light, velvety blackness reclaiming the room.

Cautiously the cadet reached for the lamp beside his bed and switched it on. Everything in the room looked normal and instinct told the young man he was quite alone. He climbed out of bed, crossed over to the table, moved the pencil box and nervously picked up the paper. As he unfolded it he realised it was not one sheet but three all covered in crudely scrawled words.

Some of what the cadet read was familiar to him and some was not. It was not until the following day when he was issued with his examination papers that he realised that what he had read were the correct answers to every question on the exam.

The cadet might have been wiser to have kept quiet about his nocturnal visitor and the reason he did so well in the exam, for the officers investigating the claims of cheating were not inclined to believe a word of his explanation. 'And where is this *miraculous* epistle?' a senior officer asked.

'In my room, sir,' the cadet replied, 'pinned to the back of my calendar.'

'Well, sir, you had better go and get it then!' the officer retorted.

Under guard the cadet was marched to his room, retrieved the sheets of paper and presented them to the investigating officers. Remarkably the paper, the ink and the writing seemed to have aged overnight. The paper was now yellowed and brittle, the blue ink turned brown and the writing faded, but the content of the words was still convincingly clear. The investigators decided to give the cadet the benefit of the doubt and he passed his examination — top of the class.

So numerous were the reports of Charlie's activities that an investigation was undertaken in 1972 by two lieutenant colonels from the Australian army with the stated aim: *To obtain first-hand information for possible handling of situation when press find out* — which was a bit late, considering the press had been reporting the ghostly goings-on at the barracks for at least the previous ninety years. As one might expect the investigating officers' official findings suggested hallucinations, coincidences, pranks, electrical faults, etc., but at least one of them became a devout believer in Charlie's ghost.

In 1975 the prison where Charlie ended his life was closed and became the barracks museum but without interruption to his ghost's activities. To this day he flits about among the exhibits at night, startling security guards, alarming guard dogs and trying, so far unsuccessfully, to trap unsuspecting victims in the cells by closing the heavy steel doors.

In 1988 the army was again obliged to acknowledge the existence of ghosts in one of its historic establishments — this time Fortuna Villa, at Bendigo, Victoria, headquarters of DIGO, the Defence Imagery and Geospatial Organisation, where millions of useful maps had been produced during and since World War Two.

A zealous patriot who had read a magazine article about ghosts at Fortuna wrote to inquire what action the army was taking to eliminate the threat to our national security from our enemies finding out that Australian service personnel believed in ghosts. A spokesperson for the army very sensibly wrote back to say no action was being taken on those grounds and pointing out that soldiers are no different to anyone else in the community and prone to fear the unknown — whether it be supernatural or otherwise.

Fortuna Villa was once the home of the mining magnate Sir George Lansell, known as the Quartz King for introducing deep-shaft mining to the Bendigo goldfields. Lansell spent a fortune enlarging the house and gardens, installing ornamental lakes, a Roman-style bathing house, valuable art works, swathes of stained glass and all the latest 'mod-cons' of the Victorian era. In 1942 Fortuna was taken over by the army and stories of ghostly activity came thick and fast — attested to by numerous officers and men who served there.

In 1998 retired Major John Bloor vividly recalled the cold winter morning twenty years earlier when he came up the stairs near the ornamental lake and spotted a filmy figure in a white shroud peering into the kitchen window. The apparition sensed Bloor's approach and turned. The living and the dead stared at each other for about fifteen seconds, then the apparition faded away. When the Major met up with someone a few minutes later they said: 'What's up, John? You look like you've seen a ghost.'

'I have,' he replied.

Footsteps are heard in what was once Sir George Lansell's bedroom and in the adjoining bathroom; also in the billiard room, which became the Officers' Mess. So often were these slow, thumping sounds heard by rank and file that they ceased to cause alarm and were dismissed with casual remarks like 'There's old George banging around again.'

Female voices are clearly audible in Mrs Lansell's former bedroom at night when the room is supposedly empty; and a sergeant who put his head inside to investigate one night was asked very brusquely: 'What are you doing here?' The identity of this ghost is less clear. She may be 'old Bedella' or 'old Edith' for there were two Mrs Lansells: the first an uneducated Irish lass who did not cope well with her husband's social climbing and reportedly drank herself to death; and the second, a formidable English woman who lived on at Fortuna like a dowager queen until the 1920s.

The ghosts of a little boy in a sailor suit and a girl in a late-Victorian tea gown have also been spotted, but not all the ghosts of Fortuna Villa are necessarily of the Lansells' time. Major Bloor was told by another officer about a tragic event that occurred there during World War Two and which may account for at least one ghost. A group of soldiers were playing cards one day when a comrade walked in and asked casually if any of them had a piece of rope.

'What for?' one of the group asked.

'To hang meself, o' course,' the first soldier said and they all laughed.

'There's a bit in my kit,' said another soldier, helpfully. Half an hour later they found the first soldier's dead body dangling from 'the bit' of rope.

Fortuna was the Ancient Roman goddess of good fortune, but it seems Fortuna Villa has not always enjoyed her protection.

32.
The Headmistress's Ghost

Now droops the milk white peacock like a ghost
And like a ghost, she glimmers on me.
***The Princess*, Alfred Lord Tennyson (English poet, 1809–1892)**

Rockhampton Girls' Grammar School has a long and distinguished history. Founded in 1892 to provide a superior education for the daughters of wealthy pastoralists and the city's leading citizens, the school prospered from the outset. This was due largely to the first headmistress, an English spinster named Helen E. Downs. Miss Downs was a character; a free thinker with progressive views on female education, women's emancipation and most other subjects. At a speech day in 1898 she reminded parents that the senior classes in her school were for training cultured women who would exert an uplifting influence in social matters — and not waste their time on prettiness.

'Prettiness' was one of Miss Downs's chief dislikes. She was not pretty herself and was possibly slightly lame. She refused to allow staff or students to restrict their bodies with corsets or 'paint' their faces. Sensible clothes, sensible diet, fresh air, exercise and lots of soap and water were her recipe for building sturdy bodies and sound minds.

Helen Downs's unconventional ideas probably shocked and upset many people, but the academic achievements of her students reached such heights that she was tolerated by her critics and encouraged by the liberal-minded. The impression one gets reading about her 100-plus years later is of boundless energy, a brilliant mind and total dedication to her vocation.

It is not surprising that such a strong and controversial character should still exert a powerful influence over the school she founded, but the form that influence takes is quite unexpected. According to school legend Miss Downs's ghost lives in the school bell tower and comes down from her eyrie once a year, at 11 pm on 11 November. The ghost makes its way through the girls' dormitories, selects the girl with the longest blonde hair, produces a pair of spectral scissors and hacks off her victim's tresses.

If you don't believe this story, ask the girls (and former girls). They will tell you that they believe in the ghost of Miss Downs — and watch the mixture of excitement, embarrassment, pride and fear on their faces as they recount their experiences and express their views.

We had our mattresses in the middle of E dorm, on the night of 11 November 1995. Another girl who lives in H dorm, and had the longest, blondest hair came into our room — she was really scared that the ghost was going to chop off her beloved hair. At 11 p.m. we heard a noise in the roof. We all screamed. A mistress came in and quietened us. She said there was no such thing as ghosts and that it was probably a bandicoot in the roof. A bandicoot in the roof? I'm sure it was Miss Downs!

Miss Downs comes drifting down from her hideout and scares the living daylights out of new and old boarders. If the girl she selects puts up a fight the ghost will drag her up and down the stairs till her hair falls out — but wait, there's more. We have three student ghosts as well. One is a girl who died of scarlet fever and another is Miss Downs's first victim. She wanders up and down the stairs trying to warn us.

I was told Miss Downs was a nice ghost who goes around at night checking that we are looking after her school, tucks us in and gives us a kiss on the cheek. I think she is far too nice to hurt anyone.

The story of the ghost of Helen Downs was first published in another book of mine in 1998 and soon after that I received a letter from an old lady who had been a pupil at Rockhampton Girls' Grammar in the 1930s. She wrote that she had read with interest my account of the ghost's activities and the impressions of the current batch of students, but felt that it was unlikely any of these younger girls had actually seen the ghost. She, on the other hand, had — or so she assured me.

The lady explained that she remembered taking part in the annual ritual on 11 November every year while she was a boarder at the school, getting (like all her classmates) overexcited with anticipation and fear when the fateful hour approached and then, in her case, deeply disappointed because she did not get to see the spectre charging down the stairs wielding a giant pair of scissors and shearing off golden locks from screaming little girls.

By her second or third year at the school, my correspondent said she was convinced the whole story was a myth — a great way for impressionable girls to 'let off steam' — but nothing more. Then, she said, in her third year at the school and 200-odd kilometres from Rockhampton something happened which made her change her mind.

A few days after her thirteenth birthday, the lady said, she was summoned to the principal's office and the news broken to her that her father had died as the result of an accident on their family property near Emerald, west of Rockhampton. It was also explained that it had been arranged for her to go home for a few days, to be with her mother and her siblings and to attend her father's funeral. A teacher, the principal told her, had been assigned to take her to the Rockhampton railway station the following day and put her on the Emerald train and that her mother or another relative would be waiting for her at the other end.

The girl was very upset at her father's death and she knew that the next few days would be an ordeal for her and for the rest of her family. She cried much and slept little that night. The following morning a teacher drove her to the station, helped her board the train and stow her bag in the overhead luggage rack then farewelled her.

The train was only sparsely filled and just before it pulled out of the station another woman got into the same carriage. The young girl noticed her, but did not pay her much attention. The woman smiled as she passed and the young girl thought the woman's face seemed vaguely familiar.

The journey took several hours and on arrival at Emerald the girl was met by her two older brothers and driven home. The next few days were taken up with all the activities that surround a death in any family — visits from relatives and friends, funeral arrangements, choosing flowers, choosing mourning clothes, a lot of handshaking and hugging and many tears. The young girl thought no more about the woman on the train or about school or her classmates, who at the time seemed far away and belonging to a different world.

The funeral was held in the Anglican church in a little town outside Emerald. The day was hot and the air filled with smoke from distant bushfires.

The church was packed and for every seated mourner there were a hundred buzzing flies. The flowers on the altar and on the coffin wilted. Men discreetly loosened their collars and ladies fanned themselves with prayer books when they thought no one was looking. The minister sweltered in his robes and had rivulets of sweat running down his forehead, cheeks and jowls.

The young girl from Rockhampton Girls' Grammar had been brave during the preceding days, but with the sudden realisation that her father's dead body lay in a box just metres away from her and that she would never see him again made her eyes fill with unbidden tears. At almost the same moment her brothers and her mother (all sitting on her left) also began to weep, setting up a chorus of quiet sniffling.

Through her tears the young woman noticed a figure moving rapidly down the outside aisle of the church. The figure stopped at the end of the family's pew and slid in beside her. A gentle hand reached out and took the girl's and a quiet voice whispered: 'Be brave, little one, I'm here for you.'

The girl recognised the lady who had smiled at her on the train and now, at close range, she also recognised the face from an old portrait she had seen at school. She swallowed her tears and whispered: 'You're Miss Downs, aren't you?' The lady smiled and nodded. Then the young girl's expression changed to alarm.

'You haven't come to cut off my hair, have you?' she asked.

'Of course not, my dear,' came the gentle reply.

At that moment the service began and for the next thirty minutes the ghost of Helen Downs sat quietly beside the girl, her presence bestowing courage and a warm sense of solace on the child. When hymns were announced the kind spirit helped the girl to her feet and joined in the singing with a soft, deep voice.

After six local lads carried the coffin from the church to be loaded onto a hearse and taken to the cemetery, the minister gathered the family together to offer his condolences and accept their thanks for the service. The girl's mother introduced her to the minister, explaining that she was a pupil of Rockhampton Girls' Grammar and had come home to be with the family.

The minister reached out and put his hand on the girl's shoulder and said he felt sure both her father and her school would have been proud of how splendidly she had conducted herself during the service. 'You were a model of propriety, my dear,' he said.

At the first opportunity the girl turned to where her companion had been sitting, but the pew was empty. As is the custom, no one left the church until the family did. Miss Downs had not 'left'; she had simply vanished and it seemed from conversations the girl had with others after the funeral that she had not made herself visible to anyone else.

Even now, more than sixty years later' my correspondent wrote, *I feel a fool for having asked Miss Downs if she had come to cut off my hair, but I'm sure she didn't mind. She was too kind and too understanding to take offence at that. I never saw her again, but I sincerely hope her spirit is still lingering around Rockhampton Girls' Grammar, keeping an eye on the welfare of her girls and probably having a good chuckle on the eleventh of November every year.*

33.
The Luna Park Ghost: Not a Joking Matter

If a ghost is really the spirit of a dead man, then it ought to appear nude because garments have no spirits.

Wang Ch'ung (Chinese philosopher, first century AD)

For generations of Melburnians, Luna Park at St Kilda has epitomised all that was fun and carefree; it's a place where they can leave inhibitions behind and abandon themselves to pleasure. There were, however, stories of a terrifying, joker-like spectre prowling the park a little over half a century ago, materialising in the path of cars on the roller coaster, sharing cages with patrons on the Ferris wheel and causing general panic. Most people thought the Joker was a publicity stunt, but not those who encountered it.

One such couple had a terrifying story to tell after they encountered the Joker on the Ferris wheel. The year was 1957 and the young man, Roy, and his girlfriend, Heather, were both nineteen. Their families lived a few streets apart in the Melbourne suburb of Footscray and Roy had invited Heather to Luna Park to celebrate a pay rise he had received.

It was a Saturday night and cold, with the smell of rain in the air. The young couple caught a tram out to Luna Park and as the tram clattered along St Kilda Road they could see occasional flashes of lightning across Port Philip Bay. They wondered if their journey would be in vain and if they would find the park closed, but when they alighted on the St Kilda esplanade Luna Park was a hive of activity. The sound of music and laughter wafted over them and thousands of sparkling coloured lights made the place look like fairyland, the brightness intensified by a moonless night and low clouds. Heather giggled with excitement and Roy gave her an encouraging hug as they entered the park through the mouth of the giant, smiling face. Inside the noise was like bedlam and the tempting smells of popcorn, hot dogs and ice cream swirled around them.

Heather was afraid of heights so they began the evening with rides on some of the less taxing attractions, working their way up to the big slide, the roller coaster and the towering Ferris wheel. The rain stayed away and excitement kept the cold at bay.

'Come on, love, please, I really wanna have a go on the Ferris wheel,' Roy pleaded. Heather hesitated for just a moment then, looking at the excited expression on her boyfriend's face, she gave in. Roy got the tickets just as passengers were boarding the giant, graceful wheel. Within moments they were installed in a cage that slowly rose as the wheel rotated.

Roy put his arm around Heather's shoulders and she soon forgot her nerves as the incredible vista revealed itself. Figures on the ground below shrank until they looked like ants, the lights of the city glittered in the distance and the sparkling waters of the bay seemed to stretch forever. Banks of heavy cloud rolled along the horizon, streaked with lightning, and the distant rumble of thunder echoed around them. The slow, smooth motion of the wheel made the couple feel as if they were magically flying together through the inky sky.

'Blimey, this is great, eh?' Roy whispered to Heather.

'It's *beautiful*,' Heather whispered back.

At that moment a particularly bright flash of lightning lit the wheel, making the white-painted spokes and dangling cages appear like a giant skeleton. A crash of deafening thunder followed. Roy and Heather were temporarily blinded by the lightning, but when their eyes adjusted they both screamed and clung to each other for dear life — and good reason they had to do so, for suddenly, almost a 100 metres in the air and without any warning, they found themselves sharing their cage *with a third person.*

Sitting casually on the restraining bar of the cage, just a few centimetres from them, was a life-size male figure dressed in the costume of a court jester — a three-pointed hat (red, yellow and black, with a golden bell on each point), a tight jacket in the same colours, tight breeches (one leg red, the other black), a yellow codpiece and pointed yellow shoes, also trimmed with golden bells.

If the creature's sudden arrival and its bizarre costume were not enough to terrify Roy and Heather then its face and form were. There was an ageless, sinuous strength to its body and its lean face wore a leering smile; its eyes smouldered, fixed on Roy and Heather, lips drawn back to reveal elongated, pointed teeth.

Another flash of lightning followed the first and lit the points of the creature's teeth and the whites of its eyes, making them shine like incandescent stars. The creature leaned towards the terrified couple and they shrank back as its face loomed nearer and nearer theirs. At close range they could hear the tinkling of the bells on the hat and shoes. One bony, red-gloved hand reached out towards Heather and a long, thin finger caressed her cheek then was quickly withdrawn. The creature then leaned back so that most of its body was outside the cage. The bells on its hat jangled wildly in the wind and from its mouth came a devilish sound, half laugh and half howl, that seemed to make the air around the cage vibrate. Just as the sound reached a deafening crescendo the monstrous vision vanished. Where a split second before the colours of its gaudy costume had been dancing before their eyes and its eyes and teeth flashing there was nothing but air and velvety blackness.

'What the *hell* was that?' mumbled Roy.

'I don't know,' said Heather, 'and I don't *want* to know!'

Roy's masculine instincts took over from his fear. 'We'll be down in a sec, love, and boy am I gonna give the people who run this joint a piece of my mind. They shouldn't allow that to happen to anyone!'

Heather's more practical female instincts were also returning to her. She took Roy's hand and looked up into his face. 'I don't think I'd bother if I was you, Roy.'

Heather and Roy made a pact to tell no one about their strange and horrifying experience and twenty years passed before, as husband and wife and clinging to one another as they had that night to ward off the echoes of their terror, they finally broke their silence.

'I was so scared I nearly wet meself,' Roy admitted.

Heather added: 'I *did* actually.'

The figure Roy and Heather referred to as 'The Joker' was seen by others. A group of ten riders on the Scenic Railway roller coaster, who were already screaming with excitement, screamed in horror when it appeared on the track just in front of their car. In a split second the roller-coaster cars passed over (or through) the figure, without the impact and crash the riders all expected and feared.

When this group complained to the operators of the ride, they were told they must have imagined the figure; or that it had been a large seabird or a trick of the light, but the group remained unconvinced. So did the management of Luna Park, until another patron complained one afternoon about a week later that the Joker had pushed her child off one of the horses on the carousel.

'It's just not good enough!' the angry woman shrieked. 'It might be a bit of fun to have your staff dressed up like that ... but that man's behaviour was unacceptable. I paid good money for Betty to ride on the merry-go-round and we waited until the horse she liked best was free. I sat her on the horse, took her fairy floss to mind it and showed her how to hang onto the pole. She was as happy as Larry when the music started.

'Then that *monster* appeared beside her. I don't know where he came from. I didn't see him arrive. He must have been behind the machinery in the middle. I saw him lurch towards Betty and jam his face right into hers. Betty screamed and I leaped onto the merry-go-round to grab her ... then he *shoved* her *right off the horse*. Luckily I caught her as she fell. The *thing* swung his leg over *her* horse as the merry-go-round started to move. He gave us this horrible smile and waved as he rode off ... and above the music I swear the bastard was laughing at us!'

The woman described how her daughter was hysterical, the fairy floss lay in the dust and her own anger was making her tremble. She waited until the carousel made its first full rotation, intending to take a swipe at the 'bastard' with her handbag as he came past, but when the distinctive horse her daughter had chosen came by again, gently rising and falling in time to the music, it was riderless.

Stories about the Joker leaked out and the management of the park responded with 'no comment', afraid that the publicity would drive business *away* rather than attract it. They hoped the stories would be quickly forgotten and their hopes were fulfilled. The Luna Park ghost (if that it was) had a very short career. The last report came barely a year after the first and all has been silence since. The giant, grinning face still welcomes visitors, the lights still dazzle, the music and the shrieks of delighted children still ring through the complex, but the Joker seems to have departed. Might he, I wonder, have transported himself to Hollywood, to act as an unpaid consultant to the parade of notable actors who have portrayed his character so memorably in film and on television?

34.
The Ghosts of Garth and Graham's Castle

> *For who can wonder that man should feel a vague belief in tales of disembodied spirits wandering those places which they once dearly affected, when he himself, scarcely less separated from his old world than they, is for ever lingering upon past emotions and by-gone times, and hovering, the ghost of his former self, about the places and people that warmed his heart of old?*
>
> ***Master Humphrey's Clock*, Charles Dickens**

Near the village of Avoca in the Fingal Valley in Tasmania stand the ruins of a house called Garth. What began as an imposing, two-storey residence 160 years ago is now reduced to a few crumbling fragments of wall, a broken chimney and a scatter of rubble. On bright summer days when the sun warms the smooth blocks of sandstone there is little evidence to support the building's grim reputation, but when winter shrouds the valley a gloomier place would be hard to imagine.

If you're hardy (or foolhardy) enough to spend a night there you may see and hear things that make you forget the cold and discomfort. If you hear a moaning sound it will probably be the wind whistling around the ruined walls; a shriek will almost certainly be the call of a startled owl and strange shapes on the frosty ground nothing more that the shadows of clouds scudding across the moon — or it might be the ghosts of Garth, for this stark old ruin is all that remains of what is still called Tasmania's most haunted house.

Truth and fiction are so entwined in the story of Garth that it is hard to separate them. The few historical facts that survive about the property conflict with the popular stories but are just as tragic and disturbing. According to the popular version, the land on which the house stands was granted in the 1830s to a young Englishman who had left his fiancée behind in England. The plan was for him to establish himself, then for her to join him. Using convict labour the young man set about building a house worthy of his future bride but, when the building was only partially completed, he became impatient and took ship for England to fetch her. When he arrived he discovered that during his absence the young lady's feelings towards him had not grown fonder. Quite the opposite: she had married someone else and had not bothered to let him know.

In despair the betrayed lover returned to Van Diemen's Land and to Avoca. The hopes and dreams that had sustained him through the years of hardship were dashed and the house he had built with such loving care now seemed as barren and gloomy as his future. In a fit of anguish the young man hanged himself in the courtyard of the unfinished house. His ghost, it is said, still wanders the property bemoaning his fate.

Sometime later (so the story goes) the building was occupied by a family with a small daughter and a convict nursemaid. The nursemaid was strict and fond of scolding her charge until one day the child threw herself into a well to escape. The nursemaid dived in to rescue the little girl but both drowned. Thereafter the ghost of the little girl joined the betrayed lover in stalking the blighted rooms of Garth.

The house stood unoccupied for decades and stories of the ghosts accumulated. Locals reported seeing the young man (his head twisted and livid rope burns scarring his throat) and the little girl, dressed in a lace-trimmed pinafore and waving to passers-by from the empty windows of the house. Heartrending screams were heard echoing through the building and the hoof beats of unseen horses rang on the hard ground in front of the house and from within the courtyard. Animals which had apparently wandered up to the house innocently were reported as racing away lathered with fear as if all the hounds in hell were nipping at their heels. When developed, a photograph taken at Garth by curious visitors with their trusty Box Brownie showed the shadowy figure of the little girl smiling shyly beside the person who was being photographed. Whispers spread like wildfire that the property was cursed and it was said that anyone who disturbed the stones at Garth would meet a dreadful end.

The true history of the property is quite different. The earliest maps still in existence show the land belonging to a Charles Peters and his wife Susannah. Devotees of the story of the betrayed lover claim that Peters took over the partially completed house after the young man's suicide, but local historians doubt there was a previous owner. Charles and Susannah Peters named their house Garth after their family home in Scotland, and if they shared it with the ghost of a previous owner they left no record of it.

Tragedy struck the Peters family on Friday, 18 September 1840 while Charles and Susannah were entertaining a friend in the parlour. Their little daughter, Anne, aged two and a half, came to the parlour door screaming hysterically, her clothes and hair on fire. She had apparently been watching the cook making jam in the kitchen and had stood too close to the stove. The child was terribly burned and, although her parents anointed her burns with oil and lime water and the local doctor did what he could to relieve her suffering, poor little Anne died two days later. The details of this tragic event are preserved in the coroner's report and the evidence of the distraught father and guest dutifully recorded and dated. Anne Peters was buried near the house and her grave remains visible to this day.

The Peters retained ownership of Garth but moved to the nearby town of Fingal after their daughter's death. The house remained empty until 1851, when they leased it to James and Charlotte Grant, but five months after the tenants moved in the house was completely gutted by fire. No one lived at Garth after that — except the spirits.

Sceptics in the district will tell you that the stories of ghosts were invented to keep trespassers out of the ruined house. Believers will tell you that the ghosts had exactly that effect and that they would not spend a night at Garth for a million dollars. Perhaps the young man who supposedly hanged himself there never existed, or maybe time simply erased records of him. Perhaps the little girl whose ghost likes to be photographed did not die in the well, although the remains of a well are still there. Could it be the ghost of little Anne Peters? Only the old house knows the truth and it keeps its secrets to itself.

The distinction of bearing the title 'South Australia's most haunted house' goes to a building that is also no longer there. Unlike Garth there are not even a few stones left to help us remember a house known in its day as Graham's Castle.

A wealthy Englishman named John Richmond arrived in Adelaide in 1838 with this wife, four children, fourteen servants and the servants' families. To accommodate such a large retinue, Richmond purchased fifty-two acres (twenty hectares) of land facing Prospect Road in what was then called Prospect Village, four kilometres north of the Adelaide GPO.

In the centre of it he built a large house and surrounded it with gardens and orchards, but the Richmonds remained less than ten years in what they called Prospect House. In 1846 the property was bought by an enterprising bachelor named John Benjamin Graham. From that time the house was known locally as Graham's Castle.

There's some doubt as to whether the house reached its final form during Richmond's or Graham's time, but whichever of these men was responsible for choosing its design had more money than taste. Prospect House or Graham's Castle was an architectural monstrosity — a stark white limestone box topped with a crenellated parapet that made it look like a bad copy of an English castle. A massive front door with two cast-iron lion's head knockers (why two?) and a high stone wall topped with broken glass encircling the property made it about as warm and inviting as a mausoleum.

Graham came to Adelaide as an undistinguished migrant, took a job as a shop assistant in an ironmonger's, soon owned the business then mortgaged it to buy shares in the new Burra copper mine. Within a few years he was a millionaire. During his time at Prospect House Graham was not exactly a recluse, but his stern character and Spartan lifestyle suited the house. He visited Europe in 1848, where he acquired a genuine castle near Heidelberg in Germany and a severe English wife.

Graham sold Prospect House in 1853 to a brewer named Clark, who in turn sold it to Nathaniel Oldham and it was during the latter's time that the house began to gain its reputation for being haunted. The ghost of a woman dressed entirely in black was often seen on the stairs and, seventy years later, Oldham's sons could still vividly recall their separate encounters with her. Some people suggested it was Mrs Graham and that she had been murdered in the house by

Mr Graham, but as both ended their days peacefully in their German *schloss* that theory is easily disproved.

Another ghost, this time a lady fashionably dressed in white satin began to visit the house. Occupants would hear a coach approaching on the gravel driveway and then the white figure would appear at a window tapping on the glass and motioning to be let in. She would then suddenly disappear, leaving her audience aghast. Moments later, delicate footsteps would be heard mounting the empty stairs. A third spectre, reputed to be the ghost of a servant who hanged himself in his bedroom, caused general panic whenever he appeared on the parapet walk; he was immaculately dressed but headless.

As well as these phantom figures the old house was plagued by strange noises: bumps and creaks, mysterious tapping, groans and terrifying shrieks that hauled sleepers from their beds. Neighbours always avoided the house at night, taking long detours rather than pass its gloomy gates.

Not surprisingly, the house changed hands many times during the remaining years of the nineteenth century, a succession of owners driven out by the ghosts or the difficulty of getting servants to stay. For a while it was leased by North Adelaide Grammar and used as a dormitory for an overflow of boarders, but the combination of its ugliness and lurid reputation meant the house finally lay vacant. Decay set in and by 1912 the old house was fit only for demolition.

Neither the residents of Prospect or of Fingal in Tasmania regretted the passing of these notorious old houses, but maybe the spirits that occupied them did.

35.
Keepers of the Flame

Down in the south, by the waste without sail on it,
Far from the zone of the blossom and tree,
Lieth, with winter and whirlwind and wail on it,
Ghost of a land by the ghost of a sea.

***Beyond Kerguelen*, Henry Kendall (Australian poet 1839–1882)**

There's a quality of mystery and romance about lighthouses that no other buildings possess. It may be their graceful shape, their picturesque locations or the comforting beams of light they project over treacherous waters at night. Whatever their charm to observers (and in particular to seafarers), one suspects it is soon lost on those charged with maintaining them and on their families, condemned to lonely lives in remote, windswept and wave-washed locations. At last count there were about a dozen lighthouses around the coast of Australia laying claim to being haunted. The following is a sampling of their spooky stories.

The 138-year-old lighthouse that overlooks Belmore Basin at Wollongong is the haunt of two ghosts. Pilot William Edwards, who guided thousands of vessels in and out of Wollongong Harbour and who drowned when his boat capsized during a storm, is said to walk the observation deck at the top of the lighthouse on stormy nights, watching out for ships in distress.

His companion is George Smith, lighthouse keeper during the 1920s and 30s. Smith was a familiar figure in the streets of Wollongong during his lifetime: tall, straight-backed even in old age and always willing to tell anyone who asked how he lost one hand and forearm while working as a sugar-cane cutter in Queensland.

Every evening at dusk George would climb the spiral stairs to light the enormous revolving lantern at the top of the lighthouse, content in the knowledge that his work was averting disaster and saving lives. George Smith died sixty-odd years ago, but some say he still climbs the stairs every evening. Hollow footsteps slowly climbing upwards have been heard many times and wet footprints found on the stairs when the lighthouse has been securely locked. That William Edwards is seen and not heard, and George Smith heard but not seen may account for why these two salty spirits seem happy to share their confined haunt.

Split Point Lighthouse at Aireys Inlet on the coast of Western Victoria has a much longer reputation for ghostly goings-on and, given its colourful history, that is no surprise. The first lighthouse keeper (another George, but this time with a less common surname — Bardin) came from the Channel Islands and broke both his legs when he fell from the crow's-nest of the ship that brought him to Australia. Just what passenger Bardin was doing 'aloft' on the long journey is not recorded. Perhaps he was trying to get used to heights in preparation for the job that awaited him on his arrival. While recovering in Williamstown Hospital, rats ate away most of both Bardin's heels, so it was a wonder that he ever managed to report for duty.

A later keeper, Richard Baker (with the odd middle name of 'Joy') also assured himself a place in local history by devising a way of spending his evenings in the local pub instead of keeping the light. Baker scratched a hole in the black paint at the back of the lamp glass in line with the Aireys Inlet pub, so that each time the light rotated it 'winked' in that direction. Baker could thus relax with his mates over a few ales and check the light was still burning and revolving.

The ghost of Split Point Lighthouse is not, however, either of these colourful characters, but the unmarried daughter of one of them, or of another lighthouse keeper. Local legend has it that the young woman went out fishing in a small boat with her dad one day and chose that time to tell him that she was pregnant. The father got agitated, the boat rocked and the daughter fell into the ocean and drowned. Her fetching ghost, it is claimed, rises out of the surf below the lighthouse and calls to young men on the shore to join her in the water, and that until one gullible guy obliges, her restless spirit will find no rest. Well, that's how the story goes and the fact that there are no records of the death by drowning of a lighthouse keeper's daughter, has not stopped it flourishing or several young men swearing that they almost succumbed to the ghost's sexy, watery allure.

Of all the haunted lighthouse stories, two from Queensland take the prizes for atmosphere and all-round spookiness. The first concerns the light that once stood on Pine Islet and if you've never heard of this place you can be forgiven. Pine Islet is a single, steep, granite rock, just 800 metres in length, part of the remote Percy Islands group, south-east of Mackay.

In 1927 Pine Islet was the scene of a gruesome ceremony. The authorities decided to build a new lighthouse keeper's cottage on the island that year and the only available flat land was a grave site. An order was obtained to exhume the body and relocate the grave.

The headstone identified the grave as that of Dorothea McKay, wife of a lighthouse keeper, who had died of cancer in 1895. When the grave was opened the coffin was found to have rotted away. The workmen collected some loose bones, a set of false teeth and a wedding ring and duly reburied them some distance away. Everyone seemed satisfied with the arrangement — except Dorothea.

When the lighthouse keeper moved into the new cottage, built over the old grave, strange things began to happen. Invisible knuckles rapped loudly on the front door, then footsteps and faint muttering sounds (indecipherable but clearly angry) were heard inside the cottage.

In the 1980s the lighthouse was automated and the last lighthouse keeper departed, but right up until then the ghost's visits continued. In July 1985 keeper Darrell Roche was reported as saying: 'The last time she came was about eighteen months ago. There was a knock on the door, then footsteps through the cottage into the lounge room. There she stopped — above her original grave — and we've never heard anything from her since.'

Perhaps Dorothea McKay was satisfied when she heard that she was going to be left in peace. Maybe she found her way back to her original resting place that night in 1985. Darrell Roche and many others hope so. She is unlikely to be disturbed again, for when the lighthouse became redundant a few years back it was dismantled, shipped to the mainland and reconstructed beside Mackay Harbour as a tourist attraction.

400 kilometres south of Pine Islet lies Lady Elliot Island. As well as a lighthouse, there's a popular resort on Lady Elliot; not as glamorous (or as expensive) as most Barrier Reef resorts, but richly endowed with natural attractions — and some unnatural ones.

One of the conducted walks on Lady Elliot Island takes guests up a narrow track to the centre of the island after dark, to visit a tiny well-kept graveyard. There are only two graves there but each headstone tells a tragic story. One is the last resting place of thirty-year-old Phoebe Jane Phillips, daughter of the lighthouse keeper during the last decade of the nineteenth century. Phoebe lived a sheltered life on the island with only her parents for company before dying of pneumonia in 1896.

The other grave is that of Susannah McKee, wife of a later lighthouse keeper. Susannah McKee came from Ballyganaway in Ireland and bore her husband, Tom, four sons before accompanying him to Lady Elliot Island. Susannah found living conditions on the island harsher than she expected. Supplies had to be brought by ship and were invariably late. Meat and other perishables would not keep. The living quarters were cramped, Spartan and windswept. Medical attention was unavailable. Loneliness, boredom and the sense of isolation weighed heavily on Susannah's mind. After her youngest son went off to boarding school in Rockhampton, she decided she could stand the conditions no longer. On 23 April 1907 she put on her best dress, her good shoes and her favourite hat, walked out onto the guano-loading jetty below the lighthouse and threw herself into the sea.

There were rumours at the time that Tom McKee had pushed his wife off the jetty, but no one could prove murder. Tom recovered his wife's body and buried her beside Phoebe Phillips on the hilltop but, for some reason, Susannah McKee did not rest easy in her grave. The first recorded sighting of a woman fitting Susannah's description dates from the late 1930s. The keeper at that time, Arthur Brumpton, looked down from the lighthouse balcony one evening and saw a female figure dressed in turn-of-the-century clothing walking between the lighthouse and the three cottages behind it.

Brumpton's young daughter Margaret also recalled, years later: 'I often felt the presence of a stranger who I sensed was a woman, watching me or following me about during all our years on the island and I heard sharp, light, ghostly footsteps echoing in the lighthouse so many times I lost count. I grew up fearing that one day whoever it was that was watching me and making those eerie sounds would chase me up the stairs and push me off the balcony at the top of the lighthouse!'

Fortunately that didn't happen, but the Brumptons' story had a curious sequel. When the family were returning to Brisbane in 1940 the captain of the ship they travelled on showed them some of photos of people who had lived on Lady Elliot Island at different times. When he produced a photograph of Susannah McKee, Arthur Brumpton recognised the woman he had seen.*

Like the one on Pine Islet the Lady Elliot lighthouse was automated in 1985 and staff at the newly established resort took over the few duties that were needed to maintain it. The last lighthouse keeper handed over the three cottages to the resort's operations manager and a multitude of strange things have occurred ever since then.

The operations manager told how, on the night of the handover, he and the lighthouse keeper heard strange footsteps in one of the abandoned cottages. Two of the resort staff moved into the same cottage soon after: a groundsman and a chef. After they finished moving their furniture in the two men decided to take a break and sat on a tractor parked in front of the cottage. It was an unusually still afternoon with hardly enough wind to stir nearby trees. Suddenly an empty plastic ice-cream container came flying out of the front door

---

* Readers interested in seeing that photograph will find it on the Lady Elliot Island Resort's website.

of the unoccupied cottage and landed at their feet. At dinner that evening the pair told their workmates about the flying container and were told the story of the mysterious footsteps. The groundsman laughed and said he didn't believe in ghosts. That night he was hurled bodily from his bed in the cottage and landed on the floor with a bone-shaking thud. After that he slept on the verandah.

A few nights later he woke around 1 am and, to his horror, could clearly see the transparent figure of a woman standing in the cottage doorway. 'She was staring at me with big, unblinking eyes. Instantly I felt cold all over. Goosebumps rose on my skin and the hair on my arms and legs stood up like bristles on a brush. I also had the strange feeling that I was fixed like a specimen on a microscope slide and that this "thing" was studying me like *I* was some kind of freak. I was so scared I couldn't even cry out. I just lay there until the figure faded and disappeared.'

The ghost of Susannah McKee has also been seen peering out of the cottage windows and striding across the island's small airstrip — and not always alone. On some occasions she has been accompanied by a young woman (Phoebe Phillips?) and an old man wearing blue overalls. A boy wearing a Stetson hat has also been seen by staff and guests, leaning against an Indian almond tree between two of the cottages. Mysterious bloodstains have appeared from time to time on the fourth step of the staircase inside the lighthouse; and the plaintive voice of a little girl calling for her mother has been heard. All of which suggests that there are dark secrets, unrecorded, in the island's history.

Crank-started generators that supplied all the power to the resort in pre-solar days were housed in a locked room. Once they stopped suddenly, plunging the whole complex into darkness, but before anyone reached the locked room they started up again. Some old kerosene tins stored in the generator room were heard rattling and crashing about. A team of painters contracted to repaint the old lighthouse cottages found that every time they climbed their scaffolding it began to shake violently, but when they got down the shaking stopped. A female guest camping alone one night woke to hear the zippers on her tent opening and closing. She got up and looked around, but there was no one outside. As she returned to her bed she realised to her alarm that the zippers were on the inside. In the bar of the resort a glass tumbler spontaneously imploded moments after a guest finished drinking from it. The same guest had laughed as he swallowed the last mouthful of his drink and declared loudly to the assembly in the bar that he didn't believe in ghosts. 'Ghost stories are a load of bullshit,' he said. He, like many other sceptics who have stayed on the island, is now a convert.

The ghost walks up to the little hilltop cemetery are very popular with guests. Perhaps after a day spent diving or snorkelling in the emerald waters, paddling across the colourful reef flats that fringe the island or simply basking in the sun on the glorious golden beach a ghost story or (for the lucky one) an actual encounter is the ideal way to round off a perfect day.

36.
The Mysteries of Monte Cristo

Thus she spake and I longed to embrace my mother's dead ghost. Thrice I tried to clasp her image, and thrice it slipped through my hands, like a shadow, like a dream.

***The Iliad*, Homer (Greek poet, 8th Century BC)**

When rich pastoralist and land speculator Christopher Crawley built a stately mansion near the town of Junee NSW in 1884 he called it Monte Cristo — Mount of Christ — but if he hoped the name would protect his home he was mistaken. Dark forces have been at work at Monte Cristo for over a century. The building's history is marred by strange events that have left a legacy of supernatural activity probably unparalleled in any house standing in Australia today.

Christopher Crawley died at Monte Cristo in 1910 after a carbuncle on his neck caused by the high, starched collars he wore became infected. His widow, Elizabeth, lived on in the great house for another twenty-three years, leaving it on only two occasions. After her death, family and servants remained for a few years then the house was left unoccupied for a long period. Thieves, vandals and the elements almost destroyed it and then in 1963 it was bought by Reg and Olive Ryan, who took on the enormous task of first making the house habitable for themselves and their young family, then restoring it to its former glory. Reg Ryan says: 'The day I first saw Monte Cristo I knew without a doubt I would one day live there. I truly believed something supernatural led me to the homestead and that I was somehow meant to be the guardian, keeper and protector of this piece of Australian history that was so nearly lost.'

If Reg Ryan was led by a supernatural force to Monte Cristo he and his family were unprepared for the barrage of other supernatural events that occurred (and still occur almost daily) in and around this deceptively peaceful-looking old building. Just three days after they moved in the Ryans had their first strange experience. Electricity had not been connected, there was one kerosene lamp, unlit, in the house and not a single pane of glass in any window yet, as they drove back from a brief shopping trip to Junee that evening, they found bright light streaming from every window in the building. Just as mysteriously, the lights disappeared as they drove through the gateway. Many times since, after the Ryans have spent an evening in only one or two lighted rooms at the back of the house, residents of the town have asked them the next morning why their house was ablaze with light the previous night.

As the years passed and the Ryan's hard work slowly brought the old house back to life, they endured experiences that would have frightened off less dedicated people. Their attempts to keep pets at Monte Cristo always ended in tragedy. Most animals would not enter the house and those that did went crazy with fear. Others died mysteriously, including a kitten found in the kitchen disembowelled and with its eyes gouged out. Chickens were found with their necks wrung and a pair of caged finches, healthy and chirpy one minute, were dead the next.

The Ryans soon realised that they shared their home with a whole company of spirits, not all of whom were benign. Perhaps the love and care they lavish on the old house protects them. 'I have never felt threatened or frightened,' says Reg, but relatives, boarders, tradespeople and visitors have, many vowing never to return. Mediums who visit the house pick up echoes of tragedy and sorrow and sense the evil that pervades its beautifully furnished rooms and carefully restored outbuildings.

When you step through the front doorway at Monte Cristo you enter a hallway that runs the length of the house with a staircase leading to the upper floor. Small children often feel distressed for no apparent reason when they approach the stairs and one of the three mediums employed by the ABC during the making of a documentary about Monte Cristo announced that she had a strong feeling that some tragedy had occurred there. Records show that a little girl was dropped by her nanny and fell to her death in the stairwell. The nanny claimed some unseen force had pushed the child from her arms.

The first door on the left of the hallway is the sitting room, charmingly furnished with period furniture and a piano. The Crawley family also kept a piano in this room. The sound of a piano being played has been heard coming from the sitting room at night when the room is in darkness and apparently empty. Then there's the drawing room, where a Catholic priest once entered, stopped in his tracks, crossed himself vigorously and backed hastily out. Other people get visibly distressed when they enter the drawing room, one elderly lady crying uncontrollably until she was led from the room — a teacher who visited the house on a school excursion in 2010 reacted the same way. Objects move about mysteriously here; tapestries carefully hung one day are found rolled up against the wall the next and expensive ornaments from the mantelpiece have been found on the floor beside the door.

In one small bedroom the figure of an old lady dressed in black has been seen by one of the Ryans' daughters and by another of the three mediums, who described the old lady as standing beside a large silver cross. The reminiscences of a former servant who came forwards after the television documentary was aired revealed that the room had originally been a box room but, after the master's death, Mrs Crawley had had it converted into a private chapel. The medium was convinced it was the ghost of Elizabeth Crawley he had seen and said that she had ordered him to get out of her house.

The boys' bedroom nearby also has an alarming effect on people who enter it. Children put to bed there have difficulty settling and a boarder who slept in the room was found by Reg in the middle of the night standing on his bed shaking with terror and crying out that there was someone or something in his room with him. What frightened the boarder may have been the ghost of a young man in working clothes whose face appears at windows from time to time and whom one of the Ryans' daughters found standing over the bed in the boys' room one night, staring down at her small brother, who was sleeping peacefully.

The figure of a woman dressed in white has appeared to at least two people in another bedroom, floating across the room and disappearing through a closed window. On another occasion in the same room the detached head of a woman appeared above the foot of the bed to the amazement and horror of a guest. The same woman in white (or another with a similar taste in gowns) appeared at the top of the stairs one night, calling out very clearly, twice, 'Don't worry, it will be all right!' to two startled house guests. Yet another ghost was seen by a small boy who visited the house with his mother and asked after being taken on a tour of the house: 'Who was that old man with the beard in the brown clothes who followed us around?' No one else had seen him.

The first-floor balcony also has its share of strange happenings. One of the mediums claimed that a girl had died by falling from the balcony and, although efforts to find records of this have so far been unsuccessful, older residents of the district recall the story of a girl being thrown from the spot. The Ryans have heard footsteps on the balcony and connecting doors opening and closing when there has been no one upstairs. Lights have been seen moving mysteriously along the balcony at night and, in September 1995, a local woman driving away from the house reported seeing a transparent figure in an old-fashioned dark-coloured dress walking there.

Despite all the supernatural activity inside the house, mediums and sensitive visitors all agree that the feeling of evil that hangs over the whole property is strongest in two of the outbuildings: the stables and the dairy and, given the gruesome history of these innocent-looking structures, that is hardly surprising. Many years ago (and long before the Ryans came along) a young man named Morris worked at Monte Cristo and slept in the stables. One day he complained of being too ill to work, but his boss thought he was shirking and rashly put a match to the straw mattress the boy lay on. Morris was genuinely ill and unable to get up. He burned to death. One of the three mediums, without any knowledge of this event, came rushing out of the stables, badly shaken and claiming he could smell the stench of a fiery death inside.

Beside the door of the dairy is a small hole in the brick wall. That hole was made by a chain that held a mentally disabled man named Harold Steel prisoner for forty years. Steel's mother was housekeeper in Mrs Crawley's time and rather than put her son into an institution she kept him chained up in the dairy. After Mrs Crawley's death the housekeeper was allowed to stay on alone in the house but she died of a heart attack and her absence was not noticed for several days. When the police investigated they found Mrs Steel's body and Harold, in a wretched state, distressed, hungry and thirsty curled up on the ground at the end of his chain. He could not speak; his hair was long and matted and his overgrown fingernails had curled back into the palms of his hands. He was taken to an asylum in Goulburn but died soon after.

A few years later a local youth who had been to see the Hitchcock thriller *Psycho* three times came up to the house one night, found the caretaker, Jack Simpson, in the dairy and shot him dead. To this day the macabre message the murderer or someone else scratched on the dairy wall, *Die Jack Ha Ha*, can be clearly read.

When the ABC crew were filming the dairy at night they set up floodlights around the building. Because it was such a cold night the Ryans lit a fire in the dining-room fireplace, but within minutes they and the ABC crew were gathered outside, oblivious to the cold, witnessing an amazing sight. In the bright glare of the floodlights, smoke was rising from the second-floor chimney of the house, curling neatly in the air and then being sucked directly down the chimney of the dairy.

And the strange events keep happening. A Sydney man drove into the car park one day with his family. Even before he got out of his car the man complained that something invisible had attached itself to his chest and was clutching him painfully. After viewing the house the man said he was feeling very ill. For several weeks he could not rid himself of the strange sensation. Back home he went to a doctor, who could find nothing physically wrong with him and, surprisingly, suggested an exorcist. Suddenly one night, while he lay in bed, whatever it was that had attached itself to him let go and the pain ceased. The man was enormously relieved but horrified to see whatever it was had not gone very far. Both he and his wife could see a faint and indistinct form clinging to their bedroom wall beside the light switch.

Even as recently as 2010, a group of professional ghost-busters visited Monte Cristo and got more than they bargained for. When they mentioned that they hoped to be able to communicate with a spirit and record its voice a clear response — 'Pick me!' — came out of nowhere and when the ghost of Mrs Crawley repeated her oft-heard order to leave her house, her voice was captured on tape for the first time. Mrs C was also held responsible for violently rattling a firmly closed window when the group entered her former chapel and for the series of loud bangs that echoed through the house each time one of the group asked if there were spirits present.

There are many more stories about Monte Cristo — too many to retell here and more than enough to earn Monte Cristo a sinister reputation. Since the demolition of Bungaribee at Eastern Creek in 1958, the title Australia's Most Haunted House deservedly belongs to the Junee attraction. The mysterious old house is a popular tourist destination and deserves to be visited by everyone who travels to the town, not least for the proof it provides of what can be achieved by private individuals dedicated to preserving our national heritage. The extensive collection of beautifully restored horse-drawn vehicles displayed in the coach house should also not be missed, but if you experience any strange feelings or witness anything that defies explanation while visiting don't be surprised — it's all part of the mystery and fascination of old 'Monte Cristo'.

A Final Word from the Author

I acknowledge that stories of ghosts and spirits (equal in richness and diversity to any in this collection) abound in the traditional culture of Aboriginal Australians, but to do justice to them in printed words requires specialised knowledge and understanding greater than I possess.

I also offer an apology to any reader who might have been offended by the occasional use of discriminatory terms like 'blackfellow', 'Chinaman' or 'spinster' on the preceding pages. Such terms reflect the customs and attitudes of the times in which many of these stories are set, and in the interests of verisimilitude I have retained them in the retelling, when under normal circumstances I would not use them.

All stories in this collection are presented in good faith. I make no claim as to the authenticity or accuracy of any of these stories and would like to make it clear that although positive statements may be made — 'the house is haunted', 'he or she said', as examples — they should be taken to mean that the location is reputed, supposed or believed to be haunted and the individual was reported as saying.

Readers should also be aware that the sites of many of these stories are on private property. The inclusion of a story in this collection does not mean that the protagonists in the story, or owners or occupiers of the premises, believe in ghosts, or are willing to answer casual inquiries, discuss the story or countenance trespass on their property.

I willingly acknowledge the generous assistance provided to me by so many people from all over Australia in the preparation of my first book about ghosts, *The Ghost Guide to Australia*, published in 1998 and which I have drawn on extensively for this volume. Thanks are also due to Brigitta Doyle of ABC Books for her support of this project and to Rochelle Fernandez at HarperCollins and Kate O'Donnell who brought her exceptional skills to editing the manuscript.

Trying to describe supernatural phenomena and convey witnesses emotions in words requires a wide vocabulary, so let's allow Dr Samuel Johnson — that roly-poly, bewigged father of the modern English dictionary, to whom all writers are indebted — to have the last word on the subject of ghosts:

> *It is wonderful that thousands of years have now elapsed since the creation of the world, and still it is undecided whether or not there has ever been an instance of the spirit of any person appearing after death. All argument is against it; but all belief is for it.*